Manuel Vázquez Montalbán lives in Barcelona where he was born in 1939. He is a journalist, novelist and creator of Pepe Carvalho, a fast-living, gourmet private detective. Montalbán has won both the Spanish Planeta Prize and French Grand Prix of Detective Fiction for his thrillers, which are translated into all major languages.

Also by Manuel Vázquez Montalbán
and published by Serpent's Tail

Murder in the Central Committee
Southern Seas
Off Side
An Olympic Death

THE ANGST-RIDDEN EXECUTIVE

MANUEL VAZQUEZ MONTALBAN

Translated by Ed Emery

Library of Congress Catalog Card Number: 2001092082

A complete catalogue record for this book can be
obtained from the British Library on request

First published as *La Soledad del Manager*
by Editorial Planeta, Barcelona, 1977

First published in 1990 by Serpent's Tail,
4 Blackstock Mews, London N4 2BT
website: www.serpentstail.com

This 5-star edition first published in 2002

Printed by Mackays of Chatham plc

10 9 8 7 6 5 4 3 2 1

One day the member of parliament Sole Barbera asked me: 'When are you going to write another of your cops and robbers novels?' I have taken him at his word, and would like to dedicate *The Angst-Ridden Executive* to him.

He'd not so much requested as demanded a window seat. The girl at the Western Air Lines check-in desk looked at the card he flashed, and complied, albeit with an air of puzzlement.

What reason could there possibly be for a CIA agent to insist on a window seat on a flight from Las Vegas to San Francisco? The girl had heard rumours about special training camps that were supposedly located somewhere in the Mojave Desert, but surely the CIA had their own reconnaissance planes. Carvalho sensed a battle of conflicting logics raging behind the girl's artificially tanned forehead as she checked his ticket. Then he had to produce the card a second time, when two policemen came up to search him. They let him pass, with a gesture that represented either total subservience or total contempt.

As Carvalho settled into his seat, he felt a sense of pleasure that was on a par with that of a child awaiting a treat. A settled sort of contentment, in which your body is master of the situation but your legs want to run to meet the experience head-on. Carvalho concentrated on the take-off, on Las Vegas as it disappeared rapidly into the distance, looking like a cardboard cut-out sticking out of the desert, and on preparing himself for the moment when they would fly over Death Valley and Zabriskie Point. Carvalho had made repeated pilgrimages to this part of the world. He was drawn by the aesthetic appeal of the blunt, white hills, which turned slowly to purple in the evening light, and he was attracted by Death Valley's reputation for treachery, and by its sulphurized waters and the glitter of its salty crust. From the plane one could appreciate the absurd grandeur of this landscape, which may have been a geological leftover, but which had always made a profound impression on Carvalho. It would be wonderful to jump out with a parachute, together with a knapsack filled with the kind of wonders that came out of knapsacks in Hemingway: tins of beans and smoked bacon. Something, however, was preventing Carvalho from indulging his secret and solitary vice. Something in his immediate vicinity that was like radio interference. Something that was being said, or sounded like it was being said. The source of the disturbance was very close. Right next to him, in fact. The passengers in the seats next to him were talking about Spain, and one of them was speaking English with a heavy Catalan accent.

'I find it strange that you could spend eight years at the Rota base and not learn Spanish.'

'The bases have a life of their own. We only use local people for cleaning the place, and for...'

With a knowing guffaw, the American made a lewd gesture that he had probably picked up in some bar in Cadiz. The Catalan chose to ignore it and continued with the conversation as between two businessmen. The American was apparently the boss of a small sports goods factory, and was discussing his franchises. For him the world was divided between people who bought from him and people who didn't. He even had a high opinion of communist China, because they bought his hiking gear, importing it via Hong Kong. On the other hand he couldn't stand the Cubans, the Brazilians, or the French. As he praised the ethical and consumerist capacities of each individual nation, the American accompanied his observations with a clap of his hands and a shout of 'Olé', evidently intended as a linguistic homage to his travelling companion. The Spaniard, for his part, gave a brief resumé of his circumstances. He was a manager working for Petnay, one of the biggest multinationals in the world. His main area of responsibility was Spain and part of Latin America, but he often came to the US in order to talk with head office and to get an update on the latest techniques in marketing.

'We Americans know how to sell.'

'I don't agree. The truth is simply that you have the political power to force your products onto large numbers of people.'

'That's history for you, friend! You people used to have an empire too, as I recall — and whatever became of that?! Not to mention the Romans. And what about the Apaches — they had a little empire too, didn't they? One day maybe the whole of American civilization will disappear, and our whole country will end up looking like that out there...'

The American gestured towards the arid Death Valley landscape. At this point Carvalho spoke up, in Spanish.

'Imagine the number of drink-flasks our friend would be able to sell then!'

The Catalan spun round to see where the voice was coming from. He chuckled.

'The world's a small place! It seems I'm sitting next to a Spaniard. Allow me to introduce myself — Antonio Jauma — I'm in management.'

'Pepe Carvalho. I'm a travelling salesman.'

The Catalan introduced Carvalho to the American, who shook his hand and launched into a string of ad hoc Hispanicisms:

'España... Bonita... Olé... Manzanilla... Puerta de Santa Maria...'

'Si, señor.'

'What's your line of business?' Jauma inquired.

He was a thin man, medium-built, with the unmistakable features of a Sephardic Jew. The nose of an Istanbul antique dealer; dark, shiny eyes that suggested a measure of ruthlessness; and a shock of thick, black hair, with a wide parting that hinted at incipient hair loss.

'One-armed bandits. That's what brings me to Vegas so often.'

'Do you live in San Francisco?'

'Berkeley. I'm doing a part-time urban studies course at

the university.'

'What part of Spain are you from?'

'Born in Galicia, but spent most of my life in Barcelona.'

'Well, we're two of a kind! This gentleman and I are fellow countrymen...' He conveyed this information to the American, who received it with an air of comic gravity.

Jauma gave Carvalho a potted account of himself. He had studied law at university. Then a trip to the USA, where he'd spent his time building highways and serving hot dogs in snack bars in the Bronx. He'd married a fellow student from his university days. They had come through hard times together.

'Some nights we had to make do with an omelette and a finger of whiskey between us.'

All of a sudden — via one of his wife's relations who was a military attaché at the Spanish embassy in Washington — Jauma had landed a job with Petnay. Within a few months he'd become their representative in Spain.

'And, as Groucho Marx might say, that's the way my career has gone — from absolute poverty to nothing at all.'

'Nothing at all?'

'Exactly. Nothing at all. A manager never makes enough money to just pack his bags and quit. What's more, he's always at the mercy of last year's trading figures and people trying to stab him in the back. I've had enough of it. Last night I had to attend a fraternity dinner for managers from all over the world. You can imagine the scene — America in full dress. The jewellery at that gathering would have put Ali Baba to shame. Anyway, on the one hand you've got this rabble sitting over your head. And on the other you've got the pressure of the workers from below. You have no idea what it's like trying to run a business with the present labour situation in Spain and Latin America. You need nerves of steel.'

'How are things going?'

'Well, for the moment. The company pays salaries that are a bit higher than the prevailing local rate, and in return it earns dollar-level profits. The only thing that worries me is the idea of a crisis looming, and my having to start behaving like a foreman. You know what I mean?'

'You have the morality of a pinko.'

'Does that bother you?'

'Not at all. I used to be a bit that way myself, but all I'm left with these days is a set of bowels in rather good working order.'

'Bravo, Carvalho — you're a hell of a man!'

The man obviously had a histrionic streak. He waved his arms enthusiastically, thrust his sharp-featured face forward, and shouted:

'We have to celebrate this meeting! Tonight I'm inviting you to eat out at Fisherman's Wharf. You know the place?'

'Yes.'

'I'm staying at the Holiday Inn on Market Street. Why don't we arrange to meet directly at the restaurant — say at nine? Ha! Carvalho! This meeting is all the better for being unexpected. Who knows, maybe we even have friends in common, although looking at you I'd say that you're a bit younger than me. Did you study in Barcelona?'

'Yes. Philosophy.'

'And now you're a travelling rep for one-armed bandits! You're a prophet! My friend here is a prophet!'

The American nodded agreement, gave Carvalho an approving look and leaned back to take a more thorough view of him, as if searching for external signs that might give evidence of his hidden powers.

'Just imagine the things we might have in common. Let's make a list of the women we've had, and then compare them. Who knows, maybe we have a parallel sexual history.'

'Or convergent.'

'That's right — or convergent. Last night the company mobilized all the best-looking call-girls in Las Vegas, and there was a farewell party in grand style in the poolside apartments at the Sands Hotel — Sinatra's hotel. I shut myself in a bedroom with two black girls. They were a sight to see, Carvalho! What would I do if I couldn't go on one of these binges every once in a while? These Americans are superb at squeezing the work out of their personnel, and then, moments before they collapse from exhaustion, stimulating them so that they pick themselves up and carry on producing. That's the fundamental principle of Taylorism and Fordism. And I prescribe it for myself. Otherwise I'd never survive the wreckage of my everyday life. The angst. The angst of a senior executive.

It was as if the smoke of ancient volcanoes had turned into a cold, wet fog. Every morning during the winter, damp vapours rise from the grey earth and envelope the big, ageing houses on the outskirts of Vich. Driven out of the town by the breath of people's front doors opening, the fog takes it out on the whitewashed adobe houses that marked the transition between the old city and the surrounding dull, grey countryside. At this time of the morning you didn't get a full view of the scenery of this landscape of ancient prehistoric disaster, of the limited end-of-the-world that must have happened in what today is known as the Plain of Vich, an ash-coloured terrain dotted with small chimneys of petrified lava. Nor do you see the hamlet of bare, dark stone, covered by beetle-browed roofs whose purpose is to offer protection against the rain, or to emphasize the gravity of a city which one local writer has described as 'the city of saints'. The priests have not yet come out of their infinite lairs, fragrant with wax and marzipan. The only humans in sight are countrywomen on their way to market and workers leaving the town on their way to sausage factories, furniture factories, warehouses or artificial stone factories. Zigzagging bicycles are

nervously observed by the steaming eyes of car headlights
and by the enormous bulk of a lorry, like some great cuboid
animal, with only its front showing through the fog.

The fog is not the only obstacle on your way to work.
You have little chance of avoiding a more or less long wait
at the level crossing, and regular commuters treat the red
traffic light as an acceptable risk which they calculate into
their working day. Those travelling on bikes or motorbikes
put their feet on the ground and hold their machines
between their legs like sleeping animals. Those in cars
switch on the demister, or turn up the heating to clear
their windscreens. One or two leave the safety of their
vehicles to clean their windows or to pull up their aerials.
It's always amazing to discover that there are programmes
at this time of the morning, with some radio announcer,
his mouth full of coffee and the small hours, attempting to
maintain a degree of enthusiasm sufficient to sell the latest
hit single.

'What's the temperature like in La Coruña?'

'Two degrees below zero.'

'Granada? Is Granada there? Do we have Granada on
the line?'

'Bilbao?'

'Two degrees, and a wind coming in off the Bay of Biscay.'

'That's one for the seafarers — a storm on its way.'

'Barcelona? How's the temperature down there?'

'Four degrees and a relative humidity of eighty-seven per
cent.'

'What about Vich?' the man wonders. 'If Barcelona is
four degrees, I'll guarantee that Vich is below zero.' He is
surprised to find himself blowing on his fingers like when
he was a boy, and he chuckles to himself as a wave of
nostalgia brings back to him the taste of bread soaked in
milky coffee. The memory is an amazing thing! The slightest
thing is capable of setting off a whole chain of fragmented
images.

'Juan, will you stop playing about and drink your milk!'

That's what his grandfather used to tell him, in just the same tone that he now used with his own children, particularly Oriol, the lazy one.

'Oh, one day I'm going to lose my patience, and I'll give you a thick ear.'

He begins to laugh. The boy puts on the superior look of a person bowing to *force majeure*, and downs his milk with a technical perfection that also seems to express scorn. Drinking milk, in the morning, with your hands cupped round the bowl, enjoying that mysterious warmth that seems to come right from the centre of the earth. 'No, I don't want cups like that,' he had told his wife on the day she brought home a Duralex tea-set. 'I don't want that kind of cup for my milk.' 'You're full of nonsense.' 'Look, I don't know why, but if I don't drink my milk out of a bowl it doesn't taste right, especially in the mornings.' 'I'm the one who has to wash them, and the glaze always comes off earthenware, and it's a breeding place for germs... and I'm tired of waiting on you hand and foot...'

'That's enough! I'm having my milk in a bowl, and that's an end of it.'

Every now and then you have to make a stand, because if you don't people take advantage of you. I know it's a bit of an obsession, but everyone's got so many manias that one more won't do any harm. His bowl of milk was a means of re-establishing a link with his childhood, and the distant faces that were almost beyond recall. His aunt: 'Juan, you'll be late for school.' His grandfather: 'Juan, will you stop playing about?' The weak light of the first lightbulbs in Valles — fifteen and twenty watts apiece — which were carefully switched off as soon as the first daylight appeared, in the daily battle between the electric current and the countryfolk who were scared to waste the stuff. Nowadays people don't care. They leave their lights on, ten at a time, and damn the expense. They don't worry any more. Instead he takes it out on her because she gives him stick for wanting to drink his milk out of a bowl. His grandma used to tell them to lock the larder properly, because the radio announcers would come out at night and eat everything in sight. He began to laugh, and laughed till the tears ran. The red light was still showing through the fog, and he roused himself sufficiently to notice that he had a hard-on. He felt his cock with a degree of pride, and noticed a tickling sensation. He needed a piss. There was no sign of the train yet, and beyond the roadside verge he saw that the fog and the undergrowth were thick enough to conceal a man's slow, steady piss from the gaze of the cars, motorbikes, bicycles and lorries that were waiting for the train to pass. The knowledge that it was cold outside, and the possibility of the train arriving at any moment, led him to one last test. He made as if to piss, and then tried holding back, to stop the hidden flow. He only just managed it, and some drops of urine emerged like beads of golden water onto the Y-front of his underpants.

He had no choice. He got out of the car, hunched his shoulders as if shoring up his body against the weight of the cold, and crossed the verge with what he imagined was a spring in his step. He plunged into the undergrowth, looking back as he went, to check whether the people waiting on the road could still see him. The hidden stream was demanding to be liberated; it seemed to take a sadistic pleasure in the domination it was able to exert over a man who was both its master and its slave. 'There you go, there you go,' the man murmured to himself. He spotted the substantial bulk of a lime tree, and reached to unzip his fly. His hand went into his fly as if trying to get hold of a soft, live creature that was hard to get hold of. He fumbled for the slit in his underpants and grasped the warm, fleshy substance of his penis. Once again he looked to the front and behind him, then to right and left, as he extracted his appendage and dangled it with two fingers of his right hand while the other fingers made a kind of roof, or rather a canopy, for the almost religious devotion with which he pissed. As he relieved the weight on his bladder, he felt a sense of euphoria, and no longer cared whether people could see him or not. He was trying to trace a pattern with his piss on the bark of the tree, but his eye was suddenly caught by something odd on the ground — something that seemed to have been buried there, and which was slowly being uncovered by the jet of piss. Like an electric probe, the urine slowly washed the shape clean, and before the staring eyes of Juan de can Gubern there finally appeared the shape of a hand. His eyes rested on the hand momentarily, as if trying to make sense of it, and then passed to the muddied sleeve of a jacket, which seemed to contain a man's arm, and then to the entire jacket, and then to the man himself, face downwards, and half hidden by earth, hoarfrost, and weeds. Juan Gubern's member turned limp as the cold got to it, and then swiftly retracted. He thought: 'I should shout,' but he didn't, because he suddenly heard the sound of the train approaching and remembered that he had left his car blocking the road. He hurriedly retraced his steps, struggling to return his penis to its rightful place as he went.

'I was just on my way to the office. Was your business really so urgent that you had to come up to Vallvidrera?'

As he asked the question, Carvalho pointedly did not invite his visitor to sit down. The detective was irritated by the feeling of having been caught unawares in his lair, and his eyes travelled across the various signs of disorder in his household: the unwashed plates on the dinner table; the record on the turntable and its sleeve lying on the floor; the overflowing ashtray next to the sofa; and the open book on the floor, covered in ash. He first resolved the problem of the book, by shutting it and tossing it onto a shelf on the other side of the room. He kicked the ashtray under the sofa while at the same time piling up plates and glasses, and taking them to the kitchen. When he returned he found that his visitor had retrieved the book from the shelf and was flicking through it, blowing out the ash from between its pages.

'Don't worry, it's only a book.'

His visitor smiled a smile of enigmatic complicity. Forty years old, Carvalho thought to himself, but looks younger. Wearing a sweater, with the tabs of his shirt collar sticking out like little wings. 'Judging by the way he moves, he must be hooked on James Dean,' the detective decided, as he watched his visitor put his hands into his pockets, raise his shoulders and smile boyishly as he scanned the room with eyes that were shrewd and calculating.

'There are worse things in life than books, señor Carvalho. Nice place you've got here. Does it cost much to rent?'

'I think I bought it.'

'You *think*...?'

Carvalho went over to the big glass door, and as he looked out to check that the Valles countryside was still where it had been the night before, he noticed a car parked at the bottom of the garden stairs, and a man, waiting there, leaning against the bodywork.

'Have you come with a chauffeur?'

'I don't even have a car, let alone a chauffeur. What I have in this world amounts to more or less nothing. A sweater or two. A girlfriend every now and then. One or two friends. And some languages. German, for example.'

'What do you take me for — an employment agency?'

'No. I've come to see you about a mutual friend — Antonio Jauma.'

'He may be a friend of yours, but he's certainly no friend of mine. I've never heard of Antonio Jauma, although I *did* know a Jauma once — a fellow student of mine... ended up as a teacher; a tall, skinny type, a Christian socialist...

quite unforgettable. He wasn't an Antonio, though.'

'Antonio Jauma wasn't tall. He wasn't a teacher, either. He was a top executive in an international company. He wasn't a Christian, and if he was progressive it was in a human rather than a political sense. It appears that Jauma had a high opinion of you. I'll remind you when and where you met: in the United States, on a flight from Las Vegas to San Francisco.'

'The executive!'

The amused expression that appeared on Carvalho's face prompted no particular reaction from his visitor. His repeated glances in the direction of an empty chair forced Carvalho to offer him a seat, and, once seated, the visitor slowly and deliberately lit a cigarette, took a deep breath, in order to get his narrative started, and gave Carvalho a detailed resumé of his encounter with Jauma miles above the Mojave Desert. Carvalho began to wonder whether he was in the presence of some kind of oral novelist, a habitual monologist with a taste for performing to gatherings of Trappists, a cultured leftist fallen on hard times, and he sensed that the story was probably going to end with a *coup de théâtre*, a carefully weighted punchline which would tie up the threads and give meaning to the whole.

'So anyway...'

A thick exhalation of smoke emerged from the visitor's mouth and hung in the air like a grey sheet.

'...Antonio Jauma has been murdered.'

He had still not said his all, because his eyes had turned from mischievous to serious, and were searching for something — a suitable prop to enable him to complete his peroration.

'Or at any rate he's dead.'

'I have to admit that I'd be more interested if he's been murdered. The fact of his being dead is just a consequence. How did he die? When? Where?'

'Shot through the heart from behind. A perfect shot. Then they dumped his body in a wood near Vich. According to forensic it hadn't been there long — probably since about one in the morning.'

'What are the police saying?'

'That it was some pimp getting his own back. As you may know, Jauma was a bit of a womanizer, in the oldest and least pleasant sense of the term. As far as the police are concerned, it's an open and shut case. While he was out on the town, either someone tried blackmailing him and he resisted, or he fell foul of one of the hard men. The body smelt of women's perfume — of toilet water, in fact... a personal hygiene fragrance, if you know what I mean. *Eau lustrale pour l'hygiène intime*. What's more, it was dressed normally, but with one exception. No underpants. Instead they found a pair of women's knickers in his trouser pocket.'

'All of which suggests a night on the tiles. Seems clear enough.'

'I don't think so. Neither does his widow.'

'That's to be expected. She wouldn't be the first widow to refuse to believe that her husband led a double life.'

'In Concha's case you could be right. She's a proper lady, from Valladolid, and she's never taken Antonio's sexual inclinations very seriously. However, I too don't believe that things are as simple as they seem.'

'Why not?'

'Well, we've all seen enough detective films to know that criminals lay false trails to conceal the motives of their crimes... Now, what's the classic false trail scenario?'

'Pouring a bottle of whiskey or brandy down the dead man's throat so that it looks as if he was drunk.'

'Exactly, señor Carvalho. And, if you ask me, something similar happened in Jauma's case.'

'Why? Did he smell of drink?'

'No. He smelt of women's cologne. As I say, intimate cologne. As if he'd been soused in a barrel of the stuff. You take my meaning?'

'Did you tell this to the police?'

'I prefer not to have dealings with the police. I spent many years in exile in the Eastern Bloc, and my legal status in Spain is not what you'd call clear. I persuaded Concha to tell the police, though, and to get a lawyer on the case. Neither the police nor the lawyer have shown the slightest interest. So she decided to look into things herself. At that point I remembered that Jauma had mentioned your name a few times — specifically with a view to bringing you in to investigate possible instances of industrial espionage. Jauma was a very important figure. Petnay is a vast multinational, and he was their number one executive in southern Europe. They also used to send him on inspection tours of Latin America.'

'What I don't understand is why such an important person should remember someone like me — a pretty crazy chance meeting over Death Valley, followed by dinner at Fisherman's Wharf in San Francisco. And then a trip up country. And what I find even stranger is the fact that you've been able to find me, and that you know that I'm a private detective. When Jauma met me, I was still living in the States.'

'Jauma made it very easy for us. We found your phone number in his desk diary, together with three possible addresses, and instructions for one of his secretaries to get in touch with you as quickly as possible.'

'Three addresses?'

'This one, the address of your office on the Ramblas, and the address of your girlfriend, Rosario Garcia Lopez, aka Charo.'

'Why did he want to see me?'

'That's another mystery. I suspect that it was probably something to do with his company.'

'Was he the jealous sort? Maybe he thought his wife was having an affair?'

'Concha?'

For the first time the middle-aged youth in the sweater showed signs of surprise.

There had been a third party at the San Francisco dinner, one Rhomberg — Petnay's general overseer in the US. Carvalho took the Power Street cable-car to Fisherman's Wharf, and arrived sufficiently early to be able to spend some time exploring pavements that were peopled with underground newsvendors, folk singers and long-haired practitioners of a variety of cheap and pointless crafts: manufacturers of sunflower seed necklaces, brass jewellery-makers, xerox poets, and spaced-out painters who ventured beyond the Golden Gate as if by an act of voluntary self-immolation. Carvalho resisted the temptation to try a portion of crayfish from a street stall. He could feel the tension in his stomach mounting at the prospect of serious eating. There were all kinds of stalls offering the passer-by a variety of ready-packed seafoods, either as consolation for the fact of not being able to afford to eat in the plush restaurants that stood nearby, or by way of an incitement to move on to greater things. Carvalho didn't have time to decide. Out of a taxi stepped Jauma, in the company of a man who was clearly a German. His feet had barely touched the ground when he frightened the life out of the aforementioned hippies with a loud display of histrionics and a cry of:

'Carvalho — For lobsters, and for the Love of God!'

The German was also introduced with a characteristic Jauma flourish:

'Dieter Rhomberg. Petnay's number three man in the sectors that I'm involved with. In other words, a man who's more powerful than Franco. Tonight's meal is on him.'

'It is?'

The German appeared more surprised than annoyed.

'We should celebrate the fact that your people have won the elections. Rhomberg might look like one hell of an executive, but in fact he's a socialist. Left-wing, too. Supports the Young Socialist wing of the SPD.'

'I can't imagine that your friend's particularly interested...' the German exclaimed, in a tone that was half civility and half irritation.

'Our friend's in the CIA...'

Carvalho's stomach gave a heave. He realized that Jauma was saying it for a joke, but he had still said it.

'...Sure, the CIA. What other explanation can there be for a Galician who spends his time travelling between San Francisco and Vegas?'

'Maybe he's a croupier?'

'Sure. A CIA croupier.'

'Why does he have to be CIA?'

'Because in Spain the CIA only recruits Galicians. I read it in *Readers' Digest*.'

Jauma laughed at his own joke, and ushered them towards the restaurant.

'For the love of God...! For Lobsters...! For Justice and for the Fatherland!'

Half an hour later there was still no sign of oyster soup and the lobster Thermidor that Jauma had recommended, or rather chosen on their behalf. During that time they drank two bottles of chilled Riesling, while Jauma and Rhomberg immersed themselves in an extremely technical discussion of the problems of the North American market and the necessity of adapting the packaging of some of their products to suit the taste of shop-windows in San Francisco.

'I still reserve judgment until I've had a look round the Hollywood stores. In a couple of streets at the bottom of Beverly Hills you have the biggest concentration of luxury-goods shops anywhere in the world. Even bigger than Paris or New York.'

'What does Petnay make?'

'Perfumes, alcoholic spirits and pharmaceutical products.'

The German seemed inclined to stop there. Jauma, however, continued the list.

'Fighter planes, bombers, high-tech communications systems, all highly "sophisticated", as they say... as well as newspapers, magazines, dailies, politicians, and revolutionaries... Petnay makes them all. Even the lobster that we are about to eat, if it's a frozen one, was very probably packed by Petnay. They own one of the biggest fishing fleets in the world, with operations in Japan, Greenland, Senegal, Morocco and the United States. In this restaurant there's not a thing that couldn't have been made by Petnay — from the fake French Californian wines down to Herr Rhomberg and myself.'

In Jauma's opinion, the oyster soup was out of a packet. Carvalho corrected him: 'Tinned.'

'There's no such thing as oyster soup out of a packet.'

Carvalho and Jauma stuck to the rules and refrained from drinking wine with the soup. Rhomberg made up for them by polishing off a bottle all by himself — one glass of chilled white wine for each spoonful of soup. Jauma justified his choice of lobster Thermidor on the grounds that this particular recipe best concealed the insipid taste of American lobsters.

'Big, but tasteless. You, Carvalho, will be my guest at my estate in Port de la Selva on the Costa Brava. We'll go to the fish market at Llansa. They sell terrific lobsters there — live, red ones, not very large, but properly fished — not farmed. Angry lobsters. To be cut up very carefully. Do you know why, Carvalho?'

'So that they don't lose their waters, in other words their blood. That's what gives them their flavour. You also have to pull their stomach out in one piece. It comes away very easily if you pull on the intestine that comes out under the central fin of the lobster's tail.'

'Amazing!'

The German's face had been turned bright red by the effects of the wine. He laughed.

'It was only women and good food that saved us all from going mad under Franco.'

Jauma shouted this out loud, to the general consternation of the surrounding tables. He repeated the statement in English, directing it at a crowded table consisting of four married couples, all white, with all the men dressed in green Prince of Wales check suits and the women dressed like Piper Laurie in a Hollywood comedy of manners.

By now Rhomberg was sufficiently drunk not to feel embarrassed. He gave three cheers for socialism and drank to the forthcoming downfall of Franco.

'I can't believe that you Spaniards have put up with him for as long as you have.'

This last querulous remark was directed at Carvalho.

'You should worry about the Watchdog of the West on your own doorstep — Willy Brandt.'

'You Spaniards have nothing to say on the subject of our Willy. Spaniards have nothing to say about anything. After all, putting up with Franco for thirty years...!'

'It was you Germans that landed him on us. You helped him win the war.'

Carvalho was annoyed with himself. He hated scenes. The natural masochistic inclinations of men and strong nations made it inevitable that the German would back down, and that Jauma, drunk and lascivious, would go onto the offensive, shouting:

'Tonight we'll sleep with five hundred women all at once! And Rhomberg will do the business. Have you seen the size of his organ?'

'An experience I can live without...'

'I saw it once, on a beach in Mykonos. The Super Paradise beach, it was. We were spending the Easter holiday there with our families. Where Rhomberg walks, the grass will never grow again.'

Rhomberg laughed and blushed.

'It'll be at the firm's expense. We'll go and look out five hundred chicks. Four hundred and ninety for Rhomberg, five for you, Carvalho, and five for me. Best to find chicks with no front teeth, because they do a better blow job. And if they *do* have their front teeth, we'll hire a dentist to pull them out in a civilized manner.'

Rhomberg was seriously annoyed to find that he had left his Havanas behind at the hotel. Carvalho and Jauma concurred in observing that American cigars were unsmokable, but luckily the restaurant's range of tobacco extended to a trio of Jamaican Macanudos. This prompted Carvalho to a brief sermon on the quality of their tobacco.

'They're perfectly made, but the flavour's not a patch on a Havana.'

'If you ask me, standards have fallen in Cuba. The best Cuban cigars these days are the ones that Davidoff's sell under their own label, but the traditional brands have gone way downhill. The quality of the tobacco's still incomparable, though. The feel and weight of this Macanudo is excellent, but what about the flavour, Carvalho. There's no flavour, no flavour!'

They moved on to post-prandial drinks. Rhomberg plumped for a black label whiskey, while Carvalho ordered a marc from Burgundy, and Jauma one from the Champagne region. Then they settled in for the night. In the years to come, Carvalho's main memory was of opening his eyes several hours later to find himself in a cushion-filled room where Jauma was engaged in heavy petting with three naked black women and Rhomberg was lying asleep next to a white girl who was busy trimming her nails, with her legs crossed and her breasts almost resting on her knees. Carvalho had a woman under him. She was gazing at the ceiling and humming a slow fox trot.

Concha Hijar de Jauma had breasts that looked sad and were probably veined. The former could be deduced from the way that she compensated by wearing an excessively

pointed bra. The latter he concluded from the transparency
of her skin, which revealed the blood flowing in her
forehead, her arms and her hands. The sight of the widow's
veins, together with the dark rings round her eyes,
miraculously drawn by nature in the space of a couple of
weeks, combined to produce a general effect of mourning.
She had been educated in English schools and in Spanish
barracks, under the paternal eye and tactical prudence of
a Spanish general who did little as a military man, and
even less as a member of the boards of countless companies.
The girl's upbringing had been wealthy and authoritarian.
She then went to university, in Barcelona, to study
medicine (Doctor Puigvert had removed a gall-stone for her
father), and two weeks later discovered sex, thanks to a
young student by the name of Antonio Jauma, and politics,
thanks to his friend Marcos Nuñez. In fact neither Jauma
with his sex nor Nuñez with his politics effected any
fundamental alteration in the young lady, who only
compromised herself in the most formal of senses with
either one of them.

'She's absolutely and radically a virgin.'

Marcos Nuñez had just concluded his assessment when
the drawing-room door opened wide to reveal señora
Jauma. Carvalho savoured the woman's presence and
imagined how many men must have fallen for her. While
her husband was alive it must have been stimulating,
fascinating, to invade this atmosphere of religiosity where
every pleasure came tinged with a *soupçon* of sinfulness.

'They told me you were here half an hour ago. I'm sorry
to have kept you waiting. My head must have been
somewhere else.'

What she seemed to be seeking was not so much respect
for her widowed state as respect for her right to lose her
head. When Carvalho introduced himself, she looked him
over, and was able to tell at a glance whether he was the
sort of man who wiped his lips with a serviette prior to
raising a wine-glass to his lips, and also whether the

detective viewed her as a widow with time on her hands. The discovery that Carvalho most assuredly would wipe his lips, and also that he was eyeing her with contempt but nonetheless voraciously, disconcerted the widow. She felt the need to take refuge in a more conventional role, so she introduced a moistness into her eyes, a tiredness into her hands as she pressed them together, and a note of anxiety into a soprano voice that betrayed a lack of sleep.

'Are you up to date with the facts?'

'He is. He knows everything that we know.'

'You will help us, won't you? Antonio deserves it. He was so loyal to his friends — even more than to his family or to myself.'

'He wasn't actually my friend. I think I ought to make that clear. I met him over a couple of days several years ago, and he certainly struck me as a remarkable man, but I wouldn't say he was a friend of mine.'

'You will help us, though?'

'If you're approaching me in my professional capacity, yes, I will.'

'I have money, and I want to get to the bottom of this. It's unbearable that everyone seems to be accepting the official version, and that everybody's trying to hush it all up.'

'Like who?'

'Everyone from the Petnay management to my father. My father has been moving heaven and earth to keep everything low-key. Petnay don't want to find themselves involved in some sordid scandal, so they prefer to offer me money to keep quiet. I can't agree to that. I'm doing it for my husband — for his memory, and for the memory that his children will inherit.'

According to Nuñez's explanation during the drive down from Vallvidrera, Concha Hijar had been a political militant during her student days in the school of medicine. But at forty years of age she was speaking as her mother would have spoken at forty years of age, and as she would also expect her own daughter to speak at the age of forty.

'I want you to spare no expense.'

'Have no worries on that score. My rate is two thousand pesetas a day, payable within sixty days. In cases where the insurance companies are disputing claims, I generally take a percentage of what my client will receive. However, as far as I can gather from what you've told me, we have no problems with Petnay or with the insurance.'

'No.'

'In this case, in addition to the daily rate, I would expect a bonus of one hundred thousand pesetas if I solve the case within sixty days.'

'When can you start?'

'Here and now. With you. Tell me honestly — was your husband involved in a romantic liaison that might have made him a target for revenge?'

'People don't believe this, but we women are always the last to know. Antonio was very much a ladies' man. They tell me he used to devour them with his eyes. But when it came to the real thing — absolutely nothing. He spent himself in words. People saw him as a womanizer because he was always talking about women, and with women, in a particular sort of way — "I want you...", "Don't play hard to get...", "Go to the dentist and get him to take your front teeth out..." etc, etc. I'm sure you know the sort. He was so predictable. He never talked of anything else. But words are one thing, action another.'

'When you said that you didn't believe the business about the women's perfume, what did the police have to say?'

'I'd rather not go into that. It wasn't exactly nice.'

'Please. I need to know.'

'It was disgusting: "People like your husband, if you don't mind my saying so, get up to all kinds of kinky things. Some of them like to be beaten... some like, well... to be urinated on. So why shouldn't your husband like sousing himself in toilet water?"'

'According to the forensic examination, had he had sex

that night?'

'There were signs of ejaculation, but they can't say whether this was due to sexual excitation or whether he'd actually had intercourse. The fact that he was not wearing underpants is more of a mystery.'

'And the knickers?'

'What about them?'

'How were they?'

'I don't know. I didn't ask. They just told me that they were women's knickers, that's all.'

'I need to know more about them.'

'I don't know what you mean. You want the brand-name?'

'No. I particularly need to know whether they'd been worn or not — in other words, when he put them, or when they were put, in his pocket had they just been used? Or had they been washed? Or were they new and not yet worn?'

'And how am I supposed to find that out?'

'Via his lawyer. Or your father. Or our friend here.'

Marcos Nuñez seemed to have lost interest in the business, and was sniffing around the books on the shelves. A dining-room-cum-living-room which would have held twenty rock and rollers and their partners with ease. A series of original paintings by artists who hadn't yet made it — Artigau, Llimos, Jove, Viladecans, and one who was on the point of making it — an eight-hundred-thousand-peseta Guinovart. Classical style for the seating and avant garde for the light fittings. A small stuffed crocodile and op art mobiles, and not a speck of dust in sight. From the living room you could hear the sound of a servant assiduously polishing the oak parquet. The widow Jauma was trying to imagine a pair of women's knickers that were not her own. Carvalho was trying to imagine them placed on the more precise geography of some woman's body.

Charo opened her eyes, the only part of her that was covered.

'This is no time to be sleeping.'

In a reflex action, the girl pulled the sheet over her head, but Carvalho had already flung the curtains wide open, and the room was flooded with April light.

'Pig! That's hurting my eyes!'

Charo leapt out of bed. She rushed to the bathroom, but not before giving Carvalho a punch in the stomach.

'I can't wait till you've finished in there.'

'I'll be out in a second.'

'I know you better than that... I'm leaving a photo of a man on your dressing table. I want you to try and remember if he was ever a client of yours. Maybe you could ask around among your fellow workers. Only people you know, though.'

'What do you take me for, Pepiño, darling?'

Carvalho leaned over to the talking door, gave it a playful tap, and replied:

'An expensive call-girl.'

'Thank you, Pepiño. You're so charming.'

'If you find out anything, I'll be in my office till one, and then I'll take a stroll round the billiard halls. I'll be lunching at the Amaya.'

He had no desire to hang about for a question and answer session with Charo. He left her flat intent on enjoying the morning's sunshine and getting to the Ramblas as soon as possible. He let the road carry him down to the harbour, where the April morning light was beginning to get a grip on the city. If he stood still, the heat of the sun made him feel as if he was slowly cooking inside his winter jacket and he needed to cool off. Having drawn new energy from the heat and light, he walked back up the Ramblas. With a burst of energy he went up the wooden steps two at a time. The house that had once been a brothel run by a Madam Petula was now divided into a maze of offices belonging to a variety of small enterprises: wholesalers of *eau de cologne*, solicitors catering for small-time crooks, a commercial agent, a journalist bent on plumbing the depths of the

Barrio Chino with a view to writing an urban realist novel, an ageing lady chiropodist, a dressmaker, a hairdresser's with faithful clients who had been going there since the 1929 Exposition, and a few flats occupied by pelota players from the Colon club and girls from the Barcelona by Night troupe. Carvalho's premises consisted of a small apartment measuring about thirty-five square yards. The office proper was painted green, and had a selection of nineteen-forties office furniture. There was also a tiny kitchen, with a fridge and a small toilet. The major domo of this establishment was an ex-convict by name of Biscuter, who had once shared a prison cell with Carvalho. The detective had never known his real name. Over the years he had occasionally told himself to ask, but the name 'Biscuter' seemed to serve well enough. Biscuter had had an unhealthy fascination with cars — other people's cars. Between the ages of fifteen and thirty he had spent most of his time in prison. He was very short, with the head of a forceps-baby, and was bald in a comical sort of way, with a thick blond growth protruding from above his ears. He had red cheeks and a mealy complexion, thick pendulous pink lips, and cod's eyes. He was proud of his fitness and the way his life was constantly being put to the test in Carvalho's service. They had met in the street a few blocks from the Modelo prison. He'd asked Carvalho for twenty-five pesetas.

'It's for the bus, chief. I've lost my travel card.'

'You're going to get pulled in by the police if they find you hanging around here, Biscuter. Don't you recognize me?'

'Good God — it's the student!'

That was what the prisoners used to call Carvalho when he was inside. He invited Biscuter for a meal, and they reminisced about the meals they had managed to concoct in Lerida prison, with a stove made out of a big tomato tin and a small red-pepper tin equipped with a wick and fuelled by methylated spirits.

'You even managed to make a crab bouillabaisse, chief.'

From the end of Carvalho's sentence to the present day, Biscuter had been in and out of prison many times. He'd been cured of his passion for stealing cars, but his record stuck with him. He would occasionally fall foul of a police round-up, and, being unemployed, would find himself charged under the Vagrant Persons Act.

'If only I could find a job...'

'How would you fancy working for me? You'd be in charge of a small office. You'll make me a coffee or a potato tortilla every now and then, but apart from that your time's your own.'

'I also know how to make béchamel, boss.'

'Fine. I'll even risk eating it. You can sleep in the office. You'll get board and lodging, and I'll give you a couple of thousand pesetas a month for your expenses.'

'And a letter of employment, so's they don't keep picking me up?'

'And a letter of employment!'

From that day to this Biscuter had not left the little Ramblas world that Carvalho inhabited. Occasionally he came in useful for detective work, looking as he did like a down-and-out.

'I'll keep your coffee hot, boss. Brrrm, brrrm!'

Biscuter had the curious habit of accompanying his activities with the noise of a 750cc motorbike. His speciality had been stealing big cars and reselling them in Andorra, but the only thing that Biscuter now retained of his former glories was the language. When he was happy, his lips made a sound like a car exhaust at full throttle, and when he wanted to indicate that all was not well, the 'brrrm brrrm' turned into a disconsolate 'pifff... pifff... pifff'.

'Give me three quarters of a cup, and then take a look to see if Bromide's about.'

'Straight away, boss! Brrrm, brrrm!'

Biscuter knew just how hot to make the coffee to suit Carvalho's delicate palate. His boss didn't like it over-hot. Carvalho drank the coffee slowly as he tried to get San

Francisco on the phone. It appeared that Dieter Rhomberg was out of town, but he had an appointment for a business dinner at the Fairmont that night. The picture of the revolving restaurant on the top floor of the Fairmont, with its Scandinavian buffet and its waitresses who dressed like a cross between valkyries and the girl-next-door in a rather dated musical, unfolded before him. He saw himself going up in the external lift, which looked out over the city, and which slowly unfolded its mysteries — a city seated on pine-clad hills, a city whose downward slopes rushed headlong into the bay below.

'Rhomberg is a lovely man, as long as you don't get put off by his intellectual manner.' So had said the 'lady from Valladolid'. 'He was very fond of Antonio. He'll be able to help you.'

'Bromide's gone to the doctor's, boss. He left a note saying he won't be back before one.'

'What's the matter with him?'

'I don't know. He's gone for a urine analysis.'

'He must be trying to find out about the bromides that he claims the government's putting in everything we eat and drink so as to keep us all off sex.'

'He could have a point there, boss. I haven't had a decent hard-on for months.'

Carvalho picked up the phone again:

'Is that the Urquijo Bank? Can I have the research department...? Colonel Parra, please... Sorry, I mean Pedro Parra...'

At university Pedro Parra had been known as 'Colonel' Parra. He'd been obsessed with the idea of setting up an anti-fascist resistance movement in the mountains, and he used to go training every Sunday, in the hills. He never missed a chance to do a round of press-ups to show off his physique. He would arrange secret assignations in the mountains near the city, always at places which were a sweat to get to, with half your breath spent cursing him and the other half spent trying to get your breath back.

There was not much of that Parra left now. These days he worked as an economic researcher for the Urquijo Bank, and the only hint of the call of the mountains was the triangle of suntan — the mark of the inveterate skier — which his unbuttoned shirt revealed.

'Pepiño — you still in the land of the living?'

'I need your help, Pedro.'

'Same old Pepiño — straight to the point. What's up?'

'I need you to prepare me a report on a multinational. Petnay, in fact. Their operations worldwide, and particularly in Spain. I want what's public knowledge, and what's not.'

'Read any book about the fall of Allende and you'll know all you need to know about Petnay. At least as regards the international side of things. For Spain, I should be able to help. We have people here who specialize in multinationals. What's it all about? You getting back into politics?'

'No way!'

'Maybe we can take this chance for a bit of time together? How about a trip to the mountains, for old time's sake, Ventura?'

'Ventura?'

'You don't mean you've forgotten your *nom de guerre...* ?!'

Bromide set about Carvalho's shoes, and before the detective could say a word he had them shining like new.

'You go round like a rich man, you eat like a rich man, and you spend like a rich man, but your shoes look like a dustman's sandals!'

'Dustmen don't wear sandals.'

'You know what I mean.'

'Listen. Pin back your ears and pay attention, because

this could make you rich. A man's been found dead, near Vich, with no underpants on and a pair of women's knickers in his pocket.'

'Did he run a sausage factory?'

'What do you make of it?'

'Had he been stabbed?'

'No. Shot.'

'Unusual. It sounds something to do with pimps, but usually they tend to use knives. Do we know who the knickers belonged to?'

'Wake up! If they knew whose the knickers were, they wouldn't need a private detective, would they! Keep your ears open, Bromide, and see if something turns up.'

'What kinds of girl would you say he was involved with?'

'Expensive. He was the sort of man who needed to be discreet, and he probably had two or three regular lays.'

'Pepe, I've been in this city for the best part of forty years and I know it like the back of my hand. My kidneys might be shot to hell, but I have very good eyesight. This would be the first time I've ever heard of high-class pimps using guns. Beating someone up, yes — but guns...? There's something odd about it, Pepe. If you were talking about cheap whores, OK — but not when you're talking about the classy end of the market. No, it doesn't sound right to me.'

'I want you to keep your ears open for anything you can find out.'

'As soon as I finish with you, I'll go to the gents. I'll piss what I have to piss, then I'll wash my ears out, and I'll listen all you like.'

'Why did you go to the doctor's?'

'To take him a cigar, what do you bloody think?! I went because I'm ill, very ill. Understand? My kidneys are fucked, my stomach's playing up, and look at the state of my tongue.'

Carvalho suddenly saw a tongue appear down by his knees. It had been ravaged by all the nicotine in the world, and was covered with a white and yellow film.

'Put it away — you're making me ill!'

'Here I am, telling you that I'm ill, and you don't even care! The doctor told me I had to go on a bloody diet. Grilled meat, salads and fresh fruit!'

'I ask you — me, when all I usually have is a vermouth, a tapas of this or that, and a black coffee to get me through the day. I get by on a hundred pesetas a day. If you ask me, they don't think. They wear their brains out studying to make themselves a career, and when they've finished their clients can go fuck themselves, because all they're interested in is the money. Say what you like, but that's the way it is. Look at my brother-in-law. He was feeling a bit rough, so he went to see the doctor. The doctor told him he had cancer. "Don't give me that..." says my brother-in-law. Anyway, three months later he was dead. If you ask me, the reason was just because he *knew* he had cancer. Thousands of people pop off just like that, because one minute you're fit as a fiddle, and then you go to the doctor and he tells you you've got cancer, and the next thing you know you get a cancer from worrying. They never actually cure you of anything, Pepe — particularly not when you get to my age. All they do is tell you what you're going to die of.'

'I thought you were going to see the doctor about the bromides.'

'That creep?! He's been my doctor since... let me see... since the Social Security started, since the days when concierges used to go round dressed like Marshal Goering. I've told him about the bromide hundreds of times, and he just ignores me. Why do you think so many people are dying these days? It's because of the downers the government puts in the water.'

Bromide looked round to make sure nobody was listening.

'Why do you think Franco lasted so long? Because we were all confused. Our heads were in a mess, and it was all because of the bromide they were putting in our water. And in the bread.'

'I thought you didn't like bread or water.'

'Well in the coffee, then. Anyway, what's coffee made from, wine? The water in your coffee — that's where the bromide gets you! I'm telling you, Pepiño, if I had any power in politics — which I haven't — I would make it my business to denounce the scandal of how they were using the bromides under Franco. I thought we were supposed to be living in changing times? Can you imagine a greater abuse of human rights than forcing a whole population to take bromides?'

With his brush in one hand and his rhetoric in the other, even when he was down on his knees polishing people's shoes Bromide's gestures and features took on a certain senatorial dignity.

'I'm going to put you up for the next elections. We'll collect signatures in the *barrio*, and you'll be Senator for the Ramblas.'

'And I'll represent the whores, and the tramps, and the private detectives.'

'Be careful you don't overdo the bromide business, though. They might take you for a Green.'

'What's a Green?'

'They're the people who protest about pollution... air pollution, river pollution, that sort of thing.'

'That's peanuts compared with this bromide business. Why should I worry about whether or not there's trout in the rivers? How many trout have you eaten in your life, Pepe? Come on, how many?'

'Twenty or so.'

'Jesus — and you kick up all this fuss for twenty trout!'

'Bromide, the last thing I need is an argument with you about ecology. Forget it. Let's get back to the corpse, eh?'

'I know, I know... mind your own business... That's always the way it is with you "gentlemen". The minute someone steps on your territory, it's "Hey, you, Bromide, get back where you belong." And that way people end up staying silent all their lives, even though they have things

to say. As I live and breathe, I wrote a letter to General
Muñoz Grande, because people said he was an honest man,
and he was my commanding general during the Russian
campaign. I told him — man to man, old soldier to old
soldier — everything I knew about the bromides. Well, *you*
didn't want to know, and neither did he.'

A thousand-peseta note emerged from Carvalho's pocket.
Bromide caught it without interrupting the violin-bow
action of his brush, and he gave it a look that said he would
find it a safe resting place.

'Don't worry — your word is my command.'

When the final flourishes were over, Carvalho stretched
his legs, admired his shoes, and descended from the throne.
He deposited fifty pesetas in the shoeshine's hand, and
made his way past the darkened billiard tables. A light hood
hung over the table in the corner, where the balls were
conscious of their colour as they rolled — sumptuously
faded whites and menacing reds. An ageing hustler was
chalking his cue with ritual solemnity as his frog-like eyes
lined up the next shot. He had a billiard-player's pot belly.
The sort of pot belly that has to be hoisted up before every
shot so as to get it over the edge of the table. The player
took a measured walk round the table while his opponent
sipped a glass of pastis without taking his eyes off the green
baize. There's no way of telling whether the light is coming
down from the conical metallic lampshade onto the green
baize, or vice-versa. What is certain is that this little theatre
is created by the darkness, and the fat billiard player drives
a ball, follows its crisp course, and as he watches it collide
and click against the others he raises his hand in the hope
of preventing some unforeseen deflection of the ball and in
order to reach for the magic cube of blue chalk which will
give aim and desire to the tip of his cue.

Jauma and Rhomberg were waiting for him outside the
Holiday Inn in Market Street. Carvalho took one more turn
round the parking lot in his VW and finally found a space,
whereupon he was greeted effusively by Jauma, who,
paradoxically, was claiming to be depressed.

'The prospect of a sightseeing trip doesn't really appeal
to me. Just as well that we get back to Vegas at the end of
it. I'm a born gambler. Are you a gambler, Carvalho?'

'No. I sometimes visit the casinos, but once I've lost ten
dollars in the fruit machines I call it a day. As for roulette
and that sort of thing, I don't really understand them.'

'Really?'

'They don't interest me. As I say, it's all Greek to me.'

They left Rhomberg at the Avis counter sorting out the
car hire. Jauma sat in the front passenger seat, and
Carvalho sat — or rather sprawled — in the back. Every
now and then he would interrupt Jauma to point out
something interesting about the San Francisco that they
were now leaving to go to Los Angeles, but the reluctance
with which this information was received was so obvious
that he opted for a state of silent somnolence. He awoke to
find himself being shaken by a smiling Jauma, who was
pointing at something out of the window. The car was
parked at a gas station, and the spectacle was that of Dieter
Rhomberg in conversation with the two young Chicanos
who ran the place.

'Observe the infinite patience of the pure-bred Aryan.'

Rhomberg seemed to be trying to explain something,
and the Chicanos were listening with puzzled interest.
Rhomberg's hands waved in a more or less easterly
direction, and then tried to trace a shape in the air. The
Chicanos repeated his gestures.

'He looks like an explorer trying to enlighten the natives.'

Judging by the flora and the openness of the countryside,
Carvalho concluded that they had travelled a fair way south,
and were probably approaching Carmel.

'Is it far to the beach from here?'

'No. I'd quite fancy having lunch there. Dieter! Dieter! Leave them in their state of ignorance and let's get a move on.'

Dieter shrugged his shoulders in a gesture of didactic impotence and returned to the car.

'What were you talking about?'

'They were asking me where Europe is.'

Rhomberg had an air of resignation tinged with irritation that seemed to strike Jauma as funny. He laughed until the tears ran down his cheeks.

'I don't see what's so funny. They asked me if I was in the movies, and I told them that I was from Germany. They asked me where Germany was. I couldn't believe it! "Didn't you go to school?" Yes, yes, they'd been to school. "Fine. Didn't they teach you where Germany was?" "No." "It's in Europe." Well, they'd *heard* of Europe, but it could have been in the Indian Ocean or the Arctic Circle for all they knew. "Germany, Germany!" I said. "Brandt... ! Adenauer... !" Nothing doing. "Hitler" — oh yes, they knew that Hitler was something to do with Germany. Then they asked me whether Germany is smaller than Mexico or the United States. I ask you! What kind of geography do they teach in this shit country?'

'Rhomberg's indignation reminds me of the eminent geographer Paganal in *The Sons of Captain Grant*, when he discovers that the British colonial teachers had taught their geography in such a way that the natives believed that the whole world was British. The viewpoint of the colonizer and the viewpoint of the colonized. When you work for a big multinational, the world takes on quite different geographical divisions. I could draw you a map representing Petnay's growth over the years, which would stretch over four continents. One of the managers of the British section described it to me one day, as follows: when a Petnay executive farts in Calcutta, the smell can be smelt in Chelsea. I thought it would have been the other way round. When an executive farts in Chelsea, it's a dead cert they'll smell it in Calcutta. You have no idea what goes into a company like Petnay. They gather more information than most governments, and they've got as much political pull as the State Department. The Petnay Empire. Capital: San Francisco.'

'I thought Petnay's headquarters were in London.'

'That's just for show. The real HQ is in San Francisco.'

Rhomberg looked at Jauma reproachfully, but Jauma's eyes were on the passing countryside, as if he was reading the text of his speech off it.

'I find it very relaxing to take a pleasure trip in the company of a socialistically-inclined senior executive and an intelligent fellow countryman. Did you know that Spaniards make the best foremen in the world? Would you agree that this is to be our role in the brave new world?'

'When I was younger I used to think that Spaniards were cut out to be only executioners or their victims. I wasn't aware of our role as foremen.'

'Oh there's no doubt of it. The history of Spain's economic and political emigration is full of foremen. From the nineteenth century onwards Europe and America were supplied with excellent foremen in the shape of Spanish political and economic émigrés. My father went into exile in 1939, and he was a forestry overseer in the south of France, until he had to run from the Germans, from Dieter and his pals.'

Rhomberg's grunt indicated the routine disapproval of a person reacting to an overworked joke.

'That's interesting — my father went into exile in '39 too, and he also ended up as a foreman. In a quarry near Aix-en-Provence.'

'You see? And I've got the explanation. In part it relates to your theory about Spaniards being either executioners or victims. The victim ones are particularly suited to being foremen in foreign countries. They've got the fears of a born loser, the determination of a survivor, and the hardness of a person who knows he can't turn back. I'm the same. I'm a foreman. And Dieter is an inspector of foremen.'

'Are you a loser, a survivor, a man who can't turn back?'

'I would say so, yes. Almost all the students in my year at the Law Faculty have ended up either as labour lawyers of such standing as to merit a ten-line entry in the *Encyclopaedia Sovietica*, or as affluent business lawyers. I was a wanderer, who dedicated himself neither to "defending the working class" nor to making a brilliant social career. I've got a survivor's instinct, and I've got myself a foreman's position in the most powerful multinational in the world. I can't go back. It would mean going back to square one: taking the children out of a nice school with trees round it where they learn French up to the age of ten and English from eleven onwards, not to mention having to give up my chalet, my fifteen-metre yacht, and membership of my golf club. What would Reclus and Quimet do without me?'

'Who?'

'Reclus and Quimet. They're the two sailors that I've hired for my yacht. I keep the boat in the marina at L'Estartit, and I use it once in a while to go for a quick trip to the Medas islands — which, by the way, you can reach just as easily by rowing, or even swimming.'

Spring was multiplying the flowers on the low fences surrounding the wooden houses that were built in the so-called Californian style. Houses of dark, seasoned timber, each with a seal of individuality, in contrast with the mile after mile of prefabricated chalets that they had left behind on entering Carmel. The eucalyptus, orange and lemon trees would have given the place an almost Mediterranean air were it not for the more northerly light, which gave things a sharper edge. As far as Carvalho was concerned, the way this landscape ran down to great long beaches and white sand was as mock as Californian or New York State champagne — a sea and beach that seemed to go on forever, in a bright, unbroken stretch of blue, with rhythmic rolling waves which the arrival of spring would convert into mobile tracks for surfboarders. The beauty of the scenery was also an obstacle to an imaginative transfer to the Mediterranean. Beautiful sands, with not a scrap of litter in sight; beautiful gardens, watered daily; beautiful Anglo-Saxons, white as the sand on the seashore, and always casually dressed, as if life for them was always casual.

The outcome of the phone call to San Francisco was that Carvalho opened the fridge in his office and downed a glass of chilled *orujo*.

'Rhomberg doesn't live here any more.'

'Since last night?'

'Not for several months.'

'I rang last night and someone told me that he'd gone out, but that he'd be back to sleep.'

'Error. He left for an unknown destination.'

'Are we talking about the same person? Dieter Rhomberg. He works for Petnay as an inspector.'

'*Used* to work. He stopped working for Petnay as of two months ago and left for an unknown destination.'

'Didn't he leave a forwarding address?'

'No.'

'Who are you? Who am I talking with?'

'That is none of your business, sir.'

And she hung up on him. The woman's voice was different to the one that had spoken to him the night before. Dieter Rhomberg had disappeared in the space of twenty-four hours, which had now turned into two months. Another glass of *orujo* made it clear that he should not venture a third. Concha Hijar was quite surprised to hear of Dieter Rhomberg's sudden disappearance.

'The two months business is impossible. He rang from

San Francisco, not even two weeks ago, inquiring after me and the children.'

Jauma's widow sounded genuinely surprised.

'Do you have an address for him in Germany?'

'When he's not been on his round-the-world inspection trips he's lived in San Francisco. Especially since his wife died. When she was alive, they used to have an apartment in Bonn. I don't know for sure whether he kept it on, but I believe he did. He had a son who went to live with his sister, and he would go to visit them every once in a while. The sister lives in Berlin.'

One hour later Carvalho knew that Rhomberg's Bonn apartment had been empty for several weeks and that, according to his sister, he had left on a drying-out trip. Dieter had left his job profoundly depressed with his work, and had sent his sister a postcard saying that he was off on a trip round Africa 'in search of the source, not of the Nile, but more of myself'. At the risk of appearing like a TV detective, Carvalho asked Rhomberg's sister if she was sure that the card was from Dieter. The card had been typed, but the style and the signature were Dieter's, she said. At this rate the facts were mounting up, but with no obvious trail in sight. The first phone call had said that he'd popped out and would be back shortly. The second call had said that the German had been touring the world for the past two months. And according to his own sister, the Petnay inspector had sent her a card two or three weeks ago.

'When was that, exactly?'

'I don't have it with me. I gave it to the boy. He keeps all the cards his father sends. I can't ask him for it at the moment, because he's at school.'

It made little difference whether it was two weeks or three. Either the second San Francisco voice was lying, or the whole scenario had a logic which just didn't fit. A senior Petnay executive seems to quit two months previously, remains undecided for a month and a half, writes to his sister, and only finally decides to leave — abruptly — the day after Carvalho's phone call. Carvalho was suspicious as much by nature as by his profession. Rhomberg was obviously very worried about something, he thought, as the morning clouds lifted from his stomach and made way for a sizable hunger. He couldn't decide whether to ask Biscuter to improvise a meal, or whether to walk up the Ramblas in search of a suitable restaurant. A sudden telephonic idleness prevented him from ringing Charo to invite her out, whereupon a restless nervous energy took him to the Ramblas and a thoughtful deliberation regarding a possible choice of restaurant. He had a beer on Plaza Real, and pined after the long-lost tapas that used to be the speciality of the most crowded bar in the neighbourhood — squid in a spicy black pepper and nutmeg sauce. Instead he had to make do with squid floating in a brown, watery liquid, which was all that was on offer under the new management. The problem with cultures of the transient is precisely that they are transient. This restaurant had once witnessed a genius in the art of cooking squid, a man who had created the illusion of a taste that would last forever — but then he had gone, leaving a void. There was no one left who could match his genius. Once lost, a good barman is gone forever — especially these days, when all you need to be a waiter is to wear a white jacket that is dirtier than yesterday's but not as dirty as tomorrow's. As he tormented his brain in mourning for the squid of yesteryear, Carvalho decided to eat at the Agut d'Avignon, a restaurant which he appreciated for the quality of its cooking, but which disappointed by the paucity of its helpings. When Gracian wrote that 'a good experience is doubly enjoyable when it's short-lived', he can't have been thinking of food. Or, if he was, then he must have been one of those intellectuals who are happy living on alphabet soup and eggs that are as hard and egg-like as their own dull heads. More than one musty philosopher has declared that 'man should eat to live, not live to eat', a sentiment nowadays taken up by dieticians, whose principal endeavour seems to consist in the oppression of fat people.

'A soft garlic tortilla to start with, followed by a plate of pork belly, and then codfish *a la llauna*, and a portion of raspberries on their own.'

'On their own?'

'On their own.'

He enjoyed the clitoral look of raspberries, and their fleshy texture and acidity, which was less gritty on the teeth than the mulberry, and with more of a physical consistency than the strawberry. The owner of the Agut d'Avignon had the air of a 1920s dandy who had ruined himself with one mad night of gambling at baccarat and had only been saved by this restaurant, which he seemed to cherish as if it were his wife or a good fountain pen. Carvalho had a vague memory of him wandering about the university campus during the years of the Terror, with his guitar slung across his back and his moustache an irresistible attraction for girls who were wild about music. One night he must have gone into this restaurant with a gang of fellow-students, and, in between one stupid song and another, he must suddenly have realized that a restaurant is the best home that a man can have, and he must have decided to stay forever. Carvalho often saw him in the Boqueria market, casting an expert's eye over the produce, always dressed as if he were about to pose for a postcard in which a young English lord has his arm round the waist of a fresh-faced girl in some Sussex meadow, and over their heads an angel carries a scroll saying: 'I love you, milady.' The owner of the Agut d'Avignon chose the same produce that Carvalho would have chosen, with an aloof self-assurance that was probably explained by the fact that he never said anything, but just pointed at what he wanted to buy. One gesture from this dandy was sufficient for fishmongers and butchers to save the required items for him, and it meant that Carvalho could now eat the best that the market had to offer, complemented by a variety of interesting contributions from the owner's market gardens, which he

cultivated with a sense of professional dignity worthy of
the best of French restaurants. The quality of the food and
the manner in which it was served excused the smallness
of the helpings, which Carvalho attributed not so much to
the owner's meanness as to a desire that all his clients
should be as slim as himself. Even though the total failure
of this crusade was evident for all to see, the clientele
emerged from his restaurant satisfied, because he had
given them the opportunity of respecting the principle of
leaving some space for their supper. A philosophy of life
that Carvalho found abhorrent.

'I was on the point of ringing you, but idleness got the
better of me and I went to eat on my own.'

'You're too kind. And I suppose you fancy a siesta now...'

'What else?'

'Well I've just been to the hairdresser's and I don't want
you messing up my hair.'

'Don't you work on hair-do days?'

'With my clients I wear a wig. Dark brown on Mondays,
Wednesdays and Fridays. Blonde on Tuesdays, Thursdays
and Saturdays. I'll put one on, if you like.'

'No.'

Charo's annoyance turned to good humour. She took
Carvalho's head and kissed him on the lips.

'Poor dear... wicked Charo was going to deny him his
siesta... Come, my darling, come... !'

Charo went off down the corridor, stripping as she went,
and Carvalho's nerves were on edge as he watched the sun
of her arse quivering with each step she took. The half-light
of the bedroom could not hide the richness of her tanned
skin — browned under sun and sunlamps — and her lazy

nipples and a tongue which drove itself between Carvalho's teeth like a karate blow. Charo removed his clothes as if they were the wrappings of some precious gift, and settled herself on his penis while at the same time rubbing his chest with a cheek that was surprising in its smoothness. They moved towards the bedroom, slipping down the corridor together, but slowly, to enjoy the moment of distance and delay. Once in bed, Carvalho sprawled on his back and contemplated the inner passions and virginal blushes that showed in Charo's face. In the floating continuity of their efforts and their caresses, the four walls of the room receded into nothingness, the bond between their sexes became as of steel, and the entire expressive capacities of their bodies became concentrated in their lips and tongues. Lubricated by each other's juices, they thrashed about and ended up scattered, like an open book, held together by hinges of arms and legs. The peace of the ceiling descended on Carvalho as his hand touched Charo's breasts in a penultimate sign of solidarity, an ember of an intense communication that was now setting, like a late evening sun.

Charo respected Carvalho's right to first use of the bathroom, and was not surprised that he felt a sudden urge to flee after making love. As if he had to escape from the scene of a crime.

'I'll ring you,' Carvalho shouted as he pulled on his shoes, while from the other side of the door there came the drumming of the shower water. He appreciated the cooler air of the passageway that led him to the fridge, where a bottle of chilled champagne awaited him. He drank one glass greedily and felt the prickling round his gums as the cool, blond liquid reached deep into his psyche. Out in the hallway he rang Marcos Nuñez, and they made an arrangement to meet at El Sot at midnight.

'When you see fifteen or twenty people listening to someone and looking simultaneously amused and bored, that's where you'll find me. You can be sure that I'll be the one speaking.'

The street was shared between delivery vans and ageing prostitutes in angora wool sweaters. One hand clutching a handbag from which years of sweat had removed the gloss, and the other giving a come-hither gesture, or using a nail to dislodge a piece of stewing steak lodged between her incisor and first molar. This same finger served to touch up her lipstick, or to empty her ear of scurf, of things that itch, and of old ear wax. The van boys divide their time between a lazy coming and going to grocery stores and cavernous bars and the occasional question to the prostitutes:

'How come you've got such big tits, granny?'

'Because your dad used to suck them.'

A drunk is calculating the shortest distance between the roadway and the pavement. Schoolchildren are returning from some mezzanine school where the toilets perfume the whole environment and the children's horizons begin and end with an internal patio divided between the section for the dustbins, a playground for rats and cats, and a number of inside passageways where the washing lines seem to be perennially full. Pots of geraniums on rickety balconies; the occasional carnation; cages containing thin, nervous budgerigars; and butane gas bottles. Notices advertising the services of midwives and chiropodists. An office of the leftwing PSUC. Maite's hairdresser's. A vile smell of frying oil: squid *à la romana*, fried seafood, spicy potatoes, roast lambs' heads, sweetbreads, tripe, rabbit thighs, watery eyes and varicose veins. But Carvalho knew these people and their ways. They made him feel alive, and he wouldn't have changed them for the world, even though at night he preferred to flee the defeated city and make for the pinewood heights. There was nothing to beat the backstreets and alleyways that give onto the Ramblas — tributaries feeding into a river which carries the biology and the history of a city, of the entire world.

Biscuter was making a potato tortilla.

'I'm doing it the way you like it, boss. With a bit of onion and a touch of garlic and parsley.'

Biscuter improvised an eating space on Carvalho's office desk, and the detective applied his mind to the quarter of tortilla filling his plate. Biscuter sat in front of him, tucking into another quarter and waiting for some word of appreciation.

'You can't say that it hasn't turned out well, eh, chief? If you're still hungry I've made you a bit of brain paté with *ratatouille*. It's good, isn't it, boss?'

'True.'

'God, you're stingy, boss. I think it's brilliant. And wait till you taste the *ratatouille*. It's a treat! Oh — I forgot. There was a phone call from Pedro Parra — the "colonel", he called himself. He said: "Don't forget, tell him that the 'colonel' rang. Tell him he'll have what he was looking for tomorrow, if he calls in at the bank." And there's a telegram too. I didn't open it.'

'Am arriving Barcelona Wednesday. Rhomberg.'

'Do me a bit of the paté.'

'I suppose you won't need any supper after this, eh, boss? You eat like a pig, and you still manage to stay trim. But it all goes into your blood, you know, and you end up with cholesterol...'

'I'm surrounded by doctors! First Bromide, and now you! Stop worrying about the cholesterol and get on with your food.'

'I was only saying it for your own good.'

'And will you be eating again after this little snack?'

'Of course. The left-overs will do fine for my supper. I don't know what's up with me, boss. I'm feeling depressed. I'm sleeping badly. I've been remembering my mother.'

Biscuter dried his eyes with his serviette, but they were still brimming with tears which threatened to spill into the green and red of the *ratatouille*.

'Find yourself a girlfriend, Biscuter. Or a prostitute. Or

have a wank every now and then. You'll find it does wonders.'

'You say find a prostitute, but that's not so easy. They just treat me as a joke. When they say, "Come on, baldy, pull your willy out so that I can give it a wash," I just want to laugh. And as for wanking, as you put it, I'm at it non-stop. First with one hand, then with the other. I even use the numb-hand system. I go to bed and lie down on top of my hand, so as to cut off the circulation, and it goes all numb. Then it feels not like my hand at all, but like something else...'

'Have you ever tried it with a piece of raw meat?'

'No.'

'You've missed something.'

With one eye on Biscuter and the other on Rhomberg's telegram, Carvalho reached for the phone. This was the signal for Biscuter to clear the table. An inexplicable sense of misgiving prevented Carvalho from informing Jauma's widow of Dieter Rhomberg's unexpected resurrection.

To arrive at a bar where the principal spectacle is the clientele, and to have to go down the stairs to centre-stage, tends to endow your shoulders with the stance of the lead actor in a New York movie, and your legs with the tension of a tightrope walker. Up until two in the morning the place is populated by two or three couples trying to escape bachelorhood or married life. From two onwards it's taken over by mainstream actors from the fringe theatre and fringe actors from the mainstream, not to mention executives with a smattering of culture and sensibility, and people who would be film directors if the film industry wasn't such an industry, and writers of protest songs and the ubiquitous political cartoonist, and so on.

'To live in Barcelona is to live in Europe!'

A poet and ex-prisoner seeking in El Sot a double life that will give him back part of the twenty-five years spent in prison; an extremely young official of the workers' commissions, with grey eyes; organizational and petitional ladies of the local Left; professional night-owls of more than thirty years' standing, ever hoping for that one night in which everything will prove possible; a homosexual novelist; a concrete poet who has read Trotsky; a chairman of political round-table discussions, the owner of just the right magic gesture to make sure people take it in turns to speak, and who can conjure up a synthesis where there wasn't even a thesis to start with; the occasional sensitive intellectual who turns up in the hopes of l'amour fou — something even hardened regulars of the place have never achieved; ex-politicos still into things more or less ethical; young islanders from one or other of the islands; wild and soon-to-be-rich youth; Uruguayans fleeing the terror in Uruguay; Chileans fleeing the terror in Chile; Argentinians fleeing successive terrors in Argentina; one of Carillo's ten right-hand men; an almost young ex-industrial engineer now publishing independent and radical-Marxist thinkers; a few leftovers of the 1940s, nourished on a diet of Stefan Zweig; puritan left-wing cadres intent on coming into contact with the decadent and definitely scandalous Barcelona Left for just one night. Cocktails somewhere between the low level of a mediocre bar in Manhattan and the abysmal level of Barcelona cocktail bars. A space that is divided into functional seating areas with differing degrees of intimacy, and a bar where people strike up conversations with the owner and the bartenders with a degree of camaraderie that reflects a nightly familiarity and the certainty that afterwards there will be a whole day to wash away its after-taste.

On this particular night the gathering around Marcos Nuñez was only ten strong, and the ageing youth was holding forth with his habitual sibylline style and a narrative rhythm acquired in his university days. A tone which is capable of imbuing even the story of a broken-down bus with sublime nostalgia, or firing wicked irony into the description of a Spanish sausage. Nuñez had been a pioneer in the reconstruction of the Left in Barcelona University during the nineteen fifties. After torture, and spells in prison, he had fled to France, where he had embarked on a life that would have made him ideal material for the bureaucracy of his own party, or a doctorate in social science and an assured place in a future democratic Spain. Too cynical to be a bureaucrat and too apathetic to be an academic, he plumped for the role of an onlooker, a role which he exercised with a dedication that was half-hearted only in appearance. Nuñez was one of the old guard, and he remained attached to the vision of moral renewal held by the Left when Franco was alive. His capacity for friendship was immense, in the giving and the taking alike, both of which he executed with a hint of sadism; he was given to verbal aggression when describing friends or enemies, and there was a certain personal angst in his frenetic adjectival acrobatics.

Carvalho went down the last of the stairs separating him from the gathering, and waited in the hope that during one of his leisurely eyebrow raisings Marcos Nuñez would raise at least one eye sufficiently to notice his presence. Some of the faces were familiar to him from his university days, and he even managed to put names to them with a fair degree of success. He was aware that people were trying to work out who he was. Carvalho came closer to the group and stopped when his eyes met those of Nuñez. He guessed that he was about to invite him to join the group, and pre-empted the invitation by indicating that they needed to speak in private. Nuñez did not break off his discourse immediately; he first cropped its wings and then killed it with a few well-turned phrases which caused a lady equipped with the large eyes of a nocturnal animal to laugh.

'You're a cynic, and you like people telling you so.'

'Me? A cynic? I'm such a simple soul that you could twist me round your little finger.'

Nuñez got up and followed Carvalho to an adjoining room in which two married couples were drinking a double scotch with ice but no water, a gin and tonic, and a vodka and orange.

'You seem to keep yourself amused.'

'If I keep myself amused I don't get bored. I see it as preventive medicine.'

'I was wondering whether you could help me with an inquiry. I've been trying to track down a man who was an inspector for Petnay — a friend of Antonio Jauma — Dieter Rhomberg. Do you know him?'

'I know the name. Jauma used to say that he had the biggest penis in the world.'

'The day before yesterday he was in San Francisco. But then, this morning, they told me that he'd disappeared two months ago, and that his whereabouts were unknown.'

'Are you sure he was in San Francisco?'

'A voice told me, "He's gone for dinner at the Fairmont, and he'll be back later." Then, the day after, another voice told me that he'd gone on leave and disappeared. Anyway, you've hardly told me anything about Jauma's life and habits. What sort of people did he mix with?'

'In part old friends from the university, particularly the ones who had achieved a social status similar to his own. Not because this was what Jauma particularly wanted, but because circumstances dictated it. Of those of us who haven't made it, only I and one other ex-comrade still have dealings with him.'

'As friends? Or politically?'

'Jauma's only remaining link with politics was financial. He used to contribute to Party funds. Occasionally we would discuss things to do with the unions and the labour movement. He didn't want problems with his workers, and he used to ask our advice. The last political talk we had together was when the embryo of new organizations began appearing in his firm, operating outside the Comisiones Obreras. Anarchists for the most part.

'Had he had labour problems recently?'

'No. But he would have had, sooner or later. He usually showed his face in only a small number of the concerns under his control, but he always took special care in choosing his personnel managers, and he would follow every dispute, however small, very closely.'

'Because he had a moral itch?'

'Partly. He had a particular conception of history that he couldn't get rid of, if you know what I mean. In other words, his political upbringing told him that the working class was always right, and that he was an administrator of a capitalism that was on the defensive. He also had an image problem. He didn't want to lose the image that he had of himself, but the image was in contradiction with the reality — that he was an exploiter. Inevitably he became paternalistic. He would go to his employees' weddings. Or when he saw that one of his workers was having a hard time with domestic problems, he would give him a couple of days off.'

'Curious — a manager in a multinational company behaving like he was the boss of a family firm. Tell me, did you think highly of him?'

Nuñez laughed a controlled laugh.

'I'll show you a photograph of our year at university. In it you'll see six students who were inseparable. I would say that, in some ways, we'll always be dependent on each other for our identities. Each one of those other five holds a part of my identity, and I hold a part of theirs. It's like a jigsaw puzzle. Between us we could do a reconstruction of what were the best years of our lives — if you leave aside the political persecution, the brutality that you laid yourself open to, and the darkness ruling the country. We could go for years without seeing each other, and then we could meet and just pick up where we'd left off. Not completely, obviously, but in relation to the past, yes.'

'Were you the hero?'

'The martyr. They idealized me during the period when I was in exile. They didn't expect me to return in such a cynical frame of mind. They found it a bit of a disappointment, and reacted rather bitterly. But in the end they accepted me for what I was. Partly because I offered them the certainty that I would never take from them anything they had, and that I lead a modest life, with just one sweater, two pairs of jeans, and a couple of shirts. Perhaps they would have preferred me to have had more power. *They* have power — economic, political, cultural, moral, what have you. I have no power, though. No power at all.'

'I'd be interested in seeing that photo, and who was in it. Maybe we could lunch together tomorrow. Where do you suggest?'

'There's a little French restaurant downtown, where you can eat something unique. A *confit d'oie* that the lady of the house brings in from Périgord.'

Carvalho was beginning to see Marcos Nuñez as a fellow human being.

During the drive up to his house at Vallvidrera, Carvalho was barely aware of being behind the wheel. Memories of his university days came flooding back, and in particular the memory of Marcos Nuñez's influence on the generations of students that came after him. The story of Nuñez's resistance to the Brigada Social, and how he had been the 'first red student' of the post-War period and the organizer of the first university cadres, went hand in hand with a reputation as an intellectual.

'Malibran says that he has great powers of synthesis, which complement useful powers of analysis.'

Those were the days when Professor Malibran used to apportion powers of analysis and synthesis among his students as if he were Ceres sharing out the fruits of the earth. When his judgment descended on a student, it was as if the apostolic ball of fire had passed above him. He would hear the nasal voice of the professor thunder from the heavens: 'This is my well-beloved student, in whom I have laid all my hopes in matters of analysis and/or synthesis.' Marcos Nuñez was the principal point of reference in the martyrology of the student resistance, and his travels in France and Germany were followed from Spain as if they were the voyage of one of God's apprentices to the source of definitive knowledge. By the time Carvalho came to be arrested, tried, and sentenced, the history of the resistance in the universities was still seen as having begun with Marcos Nuñez: 'I was in the fourth year after Nuñez.'

Dozens of more or less adolescent faces loomed up from the past. Those evenings at Juliana's. All of them with very little money, welcomed to a big house in the old part of Barcelona, with a portrait on the wall of Alfonso XIII standing next to a member of the family who had been a bishop, and antique furniture, and Bach and Shostakovich, and Montand singing:

C'est nous qui brisons les barreaux de prisons pour nos frères.

La Mancha cheese, cheap wine and *chorizo*, discussions about attacking first-level contradictions, furtive contacts between hands and brains. Then came the first ideological differences, and the first acts of political militancy. 'Colonel Parra' was arrested a few weeks before Carvalho, only to be set free seventy-two hours later. Then he told his epic tale, and most people found it very impressive, particularly when he told how he had deliberately stubbed out a cigarette on his hand to test how he would react to torture. 'Colonel' Parra wrote a report, and it was read religiously at all the student meetings, where it was generally well received. For Carvalho, the incident would have made an excellent sequence for an anti-German film with James Cagney and Richard Conte. Later he was to discover for himself that torture creates an entirely personal and unshareable dialectic, where the only rule that applies is one's ability to resist and not say anything that might destroy one's own dignity. Once your dignity is broken, you become a plaything in the hands of your torturers.

And what a quantity of culture! All the books that you had to have read, and the intellectual debates that had to be followed! The polemic in the French Communist Party between Naville and Lefebvre. To hell with the pair of them! The act of parking his car at the gate of his villa converted all this into a handful of broken images, as if a mental magic mirror had fallen to the floor and shattered. One hand for his mail and the other to keep his balance as he climbed the muddy steps. The first smells arising from the earth and the shrubbery with the approach of rain. He opened the door and dumped what he was carrying. Wide awake and relaxed, he contemplated the bookcase in the corridor, where an irregular array of books was taking up space, sometimes upright and tightly packed, and sometimes falling all over the place, or with their titles the wrong way up. He hunted out Sartre's *Critique of Dialectical Reason*, Sholokov's *Quietly Flows the Don* and Sacristan's *Essays on Heine*. He went over to the fireplace, tearing up the books with the relaxed expertise of one who is well practised, and arranged the dismembered tomes in a little pile, on top of which he placed dry twigs and kindling wood. The flames caught at once and spread rapidly, and as the printed matter burned it fulfilled its historical mission of fuelling fires that were more real than itself.

To eat or not to eat, that was the question.

'Cholesterol, boss...!'

Two in the morning. It was raining gently, and the night was filled with the smell of damp pine-leaves and the sound of flames crackling and the rain falling on the ivy that covered most of the garden like a green mantle.

A contortion of his bowels drove him to the toilet. As he went, he picked up a thriller by Nicholson — *The Case of the Smiling Jesuit* — and a newspaper. The advantage of living on your own is that you can shit with the toilet door open, Carvalho thought to himself as he strained his bowels. Having overcome his intestinal resistance, as he awaited a second offloading of faecal detritus he read ten lines of one of the most contrived detective stories ever written. The murder of an ex-girlfriend from his youth provides the narrator with a pretext for a long journey through his past as a British soldier in India. A dog's dinner made up of bits of Bromfield's *And the Rains Came*, Hesse's fascination with oriental religions, and Agatha Christie. A curious book altogether. Final intestinal peace coincided with his arrival at the end of a chapter. He filled the bidet and went in search of the arts review pages in the newspaper, and on recent trends in Polish theatre by Fernando Monegal, who was Carvalho's favourite, partly because of the absorbent qualities of the paper, but also because of the equally absorbent qualities of what was printed on it. One could say that a wonderful synthesis was effected between the paper and the article in leaving his arse suitably prepared for the final act of ablution in the bidet. Having taken his trousers off, Carvalho decided to go the whole hog and strip off. He grabbed a dressing gown off the toilet door and decided to broach the question of what to eat. As he gazed at a cupboardful of tinned food, he was caught between the simplicity of just having hot milk and the alchemical possibilities of actually cooking something at that hour of the night. What could he have? How about pasta? He sought out the necessary ingredients from the fridge and from the little larder next to the cupboard. The pork chop was salted slightly, and then subjected to the rigour of a small quantity of oil sizzling in the earthenware casserole. Then came a diced potato, grated onion, pepper and tomato. Once the frying was under way, Carvalho added a little salt and paprika before putting in the pasta and giving it a turn in the pan. It was time to pour in the broth, to a depth of about half an inch. When the broth began to simmer, Carvalho added four slices of thick *butifarra* sausage and just before removing the pan from the flame he gave the final touch, a pinch of garlic and pimento fried separately. He had learned this way of cooking pasta with black *butifarra* from the nuns in a convent where he had gone into hiding at the end of the 1950s after the discovery of his party's printing press. The nuns would leave his food on a long, scrubbed wooden table, the most beautiful table Carvalho had ever seen in his life. Carvalho still had a soft spot for nuns, a throwback to his childhood days, when he had attended a school run by the nuns of St Vincent of Paul.

'José, what do you want to be when you grow up?'

'A saint.'

'Like St Tarsicio?'

'Yes, like St Tarsicio. Or like St Genevieve of Brabant.'

'You'd have to be like St Tarsicio, because you're a boy. St Genevieve was a woman.'

At that time he'd had no idea that angels were one sex or the other.

'Pardon me, sir. Excuse my asking... would you happen to be going to Barcelona?'

'Yes.'

'My car's broken down. I saw you pulling in to eat, and

THE ANGST-RIDDEN EXECUTIVE

I wondered whether you could give me a lift.'

The owner of the voice was short and, in the opinion of
Dieter Rhomberg, had too much hair. He ran his eye over
the man's neatly-trimmed beard and unassuming suit.

'I'm a travelling rep for a sports equipment firm, and I've
seen everyone I had to see round here. I was on my way
home, and I thought, if it's no bother for you...'

'No, no bother at all.'

'I fancy a bite too. I'll sit at that table over there, and
when you're ready to go, you just tell me.'

'Why don't you join me at my table?'

'That's very kind of you. I'd be delighted.'

The man gave a sigh of relief as he sat down.

'You've saved my life, you know. If I don't get home
tonight I'd have a hell of a job convincing the wife that it
was because the car broke down.'

'Doesn't she trust you?'

'No. And with good reason.'

He gave a knowing wink. A huge gold signet ring and a
slender wedding ring glittered side by side on one finger.

'It's because of my job. Swimming pools, tennis courts,
and so on. Would you like my card?'

'It's unlikely that I'll ever need it. I'm a foreigner. Just
passing through.'

'I thought you sounded a bit foreign. You speak very good
Spanish, though.'

'I come here quite often.'

'Well keep my card anyway. One of these days you might
want to buy a villa in Spain. Just ring me. Juan Higueras
Fernandez, at your service.'

'Peter Herzen.'

'Peter? That sounds English.'

'I'm German. Peter's the same in English and in German.'

The waiter brought Rhomberg his steak and salad.

'I'll have just a portion of cod. I have an ulcer.'

Two different types of pill appeared on the table.

'I keep my daily dose in my pocket. That way I don't forget.

Otherwise I find I've left them in my suitcase, or left them behind somewhere, and then I'm in trouble. When you have too many things banging around in your brain, that's when you get ulcers, and worse! You look pretty healthy, though. You obviously look after yourself. Steak... salad... Do you do any sports?'

'I do what I can. Swimming, mainly.'

'Very healthy. A real all-round sport. Imagine it, though — I spend all my time round swimming pools and I can't even swim. What kind of schooling did they ever give us? A bit of reading, a bit of arithmetic, and that was that. If you wanted physical exercise, you'd get it kicking a ball around in the street. Or a tin can on a bit of open space — in the days when you could still find a bit of open space. Kids today are something else, though. My boy's taking swimming lessons. Twice a week. When we go to the beach in the summer I feel a bit of an idiot, because he takes to the water like a fish, and I'm left paddling about on the beach with my trousers rolled up.'

He ate his meal quickly so as to catch up with Rhomberg.

'There's one thing I won't give up, though — ulcer or no ulcer — and that's my coffee.'

He got up, excused himself, and went over to the waiter. Rhomberg saw him take out his wallet and point to the table, and realized that he was about to pay for their meal. The German got up to protest, but was too late to stop him.

'It's the least I can do, seeing you've just about saved my life.'

The man commented on how comfortable the BMW was.

'It's not mine. It's a hire car.'

'You've started your holidays early! It's still spring!'

'This was the only time I could get free.'

'Things don't always turn out the way we want them, do they? Listen, would you mind if I stretch out on the back seat for a bit? It's my ulcer. It helps if I can rest up for a while after a meal.'

Rhomberg settled himself at the wheel. He carefully

adjusted his seat belt and then turned around. The man fitted along the length of the seat just nicely. He had his hands folded on his stomach and gave him a contented smile.

'This is brilliant. Like travelling in a sleeper-car.'

They left the service area and joined the motorway. It was a good seventy kilometres to Barcelona. Dieter put his foot down, and glanced in the rearview mirror to check that his travelling companion wasn't alarmed by the speed. The man seemed to be absorbed in staring at the roof, or perhaps he was dozing with his eyes half closed. Dieter would have liked to get his business with Carvalho over with as soon as possible, so as not to have to spend a night in Barcelona. He wanted to reach Valencia in one haul, and then, the next day, get the car on a ferry for Oran. In his mind he mulled over the best way to approach Carvalho — giving him enough information to convince him, but not so much as to compromise himself. He felt his whole body in the grip of a fear that was compounded by his sense of personal isolation. He felt the anxiety tighten in his throat, and found himself murmuring the name of his dead wife — Gertrude — under his breath. His eyes became misty with self-pity. Then he thought of his son, and the pain became too much.

'The boy's too attached to me,' he said, more or less out loud.

He had once read of a writer who had fled the Soviet Union. Before leaving, he had made a point of mistreating his son during their last year together so that the boy would remember him with loathing and not with longing. He had done more or less the same himself. He had cut the boy out of his life as if he was an encumbrance, but the boy had repaid him with idolatry. He kept his father's letters and photos as if they were holy relics. He asked his aunt to alter his father's jackets, so that he could wear them. He'd fallen under the same spell of love as Gertrude had.

'I suppose it had to happen sooner or later.'

Later on, when he was somewhere safe, he would get

someone to call the boy. But maybe it would be too late, and he'd find that his son didn't want to know him.

'You're going too fast.'

This came from behind him. It took a moment for the exact tone of the words to sink in. Then he connected with them, got annoyed, and turned round. The man had sat up, and Dieter caught a glimpse of the muzzle of a gun which was held just out of his reach.

'Take it easy, Fritz. Slow down and pull into the next layby. You'll see a big blue P. That means "parking". No tricks, mind you, because I might just take your ear off. Just park up, nice and easy.'

'What do you want? I've hardly any money on me. I travel with travellers cheques and credit cards.'

'We'll see. You just park, and then we can have a little chat.'

Dieter clung to the hope that there might be other people parked in the layby to help him. He saw the blue P sign coming up, and he slowed down. He was heartened to see another car parked there.

'Stop right here.'

He braked abruptly, sending up a little cloud of dust. The man kept his distance, and kept the gun pointed at his head.

'You can see for yourself. I'll give you my wallet. You can look in my luggage.'

'Give me the card I gave you. Throw it over.'

There was a sign of movement from the other car. A man got out and came over towards them. The short man stayed just as he was. The other man was thickset and solidly built, and when he reached their car he leaned down to look in.

'Is that him?'

'Yes.'

'You sure?'

'Sure.'

'Are you Dieter Rhomberg?'

'Are you the police?'

The man behind him shouted — 'You — turn round!' Dieter turned to look, and as he turned he saw the flash of something in the man's hand as a razor slit his throat like a knife going through butter.

Carvalho was jerked to full wakefulness by the surprise of seeing Bromide outside of his usual habitat of the Monforte and its neighbouring bars. There he was, standing at the front door of his house in Vallvidrera, kitted out with a tie, a three-piece suit, and extra-shiny shoes. He was accompanied by an athletic-looking youth with the figure of a Florentine statue.

'Can we come in, Pepiño?'

'For God's sake, Bromide — you look like you're dressed for a first communion!'

'The occasion demands it. This is a friend of mine, to do with what you were asking me about yesterday. What's more, the weather's nice, so I thought to myself, a nice day in the country, go and pay Pepiño a visit.'

The athletic youth had the air of a professional paranoiac, because as he came into the house he first peered into every corner and then stepped back to the door to check the garden. Then he followed Carvalho and Bromide. But he wouldn't sit in an armchair; instead he leaned up against a chair and studied Carvalho, as if trying to get the measure of him.

'This friend of mine knows everything there is to know about arguments and problems between pimps, their women, troublesome customers, and so on. Anything you want to know, just ask.'

'Why — does he run a pimp's agency?'

'No. He's a pimp too. Better sort of class, though. He's a

stunt man in the movies. One of those who go round crashing cars and throwing themselves down stairs. He's an athlete. Show my friend your biceps.'

The young man fended off the temptation with a sweep of his hand, but couldn't avoid a smile.

'Sure — I know — you didn't come here to do circuit training! I presume Bromide has told you about the man they found murdered at Vich, and the women's knickers, and so on. What do you know about all this?'

'Nothing.'

'Do you think the killing had sexual motives?'

'We never kill a client. If one of them goes too far with the girls and starts getting disgusting, we might give him a bit of a fright. If he hits a girl, for instance, or something like that. OK, there are always fights between rival pimps — like when somebody's screwing somebody else's girl — but killing a client would be like killing the goose that lays the golden egg.'

'What about the knickers in his pocket?'

'There's something odd about them.'

'Do you say that because it's your personal impression, or because you've got proof?'

'What do you mean?'

'I mean, did you say what you said because that's your opinion, or have you been making inquiries among your colleagues?'

'I asked. From what they told me, nobody knows anything.'

'What about outside Barcelona?'

'Nothing happens outside Barcelona. A bit of small-time sleaze in some of the industrial towns, but there's nothing going on there that we don't find out about, sooner or later.'

'He's amazing, Carvalho. He knows everything there is to know. They call him the "Golden Hammer", because he's got a cock that strikes like a hammer and shines like gold.'

Once again Bromide's friend shrugged off the compliments, but couldn't contain a self-satisfied smile.

'Some people might think that I spend my time just screwing and pimping. I've got a trade now though, so I've started running down the business with the girls, and nowadays I only do a bit here and there.'

'He started at fairs, doing handstands on bar stools, on the edge of a coin, that sort of thing. Shame he wouldn't show you his muscles. And he used to have all the girls chasing him. So in the end he decided to have a slice of the action himself. How many girls are you running nowadays, Hammer?'

'Six or seven. You don't want to overdo it, because you find that you can't keep up with them, and there's a lot of competition about. Also, these days women aren't as easy to handle as they were in your day, Bromide. In those days, give them a wallop and they'd be good as gold. These days, you have to work on their psychology. With one of them you have to be nice to her kid. Another might need bringing into line. Another might have a mother in a wheelchair, and you have to find her a masseuse. And another might be epileptic. The girls don't tend to get knocked about so much these days, but sometimes people try worse things. You have to guarantee them a full-time protection service.'

'You'll end up running a union, Hammer.'

Carvalho could stomach just about anything, but he drew the line at pimps. For him they were like dog-ticks — loathsome little insects grown fat from feeding on someone else's blood. The athlete had the face of an evil-looking lamb, and the innocence of a micro electronic computer.

'Let's get back to the corpse. Why are the police claiming that it was a sex revenge killing?'

'I'm sure they've got their reasons. It doesn't add up, though.'

'It doesn't matter if it makes sense or not. One day they'll take one of you in and wring a confession out of him.'

'You'd have to be very stupid to own up to something like that. And anyway, people don't just own up of their own accord. When they pick up a pickpocket, they stick him with

every unsolved case in the book. But they know very well
that pimps don't kill clients. They might give a customer a
fright, or a good kick in the crutch, or blackmail him, but
even this happens only rarely, because you get a lot more out
of happy customers than you do out of blackmail. What does
happen, though, is that sometimes you get a young pimp
who's too clever for his own good, and wants to make a fast
buck. He has to be brought into line, and we take care of
that.'

'What about the knickers, then?'

'All for show. Believe me.'

'You mean it's not your style?'

'I can only think of one case. A dirty old shitter. The sort
who likes to shit on girls, or gets them to shit on him. If it's
OK by the girl, he can shit away to his heart's content. But
if she doesn't want to, he's got no right to force her. Anyway,
we had a shitter on our hands. We warned him. He tried it a
second time, with another girl. And another. One day we
took his underpants, filled them with shit, and sent them to
his home address, with a card that said: "A Souvenir from
Lulu". And he never came back.'

'How about it, Pepe, don't we get a drink?'

'What do you fancy, Bromide?'

'One of those wines you're always drinking.'

'What about yourself?'

'I don't drink, thanks. If I start in the morning, I'd be at it
all day, and I have to work at night. I'll have a glass of mineral
water. Non-fizzy. Or a pear juice, please.'

Carvalho brought up from his cellar a 1969 Côte du
Rhône, and Bromide watched him preparing to open it,
with his Adam's apple bobbing up and down in expectation
as if he was about to embark on some fantastic adventure.

'Are you opening that bottle just for me, Pepiño?! What is
it, French?'

In the morning light the wine looked a little sleepy, like
the face of a girlfriend who's still half asleep and still smells
of bed. The Valles light gave an edge to the wine's warm red

colour, and Bromide's dirty white tongue slurped the wine down.

'This is a hell of a wine, Pepiño. And how am I ever going to be able to drink another wine after this? They'll all taste like tap water!'

'Think of this as your first communion, Bromide.'

'Can I drink all of it?'

'All of it.'

'You don't owe me anything any more, Pepiño. What you've done for me here is better than all the tea in China. When I was in the Blue Division, one time they gave us a whole case of white Rhine wine. Very good it was. But we were just kids, and we didn't appreciate it. Some of them said that it wasn't a patch on Valdepeñas. The ignorance of youth! They gave it to us at Christmas, just before they sent us off to the Russian front. Then they wanted us to put on a guard of honour so that General Muñoz Grandes could review us. Well, I'm telling you, the soberest one among us was leaning like the Tower of Pisa! Anyway, Muñoz Grandes passed in front of us, stiff as a rod, and he didn't like what he saw. Some creep shouted "Arriba España", to sober us up and get us to stand straight, but instead we just fell about in heaps, pissing ourselves laughing — I mean *really* pissing ourselves! Because our bellies were hot and our peckers were cold! And that's a wicked combination, Pepiño, wicked...'

A strikingly modernist flight of steps led up to two large carved wooden doors with gilded fittings. In the reception area a porter was sitting reading Luiz Cernuda's *Reality and Desire*. Carvalho, being a man who was suspicious of life's surprises, found himself momentarily in a state of suspended animation as he read and re-read the title of the book. Thereupon the porter raised an ironic smile over the book in his hands, and murmured:

'Can I help you?'

'Pedro Parra, please.'

The porter used a bone paper-knife to mark his place, and shut the book as if it were the most precious thing in the world. He led Carvalho to a small waiting room and the detective barely had time to decide between *Cambio 16* and *Triunfo* as his reading matter before Pedro Parra appeared in the doorway, looking every inch a real colonel, with the air of someone about to give a crucial order. Despite the chilly spring weather, or possibly thanks to a de luxe central heating system, the economist-colonel was in his shirt-sleeves. He stood there, began to laugh, and slapped Carvalho on the back as if he were a lumpy mattress. The intervening years had done nothing to lessen his likeness to Rosanno Brazzi. He was greying elegantly, had the complexion of a mountain climber and skier, and beneath his shirt you could see the results of his daily work-out, one-two, one-two, in-out, in-out, in front of an open window every morning, summer or winter, rain or shine.

'All that's missing is the uniform.'

'A general's uniform. If twenty-odd years ago you used to call me "colonel", then I must surely be a general by now. It might even still happen. There'll be a guerrilla war soon, and that's a good time to go up in the world.'

'A guerrilla war? Your only chance of going up in the world would be if you went and climbed the front of the Senate House!'

'Still the same old knife-in-the-ribs Carvalho. But what have you been doing with yourself all this time? The last I heard was that when you came out of prison you went off travelling. They told me you were a private detective. Bogart-style, like in the films.'

'Nothing so glamorous. Runaway adolescents. Jealous husbands wanting their wives trailed.'

'Sounds a pretty reactionary job to me.'

'No more reactionary than gathering economic statistics for the financial oligarchy.'

'No need to get personal! Don't forget I'm gathering statistics for you too. Here, I've prepared you a rundown on Petnay's activities in Spain and its immediate ramifications. For example, part of their Latin American activities is controlled from Spain. Another part is controlled from San Francisco, and now they're setting up a third head office, in Chile, in Santiago. As regards their key personnel, I would make a distinction between the managers and the politicians. Sometimes the two coincide, but not always. Unlike other companies, Petnay almost never conducts its negotiations via state apparatuses — through diplomacy, for example. They have their own network, and only turn to the State Department in the last resort.'

'Who's in charge of things in Spain now?'

'Antonio Jauma. He represents management's public face. But somewhere close to him there must be the politico — the one who goes to talk to ministers, pulls strings and so on.'

'Well, just for a start, Antonio Jauma has been murdered, so someone else must be running the show now.'

'Our records aren't entirely up to date.'

'Carry on, then. Who's the politico?'

'Nobody knows. Or at least very few people know.'

'Who's going to be taking over from Jauma?'

'How long ago did he die?'

'A month and a half. No — a bit more...'

'It's probably a temporary stand-in. Companies like Petnay don't make this kind of decision overnight. I'll go and phone someone to find out.'

'Hang on. The porter in reception... Do you only hire porters with degrees in literature? He was reading *Reality and Desire*.'

'What's that? You know I'm just a humble economist.'

'The collected poems of Cernuda.'

'Oh, right. He's a poet. A porter poet. He's had a few books published, in fact.'

While he waited for Parra to return, Carvalho found himself thinking of other poets with unusual jobs. Emilio Prados, in exile, working as a playground supervisor for children in a secondary school in Mexico. Or the poet who ended up teaching infants in a school in Tijuana. Carvalho had met him in a bar at the border, as he was drinking tequila solos, with salt, interspersed with a sip of water and bicarbonate.

'I'm not coming back,' he had said, 'until Franco's dead. It's a question of dignity. Maybe I am nothing here — but at least I have my pride. You'll find me in a few pre-War anthologies. The name's Justo Elorza — have you ever heard of me? No? I've only just had the chance to start being published again. I went from the Argeles to Bordeaux. Then I got on a boat, to Mexico. I ended up in Tijuana. A temporary teaching job in a school. Temporary! Thirty years, my friend, thirty years! Every time I heard a rumour that Franco was ill, or that he was about to be toppled, I gave up shaving, I packed my bags, and I stopped changing the sheets, so that I had even more reason to leave. Several months ago I just gave up. I've got twenty books of unpublished poems. I went to Mexico to talk with the Era publishing house. Renau, the mural painter, is a good friend of mine. He's in East Germany now. Anyway, the woman at Era is the sister of Renau's brother-in-law. They've suggested I do an anthology. Imagine it — an anthology of poems that have never been published!'

A growth of white stubble round his chin, the looks of the poet Machado but with a stomach peppered with ulcers, one lens of his glasses more or less covered with sticking plaster so as to concentrate his vision in his one good eye, a stained shirt that had once been white but was now yellow, a rim of dirt round a frayed collar and the pervasive smell of old man's sweat, a pervasive smell of an animal which is soon to die.

'There's a standing committee of three or four Petnay inspectors who will advise the company on Jauma's successor. They'll stay here for another couple of weeks, and then they'll leave Martin Gausachs in charge. He was Jauma's second in command.'

'Do you know the man?'

'A meteoric career. He was four years behind me at university, studying law. Won all sorts of prizes as a student. Then he went to MIT and returned as a professor of business administration. A true technocrat.'

'Is he Opus Dei?'

'He probably flirted with the Opus when he was chasing promotion, but judging from the way he lives his life I'd say he's never taken vows of poverty or obedience. Or chastity either...'

'Screws like a dog, does he?'

'He's an unusual sort, Pepe. You might think he's effeminate, because he has the mannerisms of an English butler. I don't think I've ever seen him without a jacket, even in the middle of August. When he became aware that people were saying he was queer, he began hanging out with women. Dozens of them. A different one every night, and some of them pretty classy. And he keeps a couple of regulars in tow for when he needs a change.'

'Family money?'

'Not at all. He's the third son of the fifth son of the brother of the heirs to the Gausachs dynasty. Cotton manufacturers. They used to hobnob with the Guells, the Bertrans and the Valls y Taberner until the cotton crisis hit. They're only now beginning to pick up again. But Martin Gausachs has no real connection with them. His father was a lawyer who didn't have two cents to rub together. A solicitor, in fact, dealing with separations and neighbourhood quarrels.'

'Do you have all this information on your files here?'

'No. I know about the Gausachs family from when we

were doing a study of Catalonia's economy. The name came up, and since it turns out that one of the Gausachs is tied up with the far Left I was curious to find out about the rest of the family. They've got all sorts. A Maoist, and another one who's more or less a Maoist. Then there's Martin, the perfect executive. Another brother supports the nationalists. He's got a daughter who's in the Communist Party, and two young boys still at college — one studying with the Opus, and the other with the Jesuits.'

'A family that's determined to survive, come what may.'

'Correct. An inexorable law of nature. Every ruling class tends to perpetuate its power by reproducing other ruling classes, either through the mechanism of economic inheritance, or via political adaptability or cultural power.'

Not a hint of irony in all this. Parra spoke a language that was just as much jargon as Bromide's or Golden Hammer's.

'I'm leaving this bank with an impression of having got something for nothing.'

'Send a cheque to Leopoldo Calvo Sotelo, or to Trias Fargas. They're both on our board of directors.'

'How much?'

'I reckon an hour of my time is worth four hundred and sixty-six pesetas. I spent two hours on all this, so that makes nine hundred and thirty-two. I'll give you a discount — let's say eight hundred in total, or if you're feeling generous you can send my boss a cheque for a thousand.'

'Florentino — this friend of mine used to be a poet too.'

The porter looked up and stared at them to see if they were making fun of him.

'A progressive poet — one of your lot.'

'Poetry isn't progressive. Or raspberry-coloured. Or anything at all. It's just poetry, or it's nothing,' the poet said, without anger, but with all the dignity of a Flemish burgher.

Nuñez arrived on time, complete with his faithful sweater and the tips of his shirt collar floating above the crew neck like the shoots of some strange, hidden vegetable. He wore a fixed smile and a laid-back expression that was pure Actors' Studio.

'The only people who are punctual in this country are those who were active in the underground.'

Nuñez returned the menu to the *patron*.

'A *hors d'oeuvre* to start with, followed by a *confit d'oie*.'

Carvalho followed him in ordering the *confit d'oie*, but he decided on snails *à la Bourgogne* as a starter. He picked a Saint Emilion from the limited wine list, and now he and Nuñez had no further excuse for putting off their discussion. Nuñez's embarrassment formed part of his way of relating to people. Carvalho's, on the other hand, was a lingering echo of his residual respect for the man — the same respect he felt towards his old teachers, or to other people that he had admired. With a sigh, Nuñez took a photograph out of a shabby wallet in which Carvalho could see a solitary five-hundred-peseta note.

'Here, take this. It's like a family memento.'

An amateur snapshot, with a scalloped edge and worn by the passage of time. Four young men standing at the back, and two squatting in front. The year must have been about 1950, and they were all aged between eighteen and twenty, but now they seemed from some undefinable, far-distant era. They were all wearing suits and ties, except for Marcos Nuñez who was wearing a suit jacket and a roll-neck sweater. Jauma was presumably the one standing on the left. A thick head of hair, his Sephardic features accentuated by his thinness.

'Who are the others?'

'The cast, in order of appearance. Next to Jauma, Miguelito Fontanillas, a lawyer, like the rest of us, but doing very nicely thank you. In other words, he's the company lawyer for God knows how many firms, and has three houses and four swimming pools.'

Unkempt-looking, with a bit of a squint, and wearing a suit, in the photograph he looked like a young wide-boy from the *barrio* in his Sunday best.

'Tomas Biedma. Labour lawyer. The tall one, there. The one who looks a picture of seriousness and good sense. He's the biggest red of us all. Certainly more left-wing than me. He leads a small ultra-leftist group.'

There was something of the young Bourbon prince in those features, a sensuality contained by youth.

'He looks like the mayor of a big city.'

'He'll never get to be mayor of anywhere unless he manages to storm the Winter Palace first. I told you, he's on the far Left. He sees me as a revisionist and a cynic. Now, there are a lot of people who see me as a cynic, but for different reasons to Biedma. He says that I'm a cynic because I know enough not to be a revisionist, but that I'm still a revisionist for all that. The other one standing there is the novelist Dorronsoro.'

'Which one?'

'The elder of the two. Juan. The one that's just published *Weariness and the Night*. I'm one of the characters in it. Don't let that put you off, though. I come out just the way you see me now.'

'How do you know how I see you?'

'That's one of my favourite occupations. Working out how other people see me. Sometimes I help them build the picture. And sometimes I try to throw them off the scent. Not for long, though, because I get bored very quickly. Bored with everything except getting bored. Anyway, if I concentrate on one thing for too long it prevents me from being aware of what's going on round me. You'll have noticed already that I don't like over-exerting myself.'

'Who's this one here?'

Squatting next to Nuñez was a lad who looked the picture of happiness. A thick crop of hair sitting like a beret on his head, glasses with bifocal lenses, features that were small and hard but were softened in the photograph by a broad smile, and the whole weight of his body seemingly behind the clenched-fist salute that he was giving to the photographer.

'Who took the photo?'

'That's a source of some contention. Señora Biedma claims that she took it, but there's another friend, who's not in the photo, who claims *he* took it. The probability's on his side, since he is, or rather would like to be, a film director. Jacinto Vilaseca by name. He's not had a lot of luck in films. As you know, it's not an easy world to break into, and Vilaseca's not much of a stayer, really. What's more, he's on the far Left. He used to run a small political group — not the same one as Biedma, though.'

'What a bunch! Out of seven friends we've got two extreme left organizations, one executive, one society lawyer, a novelist, yourself, and what about this one, the one with the glasses? You still haven't told me his name.'

'Argemi. In those days he was well set to become the next great exponent of the grand old tradition of Catalan poetry. These days, though, he's a leading yoghurt manufacturer. He's the one I see least of, because he spends his time either abroad or at his mansion in Ampurdan — a huge seventeenth-century farm that he's converted into a hi-tech palace.'

'What are my chances of getting hold of their addresses?'

Nuñez reached into the top of his sweater, and extracted a folded piece of paper from his shirt pocket.

'Here. I thought you might be wanting them.'

'What sort of relationship did they have with Jauma?'

'Very good. But only on a one-to-one basis... Or two at the most. We've only ever all met together on two occasions. Once at a party that they gave for me when I returned from exile, and another time, about a year ago, when we were all invited by Jauma. He'd suddenly become incredibly paranoid for some reason and wanted us all to meet up. It was a disaster! On a one-to-one basis, we generally manage to find a common language and a common history. But when we were all together, all trying to sort out who remembered what about whom, we just all ended up in a mess, with everyone trying to justify what they had become. I could see from the way they looked at me that they'd expected better of me, and I suggested that perhaps I would have expected better of them. Then they started to get ratty.'

'All of them?'

'No. Not Dorronsoro. He wasn't saying a lot. I think he was sizing us up as characters for his next novel. Since he only writes ten lines a day, with us he should have enough material for a lifetime.'

'Was Jauma especially close to any of them?'

'He'd given Fontanillas a few bits of work connected with his company. He'd also used Biedma on a number of occasions, because he valued his "rationality". And he occasionally went on trips with Argemi.'

'Business or pleasure?'

'Pleasure, really. With their wives.'

'And what about the wives?'

'They were all more or less part of the same group. Most of them got engaged while they were still at university. All of them, in fact, except Argemi's wife. She was the daughter of a man who owned a small yoghurt factory. Then Argemi came along and transformed the family firm into a major industrial concern. He exports all over the world.'

'Aracata?'

'Precisely. It's apparently called that because one of the directors is from Aragon, and the other — Argemi's father-in-law — is Catalonian.'

The *confit* was excellent; it was nicely browned, and the fat had been transformed qualitatively into something quite other, full of tactile surprises. An elusive sort of flavour, with the meat slightly burned, and the skin basted with fat and with a light crispness that melted in the mouth. The meat was fibrous but not at all dried-out, and had absorbed the flavour of the herbs and spices throughout its sleeping form as it lay in the cold lard. What would you like to follow, gentlemen? Nuñez winked at Carvalho and asked:

'Bring me an Aracata yoghurt, a glass of orange juice, and a brandy. I'll mix them myself. I recommend it, Carvalho. It's Argemi's own recipe. He orders it in every restaurant he goes into, because that way he gets to sell another yoghurt.'

Nuñez had drunk in moderation and eaten without excess. Carvalho sensed that he fought hard to look younger than he really was.

'I'm going to ask you the same question that I'll be asking your friends. Give me your version of Jauma's murder.'

'I've read detective stories, so I know one has to look for a motive. The official version is that it was the result of Jauma's over-active sex life. The widow doesn't believe this. I myself have no reason not to believe it, but on the other hand it all seems a bit too clear-cut and simple — a bit stage-managed. If we abandon that version, I am not the best person to propose an alternative. In a novel Jauma might have been killed for business reasons, or by one of his workers getting his own back, or by one of his heirs, or because of a row with his wife's lover, or maybe even as a case of mistaken identity. Take your pick. None of these options has a lot going for it. You tend to get "business" killings among small businessmen, or among industrialists who have to slog it out against their competitors on a day-to-day basis. But not among senior executives. As for industrial disputes, as I told you, Jauma tended to move very carefully, and was good at defusing situations. The idea of his heirs killing him for his money would be ludicrous, partly because his children are too young to be killers, and partly because he didn't have a lot in the bank. He had plenty of possessions, but he was still paying for most of them. And anyway, an executive's salary doesn't look so big when it's converted into a widow's pension without yearly bonuses and so on. I'm sure he had a decent life insurance, but probably not enough to provide Concha with the same standard of living as when he was alive. As for the jealous wife killing for revenge, I imagine that now you've met her you'd find that as implausible as I do. So that just leaves mistaken identity. In my opinion, it was probably a case of mistaken identity.'

There was a note from Biscuter informing him that the lawyer Fontanillas had rung. Carvalho noted that important people were beginning to pursue him, and he rang the number marked as the one most likely to reach the lawyer in the middle of the afternoon. The fact that Fontanillas could only be reached via two secretaries, one after the other, testified to the man's social status, and the voice that finally came onto the line had the stressed and modulated manner of a priest, doctor or lawyer, when they try to disguise the fact that the slightest slip on their part can consign us all to kingdom come.

'Señor Carvalho! Delighted to make your acquaintance. Let's spare the formalities, since we're both busy men. Señora Jauma has given me a rather strange task — she wants me to find out whether the women's knickers found in her late husband's pockets had been used or not. As you can imagine, this isn't my normal line of thing, but since Concha asked me, and because it was to do with my great friend Jauma, I contacted friends and pulled a few strings. To cut a long story short, I now have the answer. They were unused.'

'Unused?'

'It may interest you, or amuse you, to know that they were, to be precise, completely new. I have to say that I find the whole business a bit of a bore, because a few minutes ago I had a phone call from a police inspector wanting to know why I was so interested in this particular detail. I had no choice but to explain, and unfortunately I had to bring you into it. In other words, the police now know that you're making inquiries on behalf of Jauma's widow.'

'They know more than they ought to know.'

'I had no choice. And now I must leave you, because I have people to see.'

'Don't hang up. Before you go, I need to arrange to meet you. It's important that I get to talk with Jauma's circle of friends.'

'Wait a moment.'

The emphatic voice turned silky smooth as he addressed an aside to his secretary, to ask how his diary looked for the following day.

'Do you like sport?'

'Only sports that involve the imagination. Eating and sex.'

'There, I'm afraid, I cannot oblige. However I do have a free hour between one and two o'clock tomorrow. I was thinking of calling in at the Cambridge club for a game of squash, a sauna, and a massage. I can take guests, and I would be delighted if you could make it. We can talk there. I'm afraid I have to go now. I'll see you tomorrow.'

Carvalho had his doubts about the advisedness of this sporting rendezvous, but Fontanillas gave him no chance to reply. So he put the phone down and took a few deep breaths in a parody of something he had once been capable of. He flexed his knees and squatted on his haunches, laughing to himself for no apparent reason. This was the moment that Biscuter chose to come through the door, holding it open with one knee as he struggled through with his hands full of shopping.

'You all right, boss?'

'Sure. Squatting's good for you.'

'What's it good for — the spine?'

'Good for something... I can't remember what, though.'

'I've been to the Boqueria to buy a couple of lamb's feet.

I'm going to do them with peas and artichokes, because I know that's the way you like them. The place needs a good clean-up too. It's starting to smell.'

He lifted himself off the floor and became aware of shooting pains in his legs.

'We should go into training, Biscuter.'

'Not me, boss. I do enough already. And when I don't have anything else to do, I invent something. That's what they taught me in the orphanage. Idleness is the mother of evil.'

'Shut up, Biscuter. When you start moralizing you get on my nerves.'

'Do you want a coffee, boss?'

'No. A glass of *orujo* from the fridge. I've got to go out. I want you to phone all these people for me. Make me an appointment to see each of them. I want you to pack them in so that I can see them all in one day. Be careful, though — don't book me in with two at the same time.'

He added Gausachs's name to the list that Nuñez had given him.

'And, Biscuter, try to sound a bit respectable on the phone. I don't want you screeching at them. You have to sound like a proper secretary.'

As Biscuter settled himself down with the telephone, Carvalho tried to find his bearings in the Jauma case. He was up against a blank wall with not an opening in sight. It wasn't even obvious which side of the wall he should start climbing. He'd taken a few steps, in a direction that might be right or wrong, based on the near-certainty that the motive had been falsified. All at once the disgust with which Carvalho customarily took on smaller cases — almost all a product of the moral pettiness of small-minded people — seemed preferable to the uneasiness he felt at finding himself involved in a case where he was probably out of his depth. What chance have I really got? I'll stir up a few cans of worms, and maybe I'll find the clue there. But what if I don't? Señora Jauma, those knickers can be as new as you like, but your husband was killed in a fight. Perhaps instead of asking for the ones that the girl was wearing, he had stolen a pair of new ones from her wardrobe. Or maybe he'd come up showing her a pair of new knickers:

'If you give me the knickers you're wearing, señorita, I'll give you a new pair.'

When all was said and done, there was no reason why the theory propounded by Golden Hammer shouldn't be right. Four thugs have a girl on the streets. Jauma turns up. They realize that he's loaded, so they decide to blackmail him. Jauma won't play ball, so they kill him. But why the knickers? There could only be two reasons for that particular detail. Either it's a ritual part of things when pimps kill people, or it's because someone knew Jauma well enough to know that people wouldn't be surprised to find him with a pair of women's knickers. Golden Hammer had said that the former was not a possibility, so that left the latter. It was a bit implausible, though, to set him up with a pair of knickers that were completely new. And why was everyone in such a hurry to accept this as the truth?

'There's someone to see you, boss.'

Carvalho was plucked out of his reverie by the realization that they were not alone. In the middle of his office stood two long-haired types flashing police badges at him.

'José Carvalho?'

'Yes.'

'We've been sent to ask you a few questions about the murder of Antonio Jauma.'

Biscuter went to fetch another chair from the bathroom. Cold, blue formica and metal. Carvalho unobtrusively moved the lever which enabled him to raise the height of his own chair a few inches above those of his interlocutors.

'Are you a private detective?'

Carvalho handed over his licence, but they ignored it.

'In Spain private detectives aren't supposed to stick their noses into other people's business, particularly when the police are involved.'

'As far as I knew, the Jauma case was closed.'

'So why are you re-opening it?'

'I've been asked by the widow.'

'Our boss has told us to give you a bit of advice, strictly between these four walls. If you find out anything, he expects you to tell us first. Be very careful with anything you find out before we do. A private detective's license lasts as long as we decide...'

'I'm not expecting an Oscar. Or a Nobel Prize either. All I expect is that my client pays me, and obviously as soon as I know anything I'll tell my client first. Then it's up to her what she decides to do with the information.'

Biscuter's eyes switched to and fro between his boss and the two detectives as if he was watching a game of tennis.

'Watch who you stir up and who you ruffle. They get angry with us, and then we have to cool them out. The boss says you've been seeing too many Bond movies.'

'Actually, I fancied myself more as Gregory Peck.'

'We're not joking, pal...'

The voice sounded irritated. There was a moment's silence.

'We've tried to keep this pleasant, but don't think we don't know who we're dealing with. You've got a very interesting past, and when the chief read your dossier he was kicking himself that you were ever given an investigator's licence in the first place.'

'I knew the nephew of a nephew of the man who was prime minister at the time.'

'When was that?'

'When the glorious General Franco was still alive.'

'That cuts no ice these days.'

The evening paper gave the news that a car with foreign licence plates had been found in the river Tordera. The river had been unusually swollen because of the recent rains, and evidently the current had carried the car a few yards downstream. There was no sign of the car's driver. All that was known was that it was an Avis car, and that it had been hired in Bonn by a Peter Herzen. The strange thing was that there was no sign of luggage in the car either, and it was suggested that, since he was travelling alone, he had kept his travelling bag on the back seat of the car, and that the water had swept it away.

As night settled on the Ramblas, Carvalho began to register the symptoms that marked the onset of the daily confrontation. The riot squad had begun moving into position, according to the prescribed rituals of the ongoing state of siege. Apolitical counter-cultural youth and young counter-cultural politicos maintained their customary distance from each other. At any moment a gang of ultra right-wing provocateurs might appear, and you would see the militants of this and that party disperse and head for their now legalized party offices, since they didn't want to find themselves removed from their recently acquired pedestal of legality and historical respectability by getting involved in street brawls. Between the hours of eight and ten the prostitutes, the pimps, the gays, and crooks great and small would disappear off the streets so as not to find themselves caught up in a political battle that was not of their making. Carvalho watched from his window as the tension mounted up the Ramblas, while Biscuter stood at his side complaining of the dangers the city was facing.

'And this is quiet compared with some places, boss. Imagine what things must be like in Bilbao. Or San Sebastian. Or Madrid. The ETA and GRAPO kidnapping people all over the place. The right-wing firing at demonstrators. And the shoot-out at the lawyers' office. That way they're hoping to destabilicize the situation.'

'Destabilize, Biscuter.'

'What does "destabilize" mean, boss?'

'Creating a scenario in which the authorities lose control of the situation, and the political system is incapable of guaranteeing order.'

'And who benefits from this?'

'Invariably those in power. It gives them an alibi for doing what the hell they want.'

'It's not right, boss! They should hang the lot of them! You know what I say — flogging, that's what they need! That's what I'd do with them. What a bloody mess!'

The valve on the pressure cooker had stopped hissing. Biscuter's execrations reached Carvalho at about the same time as the first shouts from the Ramblas. Within seconds the street outside became a nocturnal corral packed with stampeding humans. The riot squad swept down the street like so many lead soldiers, with their truncheons raised. All of a sudden, as if moved by a collective clockwork, they all paused, and the fleeing demonstrators slowly regrouped, their numbers reduced, but still sufficiently numerous for someone to start shouting, 'Amnesty — free the prisoners!' and for the crowd to advance defiantly towards the police again. Another charge. A Molotov cocktail exploded among the front ranks of the police, and the logical structure of their charge suddenly disintegrated. The controlled anger of the riot squad was now replaced by a destructive fury.

As the police passed by, innocent bystanders were felled by truncheons, and the riot cops with their tear gas and rubber bullets fired after the fleeing demonstrators. The noise of a gunshot set Carvalho's nerves on edge as he watched from the window. The police stopped and turned round to look down alleys and up at people's windows. One of them fired a rubber bullet at the front of a building, and people closed their shutters and balcony doors as if in expectation of a sudden downpour. Carvalho left his shutters slightly ajar, and witnessed a stylized charge and fragmented movements as the forces of order passed in front of the restricted viewpoint of the crack in his shutters.

Biscuter called from the kitchen:

'It's ready, chief. I've made the sauce.'

As the smell of the cooking made him turn his head, peace had already returned to the Ramblas. The police had resumed their previous cautious vigilance, and in the riot buses the cops had raised the plastic visors of their helmets and were relaxing.

'Are they properly cleaned?'

'There were a few hairs, but I cleaned them off. They're really tender.'

A whole culture of Catalonian cooking has been constructed on the basis of an onion and garlic base with spices, and Biscuter had learned it studiously. The little fellow ate without taking his eyes off Carvalho, in the hopes that he might let fall some word of appreciation.

'Delicious, eh, chief?'

'Correct.'

'Correct — is that the best you can say, boss?! Jesus — I'd have to do your budgie's balls in béchamel before you'd say "Very good, Biscuter! Bloody brilliant, Biscuter!"'

Minutes later Carvalho was drinking a coffee with brandy in the Café de l'Opéra, surrounded by remnants of the demonstration and the first specimens of Ramblas nightlife. Carvalho instinctively picked out the plainclothes policemen. As between plainclothes police and those who have a policeman in their heads, who was not a policeman here?! Two gays were caressing each other beneath a modernist-style mirror which reflected the tender napes of their necks. Seventeen young girls dressed as dope-smokers and runaways had just arrived from home and were ordering Evian water from the waiter. The two hundred and thirty clients of the Café de l'Opéra sat on their cinemascope island and provided a spectacle for the shy passers-by outside, out sightseeing or looking for whores. The waiters carved a passage through the customers like black and white snakes, and their evidently magnetic hands contrived to hold aloft brass trays that in the olden days had been corroded by spilt absinthes during nights of passion involving gentlemen and their mistresses in moiré.

'The drinks are on the house,' shouted a doubled-up hunchback trying to clear a way for himself. His clothes smelt of hashish and his armpits of sweat. Voices that smelt of tobacco and of sandwiches swallowed down like a fuel to sustain the body on its long voyage from nothingness to death, passing via total apathy. On the shoulders of a big-boned man, a two-year-old child is leaning over a gin and tonic and accepts a strawberry lollipop handed to him by a waiter with rosy cheeks. In a corner a pre-tubercular youth sits alone, listening to his own guitar solo, and his dirty locks of hair spill over the guitar strings. At the door two riot cops suddenly appear. They stand there, with the visors of their helmets down and their malicious smiles flattened by the transparent plastic. They show no indication of either coming or going. They just look, and probably enjoy listening to the silence they have caused, which is broken by the occasional cough or the clink of glasses being replaced on marble bar-tables. The kid starts to cry. The riot cops leave.

'Have you never been to our premises before?' 'Haven't you taken a stroll around our private woods?' 'Would you like to take a look around so as to familiarize yourself with the mansion?'

Carvalho wasn't sure whether Gausachs had actually said any of these things, or whether his tone had simply suggested them. Tall and sturdy, with a bell-shaped chest, blond hair and looking like a young patrician of the textile industry with some English engineer or his daughter among his antecedents, Gausachs was a picture of refinement, with a Greek profile somewhat bloated by excesses of food and drink. He had the gestures of a master of ceremonies, a way of looking at you with half-closed eyes, a restrained smile, and just one arm moving gently in order to indicate agreement, remembrance, forgetting, direction to, etc. He spoke a formal Spanish which deliberately avoided the drawling vowels of Catalan, a falsely pure language chosen so as to keep in with the people who mattered in Madrid. He also had the linguistic jargon of the typical young executive: 'It goes without saying...'; 'On the basis of...'; 'At the level of...'; 'Consider it done...'

'I'll be delighted to show you round, but you'll have to forgive us if the place is in a bit of a mess. We've got the builders in. Everyone to their own taste — I've decided to redesign the style of the place a bit. Especially the reception area. Poor Jauma was a creature of instinct, in this as in all things, and he gave no importance to scene-setting. Even this improvised office that you now see would have been inconceivable in his day.'

Walls panelled in beechwood, a Res Mobel table, an office refrigerator, a three-piece Oxford suite in real leather so delicate that it looked almost like human skin, an Indian rug, a Sunyer acquired at a recent auction (a present, Gausachs added) and a cocktail bar in which malt whiskey had the pride of place, next to a solid silver ice bucket.

'Then I'll show you where Jauma used to work. It looks like a warehouse office in some suburban department store. He was a man of brilliant intuitions, but he was a bit old-fashioned in his ways, even though you could say that he was still very much on the ball. When it came to running a company, he was a force to be reckoned with, but at the level of image, of packaging, he was fifty years behind the times.'

'So have you now been put in complete charge of the company?'

'I'm being advised by a committee sent from our head office in London, but they'll be leaving soon.'

'According to people who have studied Petnay — and as you know there's a lot of them about, especially since the coup in Chile — people who reach high management positions in the company — yourself, for example — always have beside them a political appointee. Something analogous to the function of a political commissar in the people's armies.'

Miraculously Gausachs managed to laugh just with his lower lip, a technical feat that Carvalho found astounding.

'I do not know whether multinational corporations will go down in the history of world economics, señor Carvalho, but it appears that they already have a special place in the history of literature — in the fairy story section. Absurd, completely absurd. I won't deny that there are areas of management that touch on politics and — more than politics — on the business of law-making. Decisions in these areas are taken at high political levels — but *I* am the one who makes them — me, Martin Gausachs Domenech — just as señor Jauma did in his day.'

'Nothing escapes the eye of a regional general manager?'

'Absolutely nothing. Each of us has three-monthly bilateral meetings with our senior management, and every six months there's a general conference. Periodically regional inspectors pass through, or general inspectors, and there's a kind of central administrative committee which functions as the main accounting brain.'

'Isn't Dieter Rhomberg the inspector for this region?'

'Indeed he is. But he's just resigned.'

'When?'

'I heard yesterday. I had a telex from head office which said that, as of two months ago, Rhomberg is no longer our regional manager. He has resigned.'

'Isn't it a bit strange that it's taken them two months to get round to announcing it?'

'Since Jauma's death things have got a bit out of synch, and a few things have tended to get overlooked, because this is a big period of re-organization and it'll be going on for a while yet. Even if big firms like this are like giant machines, the human element still counts for something. Particularly so in Jauma's case. He was very much his own man, in the sense that he kept a lot of things in his head and few in his diary. There are dozens of corners that we still haven't had time to explore. He relied on his fantastic memory, and that's something that can't be handed on. The man didn't believe in division of labour. Just imagine — this company has an amazing management team, absolutely brilliant, and a computer centre to rival the Pentagon, but Jauma felt duty-bound to take the accounts for his sector and get them checked over by some mysterious accountant friend of his.'

Again the smooth, flat laugh emerged via Gausachs's bottom lip.

'Was he suspicious of something or someone?'

'No. I don't think so. It was just the way he was. Must have come from his background — rural... provincial, rather. He was a bit provincial in some things.'

'What did you think of him?'

'He was a very capable man, in a professional sense, although I myself would have done a lot of things differently.'

'You'll get your chance, now.'

'It's made a few difficulties for me. Jauma's job involves a lot of travel. I'm having to give up my assistant lectureship at the university, and right at this moment I'm wrestling with a bit of a problem. Should I stand as an MP in the next elections? A group of my friends is pushing me into it. Catalonia needs businessmen to represent it in the upper echelons of government.'

'And the upper echelons of government need Catalonia to be represented by businessmen.'

'That's certainly true. But I'm not sure whether I'd be capable of alternating responsibilities between business and politics. I think I'm going to have to choose.'

'Which will you choose?'

'At this moment in time, as things stand, at ten in the morning, on the basis of all the available data, and strictly between ourselves, I choose Petnay. There will always be other elections, and anyway I find this job fascinating.'

'What does Petnay produce in Spain?'

'In the sense of manufacture, it makes mainly cosmetics, pharmaceuticals, fertilizers, feedstuffs, packaged food, and so on. But it also runs finishing lines for a lot of other products, and it's no secret that Petnay has a qualitatively determining stake in a lot of other Spanish companies.'

'Qualitatively determining?'

'That's a term I coined for my classes on foreign investment. A lot of the time it's not necessary for a big multinational to control a full fifty-one per cent of the shares of a given company. All it needs is to own a holding large enough to guarantee internal stability in the company concerned and its creditworthiness in relation to the banks. You follow?'

There was almost nothing left of the tousle-haired, slightly cross-eyed, but sympathetic-looking lad. He had enough hair not to appear bald, but not enough to be able to go around uncombed. The thick bifocal lenses that he wore seemed to have corrected his squint by submerging his eyes in a sea of milky distance. Wrinkles and ruts on his cheeks served as drains for the trickle of sweat that sprang from the roots of his hair, as the lawyer Fontanillas struggled to follow the trainer's movements.

'That waist — that waist — *work* that waist. That's it, that's the way, go on — be angry — one-two, one-two!'

Still panting, Fontanillas abandoned the circuit-training session and headed for the exercise bike. Meanwhile

Carvalho changed into the clothes that were provided for visitors. A vest and white shorts, and under the shorts a pair of red nylon trunks for the sauna and the pool. Carvalho did a bit of running on the spot, as if warming up for a football match. His knee-joints were creaking, but he had sufficient muscular elasticity to be able to warm up in his gym-shoes. Fontanillas, who was panting and sweating and looking like he'd just completed the Stations of the Cross, signalled to him to follow. They picked up a pair of rackets and made their way into the squash court, which was painted spring green. The first balls resounded against the hard, hollow walls. Sometimes the ball hit the metal perimeter mesh with a noise like the chattering of a lie detector. This is truly a sport for atomic fall-out shelters, because the ball has no way of escaping to the sky or disappearing behind some bank in search of a hiding place. The balls are condemned to bounce and bash around until their balding rubber ages prematurely and one day someone gives them a mighty whack which breaks them open, liberates the air inside them, and sends their rubber soul upwards to heaven.

Fontanillas had reflexes which had been tuned to this subterranean, animal style of game. Every well-placed stroke stretched his muscles to the limit, and the smile half-hidden in a gesture of fatigue indicated that he both loved and needed this minor victory. For Carvalho, the coming and going of the ball as it bounced back from the side walls or rebounded with undiminished force onto the playing-wall meant a lot of running around to not much effect. As a thin sweat began to appear on his skin, he found he was getting his eye in and he played as best he could, in the knowledge that Fontanillas was making no allowances for him. The lawyer consulted his watch and decided that he wasn't going to run for the next ball.

'Sauna now. And then the pool. We can talk in there.'

In their red trunks they made their way down the carpeted corridor, and a swing door brought them into the club's humid zone. A cold shower, a few strokes up and down the small swimming pool, which was joined to the roof by a jet of constantly-flowing water, and then drying themselves with towels before passing through a heavy wooden door to enter the ante-chamber of hell. A brazier of hot coals, wooden benches, magazines that had suffered in the heat of the place, and thermometers and hour-glasses on the walls. Their two bodies lay flat on a raised bench as if they were loaves pushed into an oven by the baker's pallet and slowly baking. Carvalho's reserves of sweat were flowing like a river in flood, and Fontanillas observed with satisfaction that Carvalho had been lucky to have had the opportunity of this experience.

'This is very good for you. Not because it helps you slim, but because it opens your pores.'

'Isn't there a less painful way of getting your pores open?'

'This is nothing — it's just the pre-sauna. That narrow door there takes you into the *real* hell. I'm having a house built in the wilds of Sarria, and I'm having a little sauna put in. I find it very refreshing. Anyway, time's running out — go ahead, say your piece.'

'No. You. You're supposed to be telling me about Jauma.'

'I suppose you want concrete facts rather than chit-chat.'

'Did Jauma ever consult you about anything that might explain why he was killed? Dodgy dealings, that sort of thing?'

'I'm a heavyweight lawyer, señor Carvalho. Field artillery, battleships and long-range bombers. I won my spurs in the law courts fighting big-company cases. I've made money for some clients, and lost money for others, but in none of my cases has anybody ever ended up dead. You might get farmers killing each other over land boundaries, or shopkeepers because they're competing for trade in the same street, but in the world of big business the rules of the game are Dante-esque, señor Carvalho, and the whole world knows it. That said, I did have occasion to advise Jauma in a couple of instances where his business life touched on his personal life, but for company matters Petnay keeps its own team of lawyers.'

'It's strange. There's Jauma, with all the resources of a major multinational right at his fingertips, and he feels the need to hire his own personal accountants and lawyers. Presumably he paid them out of his own pocket too.'

'My time was paid by Petnay, not Jauma. I'm afraid I know nothing that could be of use to you. Our discussions were very technical.'

'How would you explain Jauma's death?'

'I have no explanation other than the official one, and it surprises me that Concha isn't going along with it.'

'From what I hear, experts in pimps and prostitution don't believe the official explanation either. The detail of the knickers is too contrived. What's more, they were new. Never worn. Never been anywhere near a woman. What's the point of having women's knickers in your pocket if they don't carry the smell of a woman?'

'He doesn't *have* to have been killed by a pimp or a prostitute. Why couldn't it have been revenge by a jealous husband, or a jilted lover, or the father of one of the girls? The police looked into all this, interviewed all sorts of people, and came up with nothing. Concha was moved by pure emotion, which was understandable but less than helpful.'

'You don't want complications in this case, do you.'

'How do you mean?'

'You'd prefer it to be an open and shut case, wouldn't you. It's obvious from the way you deny any possibility of complication.'

'I don't like pointless complications. I never have, and I've found it a perfect recipe for getting on in life. Concha is looking for pointless complications, and it's all Nuñez's fault. I like Nuñez a lot, but the man's a disaster. At the age of forty-five he still goes round behaving like a budding teenager. In another five years he'll be a failed fifty-year-old. He enjoys going round looking for problems where there are none. Now he's decided to query the motives of Jauma's death. He's managed to convince Concha, and now we're all caught up in it. Why? Just because Nuñez has nothing better to do with his time. So why pick on this? So as to make up for his understandable frustration at never being able to do anything useful.'

'Like having a wife and children, and a house in the wilds of Sarria, and a sauna...'

'Don't tell me you're a politico too! I thought private detectives were men of the world and had a bit of sense... Am I to presume that you're in the private detective cell of the Communist Party?'

'No — the gastronomic cell.'

'In that case you should call round to the aforementioned sauna, because good eating makes you fat, and so does ethical smugness and political self-righteousness.'

Carvalho felt an undeniable sensation of lightness, floating, as he made his way out of the gym for out-of-shape executives. He felt as if his pores really were more open, and as he went up the stairs to the office of the labour lawyer Biedma, his legs felt as if they were trying to get there before him. In the reception area a group of workers was listening attentively to a report of something that had happened that morning at a Labour Tribunal. In a corner a secretary was typing under a poster of the Portuguese Revolution: a picture of a boy holding out his hand to take a carnation poking out of the barrel of a rifle. Forget the flower and take the gun, kid, Carvalho thought to himself, because otherwise one day someone will shoot you and you'll discover that the carnation was really a bullet. What the workers were discussing was the closure of a section of a sanitary-ware factory. He found himself in an Ensanche apartment, with decorated mosaics, a fake alabaster fireplace, embossed wooden doors that had been painted over with blue paint, and in the sea of blue a rectangular space that was occupied almost entirely by Tomas Biedma — tall, solid, with large, wide-awake eyes set in a cylindrical face. The workers fell silent and greeted him with the sort of respect they would have accorded to a doctor. Carvalho allowed himself to be swallowed up in the sea of blue, leaving Biedma behind to exchange information with the group outside. An efficient-looking office, full of 1940s bits and pieces very similar to the furniture in Carvalho's: a wooden filing cabinet with a roll-down shutter; a glass bookcase; two leatherette armchairs worn at the seat and arms. On the desk there was a degree of disorder, which seemed to lose importance when Biedma sat down, leaned forward on his elbows as if his arms were architraves for the weight of the rest of his body, and, in a voice that was slow, deep, and youthful, confirmed the air of moderation that radiated from his face — an appearance that was belied only by an intermittent tic as he frowned slightly and his gaze wandered off apparently in search of some non-existent point somewhere to the north-east.

'I've just been for a sauna with Fontanillas.'

Biedma laughed.

'Was it free, or did he make you pay?'

'He's sending you the bill.'

Biedma laughed again, and his face — which could have been that of Louis XV's elder brother — grew boyish.

'He's always been that way. When we were students we were all short of money. None of us came from wealthy families, except Vilaseca maybe, because his father was a lawyer. Most of us had to duck and dive to get money — private lessons, selling encyclopaedias and so on. It wasn't that we didn't have money to eat — we just needed extra cash to spend. And one way or another we all became small-time traders. Fontanillas especially. He'd go up to the girls in the philosophy department and try selling them nylons and contraband French perfumes. He even went and had two inside pockets stitched into his jackets so that he could open them and show his wares — watches, lighters, nylons and so on. He used to go round shouting like a street trader. "Watches! Lighters! Roll up, roll up!"'

'Now he's rich.'

'Very rich.'

'And you're not.'

'No.'

'But you will go to heaven, and he will most definitely be down for a spell in Purgatory.'

'I console myself with that thought.'

'How come you're such a red?'

Suspecting that he was being made fun of, Biedma momentarily forgot his tic and studied the slightly mocking look in Carvalho's eyes.

'Because I'm faithful to my own logic. Politically speaking, we all started from the same place. Take Fontanillas and Argemi. They played their part. They printed leaflets, and handed them out. They set up Marxist study groups — I'm not joking. It was Fontanillas who first explained to me the law of supply and demand. He was always the first to understand things, the first to try them, and the first to abandon them. If you look at my friends, they've either abandoned their politics, over time, or they've become stuck in a rut — like Nuñez, a lifelong supporter of a party which was once revolutionary but today is openly reformist. He supports the Party because he's married to it, and because he doesn't want to renounce the sentimental vows that he made thirty years ago. Thirty years, give or take...! I, for my part, have remained faithful to a logic which ties political action to a real desire to change history, in a progressive direction, and as quickly as possible, without falling into electoral agreements and compromises that merely conceal their revolutionary impotence.'

'You're not the only "red". Vilaseca sounds like a bit of a revolutionary too.'

'Pah — he's a snob. Very intelligent, but a snob. Having run through every group in the ultra-Left he's now settled on anarchism. I, on the other hand, am now what I was in 1950, applied to the historical necessities of 1977: a Marxist-Leninist.'

'So as far as you're concerned, Argemi, Fontanillas, and Jauma are traitors to the cause, Nuñez is stuck in a time-warp, and Vilaseca is a snob. You make things very easy for yourself.'

'I wouldn't say that Argemi, Fontanillas and Jauma ever actually betrayed anything. They simply followed the logic of their class positions and then went back to an assured place in the bosom of the bourgeoisie. Nuñez used his political militancy as a way of not ending up as a has-been, and Vilaseca is a curiosity, a voyeur of history and politics.'

'And Dorronsoro?'

'He's a writer, an artist, and artists should be left to their own devices unless they're out-and-out reactionaries.'

'Jauma is dead. Why did he die?'

A mist, possibly resulting from the evaporation of hidden tears, clouded Biedma's vision. He hung his head for a moment.

'It's as if it's *us* that they've mutilated. As if it was *my* life that they cut short. A man who was the life and soul of any company. He never changed — just carried on the way he was — emotional, sex-mad, crazy...'

He sank into a reverie, with his gaze fixed on a pile of duplicated pamphlets with the title *Red Notes*:

No to the Fascist Monarchy!
Down with the Status Quo!

'We had dinner together a few days before he died. He'd just got back from a trip to San Francisco and wanted me to fill him in on the labour scene, and what was happening with the coming legalization of the trade unions.'

'Did you advise him on how to deal with the union people

in his factories?'

'I'm not a business consultant, señor Carvalho. With Jauma I have always simply given my political interpretation of the situation as it stands. I never give him advice so that he can outsmart the working class. Only so that he doesn't delude himself.'

'Do you have your own ideas about why he was killed?'

'At first I accepted the police version, and for the moment I don't have enough evidence to suggest that their version is not correct. You, however, do, or so it seems.'

'Not at all. I was sitting happily at home dealing with adultery cases and over-emotional runaway teenagers when all of a sudden they wanted me to show that the official explanation of Jauma's murder actually explains nothing. So here I am. I'm a professional, and my motivation in this case is strictly economic, although I did actually meet Jauma once, years ago, in the United States. We had three days together. We travelled together through the Mojave Desert, from Los Angeles to Las Vegas. The last time I saw him he was playing roulette at Caesar's Palace. I tried to say goodbye several times, but he didn't even raise his eyes from the baize. When he did finally look up, I gave him a wave from the other side of the table, but I don't know if he even saw me.'

'He was an orderly man, who had a passionate and dangerous hobby — gambling. I, on the other hand, am a disorderly man, but I have a hobby which is soothing and relaxed, almost decadent.'

'You play the violin?'

'No. Art. I'm a specialist in second-rank artists. Do you know what separates a second-rank artist from a first-rank artist in the majority of cases?'

'No.'

'Nothing. Absolutely nothing. The history of art, and I suppose the history of literature too, is full of bitter injustices. A given era creates sacrosanct values and transmits them to the next. Nobody ever questions whether the original classification was fair in the first place. In Velazquez's studio there were at least two students who painted as well as he did. Look.'

He got up slowly and went over to a cupboard. It opened to reveal an interior filled with identical metal boxes that contained rows of slides. He took several slides from one of them and placed a viewer on the table.

'Look at these. What do you see?'

'A painting. Girls paddling in a stream.'

'Who would you say painted it?'

'It looks Dutch.'

'Well done. Carry on.'

'Rembrandt?'

'Not at all!'

With evident satisfaction that his theory had been proved, Biedma came round the table and settled down with a view to expounding his theories.

'It's by Lucas Paulus, one of Rembrandt's students. You should see the original. You won't find it in any gallery. It's part of the treasures of a tenth-rate Flemish church in Holland. If it had Rembrandt's signature on it, it would feature in every art history book in the world. Look — here's another one...'

'I'm sorry, señor Biedma. I've got a busy day ahead of me meeting all your friends. I'm on my way to see Vilaseca now. You've still not answered the question that interests me, though. When you last saw him, did Jauma show signs of being especially worried about anything?'

'He wanted to give up his job. Find another job before he reached fifty. He was very dramatic about it at first. That was during the last time we dined together. Then the conversation took a lighter turn, and by the end he was laughing at himself, and quoting Saint Teresa: "I live in myself without living in myself, etc, etc." Then he ended with his favourite phrase.'

'What phrase?'

'The angst of the senior executive.'

Compared with the youthful, parsimonious neatness of Marcos Nuñez, Vilaseca cultivated a provocative image of marginalization. Long unruly hair, a moustache, an unkempt beard, an ex-army combat jacket that probably once belonged to some hero of the Sierra Maestra, a pair of jeans that looked as if they had been rescued from a dustbin and then ironed by a steamroller, a post-war military haversack and soldiers' boots darkened with dubbin. He arrived at their rendezvous with a girl who was slim as a bamboo cane, with willowy hands, brown hair worn in an Afro, and two breasts that seemed to apologize for their smallness beneath a camisette that looked as if it had been stolen from some Museum of Slavery.

'Three people can eat as well as two, and anyone who's paying for two might as well pay for three.'

'Who's paying?!'

'You are. Goes without saying that I'm not. I've got two hundred pesetas on me, and they've got to last till tomorrow. In exchange you will have the pleasure of lunching with two celebrities — myself, and this young lady. Anna Marx. She's not related to Karl Marx. Or the Marx Brothers either. I gave her the name three months ago as a screen name. She's a muse of the silver screen.'

'You're crazy, crazy...' the girl said, with a hint of irritation at the end of her little wrinkled nose.

'You can choose the restaurant... what did you say your name was... Carvalho? Stand next to me. Let's say that north is over there, south is down this street, and this is east and that's west. To the north, behind the church of Santa Maria del Mar, we have El Borne, a restaurant run by another Barcelona film director. Self-service, with halfway decent food. French cooking and cheeses ditto. Not bad. To the south, behind this portico, we have a Galician restaurant. A bit of a dive. You know what we can expect there, and at this time of day it's bound to be packed. Continuing round to the east, we have El Raim, home cooking, local recipes, good food. Limited seating, though.

To the west, they've just opened...'

'I do know the area!'

'You choose, then.'

'El Raim will be full. Let's go to El Borne.'

'Up to you. Don't complain when they bring the bill, though.'

He gave him a wink and set off in front of him with his arm round his girlfriend's angular shoulders.

'You're crazy, crazy...'

Vilaseca was wearing the same clothes that Stanley Kubrick might have worn ten or fifteen years previously when he was shooting *Space Odyssey*. There was a certain physical resemblance too.

'I'd paint it lilac and put an Arab souk inside it,' he said, pointing at the church. They walked round it and saw the prospect of the Paseo del Borne opening before them, a broad, tree-lined avenue that contrasted with the dark, artisanal alleyways of the old mediaeval *barrio*.

'Poor Jauma.'

And his eyelids drooped like coffin lids.

'This gives me an idea for a film. How about this? A top executive gets obsessed with the myth of Gauguin and decides to leave his family and run off to Tahiti. The title could be *Gauguin 2*, or *Tahiti*. He takes the tube during the rush hour and reaches a working-class area of town. He decides to adopt the lifestyle of the Tahitians. He takes up with a girl from one of the factories, a tasty number from the industrial suburbs of Barcelona. Nobody knows his real identity. To begin with, he's happy. But then he comes up against a set of insuperable mental class barriers. The unhappiness that catches up with him also infects the people he's with. He has introduced a restlessness previously unknown to these Tahitians, and so as not to bring more unhappiness to himself and to them, he decides to commit suicide. Anna will play the young factory girl.'

He removed his arm from her shoulders and put her at arm's length as if to see her in perspective.

'I know she looks like just what she is — the daughter of a money-bags who was once a Barcelona councillor. But she plays a very good critical role on film. As for you, I'd say you'd make a good murderer. A sort of Richard Widmark *à la espagnole*. Hunch your shoulders a bit. That's the way! Now turn your hands outwards a touch. That's right. Now walk. Come on. Don't go all stiff. The trouble with Spaniards is that we all seem to be made of quick-setting concrete. We don't know how to move. It's as if we're incapable of establishing a relationship with the space surrounding us and altering it through movement. The part's yours if you want it...'

'What part?'

'The part of Jauma's murderer.'

'How do you know he didn't commit suicide?'

'Both are equally possible.'

Various people greeted Vilaseca from behind the bar, and Carvalho followed him up the narrow spiral staircase to the two upper rooms that comprised the restaurant proper. On the counter stood several pans full of wonderful-looking food, and a serving tray piled high with Basmati rice. Vilaseca dumped his haversack on a table as an indication that it was occupied, and invited Carvalho to accompany him over to the food counter. He loaded a ton of rice and civet of hare onto his plate. Carvalho went for the same, and when they returned to the table they found the girl hunched in her seat, anxiously contemplating her plate, which had on it only a teaspoon of rice and a few bits of goulash..

'I'm not at all hungry... really.'

'She never eats a thing all day! Breakfast, lunch, or supper, it's always the same — "I'm not at all hungry... really"!'

Vilaseca had assumed the curious tone of an intransigent father dealing with a recalcitrant daughter, and the girl exploded.

'So what?! I'm the one who's eating, and I eat how I like.'

'Next thing, you'll be staggering down the street groping at the walls — not in imitation of Monica Vitti, but because you'll be fainting with hunger. Hey, this food is good. What wine are you offering? I'll choose — Mumieta, red.'

'What relationship did you have with Jauma?'

With his mouth full of meat and rice, Vilaseca was unable to say anything, so he gesticulated instead. As the food commenced its downward journey, he declared:

'Paternal. It was a paternal relationship. He used to tell me off as if I was a little boy. "You ought to make a man of yourself, Vilaseca!" Or words to that effect. I used to irritate him, you see. The total freedom of my lifestyle used to irritate him, because he envied it.'

'This food makes me feel sick,' the girl said, looking at her lunch as if it was a plateful of garbage.

'Why don't you go for a walk? It's bad luck to eat next to people with no appetite. Go on — go take a walk!'

The girl left the restaurant sullenly with all the cheap dignity of a slighted character leaving a stage.

'She's horribly spoilt. But she's got a terrific temperament. Especially in front of the camera. She's ever so sexy. She might not be much to look at, but she's got that special something. And those two little tits that look like currant buns, when they're on film, they're as captivating as the breasts of Manet's *Olympia*. As soon as I get some money I'm going to start filming, and this kid's going to go a long way. Not in the bourgeois sense. I don't want to make a star of her. I want to create new icons for a new cinema, in tune with the times we live in.'

'Did you see Jauma often?'

'Not a lot, recently. I can't abide paternalism. I wouldn't tolerate it from my father, so I'm damned if I'd tolerate it from him. He was sort of nervous when I last saw him. Tetchy. Critical. More envious. He was always chatting up the chicks that I go round with, but they're women for the high seas, and every time I saw him it seemed like his life was on the rocks. Beached, run aground.'

Vilaseca insisted on accompanying Carvalho to visit
Argemi. The girl was waiting for them at the entrance to
the restaurant, lounging against one of the cars parked in
the driveway. She followed them indolently and as soon as
she had got into the car and heard what their plans were
she began raising objections. Discreetly at first, but when
Vilaseca was evasive in his replies she ended up shouting
and demanding to be let out of the car.

'Change your role. Drop the spoilt rich-kid image and
act something a bit better. How about Gloria Grahame's
dialogue with Glenn Ford in *The Big Heat*. You look like
Gloria Grahame, as I'm sure I've told you a hundred times.
Do you remember Grahame, Carvalho? She was born with
the most gorgeous expression in this world. Ambiguous,
gentle, lascivious... She had the kind of face you need, to
be able to carry on an intelligent dialogue. You look a lot
like her, Anna, seriously...'

'I want to go home. I can't stand your friends. I can't
bear the thought of having to spend five hours listening to
you talking about stupid things that only make *you* laugh,
only *you*. You are boring, and I'm bored.'

'Best pull up, Carvalho.'

The detective braked and began to park the car. The
manoeuvre was still under way when Vilaseca got out,
opened the rear door, and told the girl:

'Get out, then. Go and do what the hell you want. You've
got the day to yourself.'

The girl got out with all the style she could muster,
passed in front of Vilaseca, and pointedly ignored him as
she said:

'I'll be waiting for you at the Zeleste at eleven.'

'I'll be home within two hours.'

'Well I won't.'

'Where are you going?'

'That's my business.'

'Carvalho, I've changed my mind. I won't come and see
Argemi. Do me a favour — ask him to ring me one of these

days. I've got some interesting projects lined up.'

He leaned over more so that only Carvalho could hear him.

'Forgive me if I don't come with you. She's like a kid. I've overdone it a bit. I've spent the whole morning in meetings that are nothing to do with her. If you need me any time, feel free to phone. You should take more care of your hair, you know! Look at that receding hairline. I was on the verge of going bald myself, and I went to see the doctor just in time. Do you know what it was? Nerves. The routine of daily life. I'd have ended up bald as a coot, and fat into the bargain. So, as you see, I've decided to give up having a routine. Phone me. Don't forget.'

Vilaseca's generous personal disposition was touching. In his rear-view mirror Carvalho watched as the film-maker decomposed the gesture of a US general bidding farewell to his troops as he sends them off on a suicide mission and adopted the style of a lover concerned for the welfare of his beloved. Carvalho explored his allegedly receding hairline with the tips of his fingers, and tugged at his hair to test its roots.

'That's him all over. Full of crazy ideas.'

Argemi's assessment of Vilaseca matched the one the detective had reached as he drove back from their lunch-date. Argemi was stockily-built, with wide shoulders, a good growth of hair which was showing the first signs of greyness, and a deceptively sleepy look from behind his bifocals. He was slow in expressing himself, and had a voice which could probably be frightening when he got angry. He had the air of a man perennially caught napping, who had never got over his anger at being woken up. This impression was reinforced by the way his glasses made his eyes seem smaller, and by the slowness of his movements and his style of conversation.

'I'm only coming to sign,' he said, and looked over the top of his glasses to see what effect these words would have on Carvalho. He laughed in order to prompt a laugh from

the detective, and got a smile of solidarity. With what looked
like an extremely expensive pen he signed his name to a
series of documents that were handed to him by a secretary
who was young, modest, neatly dressed, and a virgin, as
befitted a secretary in a company producing yoghurt — a
product associated with images of purity and innocence.
Because it is white, because it is recommended for sick
people, and because it is cheap, yoghurt is a Florence
Nightingale of foods. The hand with the pen in it revealed
part of the forest of hair that spread the length and breadth
of Argemi's body, which was the body of a wolf-man with
the head of a sweet kid with glasses. The scene could have
been a country residence for ladies of leisure in the days of
roof gardens and tennis. The walls were lined with pink
satin. From the delicately stuccoed ceiling hung a glass
lamp engraved with a flight of opaque birds. The glass that
encased the cocktail cabinet was also engraved, and all it
needed was the presence of Gene Tierney offering a
Manhattan to a naval officer and asking his protection as
he leaves to conquer Germany and then again as he returns
with the world under one arm, as if he had won it in target-
shooting at a funfair. Argemi's office boasted an oak
parquet floor as solid as the well-heeled English shoes that
Argemi displayed, under a heavy wooden desk with two
banks of drawers.

He put the top on his pen and arched his eyebrows with
sufficient force to be able to keep them up for a while.

'OK, fire away. I imagine that you haven't come here just
to tell me things about the lovely but crazy Vilaseca. Crazy,
he is, quite crazy...'

Another personal and infectious laugh.

'I'd like to be able to live like that madman... He lives a
hell of a life, a hell of a life!'

He clasped his left hand with his right, sank his head
into his chest as if to concentrate better on the person
before him, and encouraged him:

'Go ahead — fire away.'

'It appears that out of all the friends of his younger days you're the one who has kept the closest links with Jauma.'

'Am I to conclude from the way you phrased that that you consider me no longer young?'

'Not *as* young...'

'Ah, that's better.'

Once again, an invitation to laugh.

'I'm involved in re-opening this case, and I want you to tell me anything that might encourage me to keep it open. In other words, anything that might verify my suspicion that Jauma was not murdered for the reasons stated in the offical version.'

A long sigh. A slow reflection. Slow movements in search of the back of the chair. A slow resting of his head against one of its wings. A slow return to his initial position.

'I'm afraid I can't really help you. I've already told the police everything I know about Jauma, and everything that I know fits perfectly logically with the facts of his unfortunate death. I knew him well, very well...'

He took a Davidoff Special from a Dunhill humidor. With a wooden spill he meticulously applied a flame to the end of the cigar, and when the sides began to catch he moved it continuously between his fingers until the whole thing was alight. Then he trimmed the other end with a silver cigar-cutter and inhaled a compact mass of smoke.

'Oh — I *am* sorry,' he said, as if suddenly annoyed with himself for an unpardonable oversight, and he passed the box of Davidoffs to Carvalho. The detective sensed that this was a deliberate manoeuvre, a test to find out whether he appreciated quality tobacco. In fact Carvalho had not taken his eyes off the Davidoff ever since it had appeared in Argemi's hand like the apple appearing in the hand of Eve. Argemi watched with evident gratification as Carvalho went through the lighting-up ritual, and when both Davidoffs were alight and their perfectly-formed tips were glowing at each other, a mutual bond of connoisseurship had been established between the detective and the entrepreneur.

Argemi fondled the beginnings of a waistline as if it was an expensive pet and observed:

'Jauma didn't smoke.'

'But he certainly liked to eat and drink.'

'And screw! And screw! Don't forget — he did like a good screw!'

Laughter and smoke arose from Argemi's half-closed lips as he leaned towards Carvalho to underline this statement, waving his cigar assertively under his nose.

'We used to go on trips a lot. Sometimes just the two of us, and sometimes with our wives. When you travel together you get to know a person. I could say a lot about Jauma's erotic obsessions. Not least, I suppose, because I share them myself.'

'Why did you travel together so often?'

'Sometimes for business and sometimes just because we enjoyed each other's company. Jauma's business and mine had aspects in common, in the sense that Petnay supplied me with particular products via one of its many subsidiaries.'

'Can you confirm my impression that Jauma had been getting particularly depressed recently?'

'Absolutely not. Not at all. He was certainly capable of swinging between euphoria and depression, but I'd not noticed any particular change in him recently. Who's been telling you that Jauma was depressed?'

'Nuñez, Vilaseca, and Biedma.'

'Oh, the left wing! They seem to take a particular delight in trying to show that Jauma, Fontanillas and myself have made a mistake in the kind of life we've chosen.'

'Have you?'

He raised the Davidoff as if it were a chalice about to be consecrated, and nodded towards the cigar in Carvalho's hand.

'Do *you* think we've made the wrong choice? The day that you reach maturity is the day when you realize that you only live once. Then you have two choices. Either you decide to live the best life you can, or you go transcendental, go for the hereafter, and turn religious like Nuñez, Vilaseca, Biedma and Santa Teresa de Jesus. Every time I get intimations of mortality, I take a plane and I head for the Princess Hotel in Acapulco. You've heard of it, I'm sure. It's the most luxurious hotel in the world. When I was young and had no money, I used to write poetry and buy myself ties. That used to get me through the depressions. Nuñez, Vilaseca and Biedma believe in the immortality of the soul — not the individual soul, but the soul of the ascendant classes. Note that — "ascendant"! According to them, the class that I belong to is on the way down. Fair enough, I say. But the soul of the bourgeoisie deserves a decent death — with its stomach awash with champagne — Dom Pérignon for preference — and its eyes veiled by the smoke of Davidoff cigars. Every morning I breakfast on three decent-sized Iranian caviar sandwiches and a glass of French champagne with orange juice. Then I go for a swim in my indoor swimming pool, or play tennis on my tennis court, or go for a game of golf. When the good weather comes, I race my yacht during the week, and at weekends I lend it to my friends, so as to enjoy the pleasure of being hopelessly envied. I never eat run-of-the-mill food, Carvalho, never! Our senses deserve better than to be subjected to a routine, because it is through our senses that we are living, sentient beings. In my house we eat *à la carte*. A choice of at least five courses every day, and at every meal. My wife and I are both on a diet, to keep in trim. Nothing miserable, though. Grilled lobster with a caper salad, or a sirloin steak, or maybe a low-fat beef stew. I've been sending my cook to special courses on dietetic cooking. You have no idea what my cook costs me! First I have to pay him enough so that he doesn't just pack his bags and leave. Then I have to shell out even more, to make sure nobody makes him an offer he can't refuse. I keep his whole family employed in my firm. But there you go... a cook is a man's best friend, Carvalho, and if my cook were ever to die I would be heartbroken. I have five thousand bottles in my cellars at Ampurdan, and about two thousand in Barcelona. Top quality, all of them. The best French vintages you can get. And a few Spanish ones — a few good white wines, because sometimes I have a hankering for a well-chilled Galician vino verde — in spring, maybe, or when I have a real thirst. Tomorrow I'm off to Paris, to dine at the Tour d'Argent, and the following day I'll be driving to Lyon, to eat chez Paul Bocuse. A voyage of gastronomic moral rearmament. So what do *you* think? Do you think I've chosen the wrong kind of life? Not a bit of it! I live a hell of a life, and I love it! I don't have a lot to worry about on the business front. I don't even have to worry about domestic competition, because I'm an exporter. D'you hear that? An exporter. Of yoghurt! The production process, incidentally, is child's play, and so is the distribution. As for my love life, I could insure it at Lloyds for a billion dollars. I have a sensible wife who knows when to be intimate and when to leave me alone, and who looks as good in a nightdress as she does in evening dress. My children are perhaps not as intelligent as I would have wished, but they're adequate, and they're healthy too. I have friendships for every occasion — from the nostalgic pleasure that I get from my university friends, to the occasional high-class wedding reception. I have girlfriends for every occasion too. An old girlfriend from my student days, with the body of a forty-year-old woman, who frees me from my adolescent hang-ups; other girls who may be a bit past their prime, but who have a convertible and a cheque book and a slight resemblance to Jacqueline Onassis that I find increasingly attractive as I get older; the wife of one of my subordinates, which provides me with that particular shot of humiliation and abuse that the sex act sometimes requires; and the wife — or the daughter — of one of my friends from the wedding receptions. You could say that I'm a collector. I'm only telling you all this because one should always tell policemen and detectives everything, and also because you know how to smoke a Davidoff. Last week I blew two hundred thousand pesetas buying shirts in London. I shall go back in September in order to replenish my supply of sweaters. I have as much as I need in life, and, thank God, I am not attracted by the sensuality of political power. For some weeks now I have noticed how increasing numbers of business people seem to be getting hooked on politics. They want to be MPs, or senators. Partly because they're worried that the politicians aren't looking after their interests. And partly because political power has a sensuality all its own. They know that history books tend to print the names of politicians and cabinet ministers, and that nobody will ever record the fact that I happened to be the owner of Aracata Ltd. This is another aspect of transcendentalism, against which, fortunately, I have been vaccinated. I have written some excellent books of poetry in Catalan, and I'm thinking of publishing them when I reach the age of sixty, for the simple pleasure of forcing the *Encyclopaedia Catalaña* to dedicate ten lines to me now — and probably thirty lines fifty years from now. Take a look at this. I've written a likely version of what they'll write about me fifty years from now. I'll do you a photocopy so that you can keep it — assuming you want to — and if you live that long you can have a look in fifty years time and see if I was far wrong.'

'Argemi Blanc, Jordi. Born Barcelona 1932, died Palausator (Gerona), 2002. A late-developing Catalan poet. His first book, *Keep the Wood on the Quay*, published in 1980, revealed a previously unknown link between the poetry of Salvat-Papasseit and Gabriel Ferrater, a poetry of personal experience which sometimes tends towards social comment (Salvat-Papasseit), and sometimes adopts a hermetic style of intimate love poetry (Ferrater). *Fruit Skin* (1985) returns to more traditional themes of love poetry, drawing on the Catullan tradition of lyric poetry to create a libretto for a rock-opera. A poet without a poetic history, and with no links with the literary movements of his time, Argemi maintained a constant development in his thematic material and his poetic forms, which culminated in his masterpiece *Yoghurt*, a Laocontian attempt to convert poetry into a synthesis of different literary genres. Some writers on Argemi have seen in *Yoghurt* (1990) symbolic elements which go beyond the formal and expressional challenge contained in it. In the words of Pedro Gimferrer, *Yoghurt* is "an attempt at poetic apprehension of the essence of a country — Catalonia — at the historic moment when, for the fourth time, its desire for independence is frustrated. In this sense, *Yoghurt* forms one part of the great triptych of Catalonia's national poetry, alongside Verdaguer's *Atlantis* and Josep Carner's *Nabi*." Between 1990 and 2002, the year of his death, Argemi's only published work was a curious book of "sensual memoirs" entitled *Capital Pleasures*. A year after his death, in 2003, a minor work was published which revealed the creative decline of the seventy-year-old poet, although it still had the characteristic linguistic inventiveness which was so typical of his writing: *The Smoke of a Davidoff* (2003). Essential bibliographic reading: *Argemi Through the Looking Glass*, ed. P. Gimferrer, La Coqueluche, 1995; *Final Poems*, Josep M. Castellet, Edicions 62, 1983; *Argemi Alone*, Françoise Wagener, Editions Gallimard, 1990.'

'All these books, of course, will have been written by myself,' Argemi concluded as he sat half-hidden behind a final puff of smoke from the Davidoff.

In a solidly modern flat located in a part of Barcelona that was high enough up a hillside to escape the hurly-burly of the urban masses and central enough to enable its owner to go on foot to any of the city's art movie houses or one of the restaurants catering for reasonably well-off cultural minorities, lived Juan Dorronsoro, the youngest son of a family whose eldest son was a poet featured in seventy-three per cent of international anthologies of Spanish poetry and whose second eldest was Pedro Dorronsoro, the best known of all Spanish novelists, who had even been mentioned in an American TV mini-series.

'Who are your favourite writers?'

'I've just finished a Hemingway, and now I'm starting something by Pedro Dorronsoro, whom I find a very interesting writer...'

While it lacked the socio-cultural representativeness of the one brother, and did not enjoy the intellectual repute of the other, the work of Juan Dorronsoro had advanced slowly but steadily in the form of just three novels, which had met with more critical than popular acclaim. He was a man who wrote ten lines a day, and he lived life as a function of his writing, in a time-scale all his own, and in a physical space limited solely to the present. He lived in the antechamber of a photographic memory that was sufficiently falsificatory to provide material for his novels and at the same time not transgress the bounds of a decent and socially desirable forgetfulness. He had the features of a young duke, the gangling walk of an adolescent, and was the living image of his mother — the classic description of young dukes in novels wherein they contract tropical diseases and impossible passions. And beneath the delicacy of features that had probably remained unchanged since puberty lay the passion of a rationalist writer whose self-imposed brief was to leave some testimony to the collective mediocrity of this city. A silk dressing gown, worn over a mohair jumper; leather slippers; culture piled high on tables and stacked up the walls, in the shape of books, files, and pieces of paper; the look of a writer who has just finished one line and is thinking about the next; and a study with the restrained lighting characteristic of the serious writer — a room where only the sun is allowed to enter without knocking, and even sunlight is only permitted in small quantities, for fear that it might impede the writer's capacities for re-inventing reality.

'I'm afraid I can't tell you a lot. My relationship with Jauma was very one-sided. He talked and I listened. I wrote, and he read what I wrote. He was a pleasant sort of chap — intelligent, wealthy, and a bit of an extrovert. But he was dangerous. He was like a character in a book who ends up endearing himself to the reader without the writer intending it.'

'Is that bad?'

'Bad in every sense. If his appeal derives from the author, it means that the author has been unacceptably partisan in expressing his personal preferences. On the other hand, if he is sympathetic despite his author, it means that the writer has lost control of the book's internal equilibrium.'

'So for you Jauma was just a character?'

'Recently, yes. I have reduced my level of receptivity to real flesh and blood people. My close friends I can handle. The rest are just characters. In the past Jauma meant something quite different to me. Now he's just a character.'

'What about the way he died?'

'Lacking in verisimilitude. It reads like a Spanish erotic novel of the 1920s — Pedro de Repide, Alvaro de Retana, or Lopez de Hoyos. The decadent aristocrat is stabbed to death, and expires on a rubbish tip, having fornicated his way through every sexual aberration known to man.'

'How would you have scripted his last days, if it had been up to you?'

'Jauma at the age of seventy. He goes to the pictures every afternoon with a view to groping girls. His name comes up in the gossip columns. His eldest son starts knocking him about, and the old man takes off to the zoo to watch the monkeys masturbate.'

'And the real facts of his death?'

'...That his death was real.'

'I mean the real causes of his death.'

'He died of real causes. A bullet, I believe.'

'But someone must have fired that bullet.'

'This is a detective novel, and generally speaking I prefer to steer clear of naturalistic literature. But if you insist on playing at detectives, at least let's divide the parts fairly. You want to be Philip Marlowe? Well, I want to be Sherlock Holmes. I'm serious. I really can't help you. It's possible that my friends will be able to help you in imagining the real causes of Jauma's death. I, however, spend my time imagining other things. Many other things. My whole job is precisely that — to create things in my imagination — but within a proper logical framework, within my narrative discourse. What happened to Jauma was terribly sad, and, believe me, I was very upset about it at the time. But I feel that to carry on raking it over now would be like arguing about the sex of angels, or whether Muhammad Ali would have beaten Rocky Marciano.'

The audience had ended. Dorronsoro uncrossed his legs and prepared to get up and show Carvalho to the door as good manners required. The detective didn't take the hint. The novelist hesitated for a moment, and then settled into a waiting mode. He stared into nothingness, to avoid letting Carvalho see the impatience in his eyes, and half absent-mindedly he opened a book that was lying on the table, and began flicking through it. In a space between two of the shelves hung a hunting rifle, which was evidently well looked after.

'Do you hunt?'

'Yes.'

'Are you any good?'

'It depends what it is. I'm good with partridge, but not so good with rabbits.'

'Ever tried big game?'

'I learned my shooting in Maresme, in the hills around San Vicente de Montalt and Arenys de Munt. They have no big game there.'

'Intellectuals aren't supposed to like violence, though...'

'Aggression is another matter. We writers are as

aggressive as anyone else, and I find that hunting releases my aggression. It enables me to contemplate other people's aggressiveness as a spectacle and then describe it.'

'But you still kill.'

'I hunt.'

'You kill.'

'Killing is something different. It's cutting a chicken's throat in a farmyard, or shooting someone, or taking an axe to your neighbour. In hunting there are rules...'

'Which the hunter imposes on an animal that has no weapons to defend itself with.'

'I suppose you'd prefer it if pigeons went around armed with shotguns? Hunting has a certain aesthetic justice. It has its own morality too. If you ask me, you're a puritan. For my part, I love animals. I'm passionate about dogs. I'll introduce you to my dogs, if you like. You've stirred my guilty conscience, and now you're making me feel like a criminal. If we carry on like this I'll end up confessing that it was me that killed Jauma, with this rifle.'

'What would have been your motive?'

'That he didn't like my latest novel.'

Now it was the novelist's turn not to want to terminate their meeting, and he began to study Carvalho as a possible character for his next book.

'Have you never killed?'

'Yes, I've killed.'

'Animals?'

'People.'

'You must have been a hit-man, or part of a firing squad, because you're too young to have been in the war.'

'I was in the CIA.'

'This is getting interesting. A double agent?'

'Treble.'

'They're the best sort. Did you kill them with your own bare hands?'

'I've trained in hand-to-hand combat. The human body has twenty-five points where you can be killed by somebody with their bare hands. But I prefer to use weapons.'

'Who did you kill? Russians? Chinese? Koreans? Vietnamese?'

'Some of each.'

'With those hands?'

Carvalho placed his hands in full view of the writer, who looked at them with mock panic.

'Your hands don't look particularly special.'

'That's because I haven't killed anyone recently.'

'If you don't practise, you'll lose the knack.'

Now the audience was over. Dorronsoro got up and stood back to enable Carvalho to leave. The detective didn't take the hint. He got up, went over to the rifle, took it down, raised it to his shoulder and aimed it at the novelist, who by now was thoroughly annoyed.

'That's not funny. Put it down.'

'Don't worry, chief, I'll put the camp bed next to the phone.'

Biscuter was prepared to stay awake all night in the event of Rhomberg's call not arriving during what was left of the day. Concha Hijar had replied to say that she could only see Carvalho after nine, because she had to feed the children first. The papers were full of their usual contradictory news items. On the one hand the police were arresting the extreme Left, and on the other they were setting them free. In the afternoon they were persecuting the extreme Right, and at night the extreme Right was given a free hand. The political parties were preparing for the forthcoming elections. The fascist International had its headquarters in Spain. There was still no sign of the driver of the BMW that had crashed into the Tordera. 'The Peter Herzen Mystery: It appears that Mr "Peter Herzen" had hired the BMW with false papers.'

'I'm going out before the trouble starts on the Ramblas.'

'I've got your dinner ready, chief. Kidneys in sherry and rice pilau.'

'What sort of rice?'

'Uncle Ben's.'

'Keep it for me till tomorrow, and keep an ear out for Rhomberg's phone call.'

'God — anyone would think I'd ever let you down, boss.'

It seemed that the stage was being set for a scene similar to the night before. The police were waiting for the demonstrators, and the demonstrators seemed to be waiting for the police to take up positions. A drunk with a face blackened by his own grime began calling to imaginary chickens: 'Here, chook... Chookie, chookie...!' And then he began to sing:

> The wine of my Asuncion
> Is neither white nor red,
> It has no colour at all.

Somewhere between his chest and his shoulders, Carvalho could feel a psychological chill. He tried to work out which of his recent experiences could be worrying him. Probably the drunk. But possibly not this drunk in particular.

> The wine of my Asuncion
> Is neither white nor red,
> It has no colour at all.

A few five-and ten-cent coins clattered down into the street. They glittered on top of the cobblestones where they fell, or down the cracks in between. The old singers gathered up their harvest, and didn't turn up their noses at a small coin that had fallen into a pile of horse-dung.

'Give him some — that one there.'

'Why that one, and not the one before?'

'Because this one's old.'

The street singers were old, and were disabled. The people of District 5 leaned over their balconies and were selective in their charity.

'He must have been wounded in the war,' his mother would say. Wounded in the war. And grown old from what? Grown old from the war? Who hadn't grown old from the war? Who wasn't war-wounded in one way or another?

'Thank you, sir.'

The drunkard took the hundred-peseta note that Carvalho passed out of the car window. Between the black of his face and the yellow that bore no relation to what should have been the whites of his naked eyes, the drunk stared uncomprehendingly, trying to resurrect a semblance of dignity in gratitude. Despite the fact that his body and his ulcerous lips were aimed towards Carvalho, he wasn't capable of looking straight ahead of him. He smelt of cheap sherry and death.

'He's asleep. He's drunk.'

'No, he's dead.'

Somebody pulled him away from the circle of onlookers surrounding the fallen body.

'It's the Murcians' son.'

When he had got out of the concentration camp, the Murcians' son had survived on the few vegetables that his parents managed to sell clandestinely, when they weren't being caught by the sergeant, who would give the old man a kick that sent him sprawling among his scattered vegetables. When the Murcians' son was drunk, he would take up a position at the junction of calle Cera and Botella, and would give a military salute and shout: 'Franco! I shit on you!'

While his mother tried to shut him up, his father would try to pull him away, and the gypsy lads at the Bar Moderno would freeze their seemingly inexhaustible hilarity, reduced to silence by the drama.

'He was dead.'

'Sssh! The boy will hear you.'

Why so much effort in concealing his death? Hours later, the silent moving line of people came up the street to the Murcians' house.

'Even with a hundred lives, they'll never pay for the vile thing they've done.'

'Who?'

'The fascists.'

Sometimes he began to doubt the reality of his neighbourhood. Looking back, he remembered it as a city that was poor and sunk in a kind of bitter-sweet syrup. People who were defeated and humiliated, forever having to apologize for the fact of having been born. The first time that Carvalho had left those narrow streets, he actually had imagined that he had freed himself forever from his existence as an animal drowning in historical misery. But he found he was carrying it with him, like a snail carrying its shell, and years later, when he belatedly decided to accept himself for who he was and what he'd done, he returned to the scene of his childhood and adolescence.

His old neighbourhood had been transformed into a waiting-room for the grave, where the older generation had been sentenced to die in its damp surroundings, while the younger generation sought refuge in cheap flats out in the suburbs. Next to ageing survivors of the pre-war period were the middle-aged ones with a sense of personal failure at not having got out in time from the tight, satanic grip of this defeated city. And then a transient population of recent immigrants from Morocco and the odd bunch of Latin Americans forced into cheap rented apartments. Carvalho braked. He pulled up at the side of the road without thinking why.

'You've hit rock-bottom,' he thought to himself, and he pulled a box of Montecristos from the glove compartment and lit one of them with speed and the anticipation of great pleasure, with his lighter, as if he was drinking the gas flame through the Havana. When I die, the memory of those times will disappear with me. And also the memory of the people who, in bringing me into this world, gave me a first-class vantage point from which to view the spectacle of their own tragedy. Carvalho hadn't just watched the spectacle. He'd made it his own, and had tried to transmit it to the younger generation. Up and down the Ramblas young and old people alike had expelled the fear that was left in them, on the day that the Dictator died. Happiness in their hearts — but silence on their lips. The shops ran out of bottles of cheap champagne that day; the streets and terraces were full of people enjoying the pleasure of being together without the great crushing shadow hanging over them. But still in silence, still with that cautiousness with words that they had learned in the years of the Terror as a guarantee of at least a mediocre survival. In some ways he understood that past. He knew its language. On the other hand the future opened by Franco's death seemed foreign to him, like the water of a river that you shouldn't drink, but that you wouldn't want to drink either. Gausachs, Fontanillas... the crooks of the new situation.

'And if there was another Civil War, the two of them would go to Burgos.'

'And Argemi? To Tahiti, via Switzerland.'

And you, Pepe Carvalho, where the hell would you go? To Vallvidrera, to make myself roast leg of lamb à la Périgord, or a meat stew. Would you cook the cabbage together with the meat? Maybe, as long as you don't put too much cabbage in. Otherwise the flavour of the cabbage drowns out everything else. And what if you didn't have the wherewithals? Then I'd make salt cod with rice. And what if there wasn't even any salt cod? Then I'd walk down the road into Barcelona, and I'd let myself be machine-gunned by a diving jet fighter. And what if they dropped a neutron bomb? It'd kill everyone on the Ramblas, and the only faces left would be the ones on the front pages of the newspapers hanging outside the kiosks. Then the conquerors would come marching in, bringing with them the seeds of their own destruction fifty years or a hundred years later.

'No, I don't have any news.' Carvalho wasn't inclined to share with the widow Jauma the news that Rhomberg was arriving, and he asked her if she had any news, in order to find out whether Rhomberg had been in touch with her too. Then she asked:

'What about you?'

'Things are moving — slowly. Now, first of all, is it true that your husband was particularly depressed, particularly worried, in recent weeks?'

'He would swing from being very cheerful to being very depressed. He was worrying about everything, and he was particularly worried that a poor year would greatly reduce the value of his shares in the company. These fears were always self-inflicted and without foundation. Recently he was worried by the effect that the changing political situation was going to have on the economy. He would say: "If harder times lie ahead, then democracy is an expensive party." Maybe that's what you're referring to?'

'I have come to the conclusion that your husband was not what one would call a trusting person. For example, we know that, in addition to the firm's own staff, he had his own private accountants.'

'He was afraid of the power-games. He had no sense of his own worth. He used to be scared of Gausachs, for example, because he used to say that he had friends in high places and a lot of ambition.'

'Did your husband go to any accountant in particular?'

A smile illuminated the widow's pale features. She repressed it as if it had been a serious lapse.

'Ah yes... his Alemany mania.'

'Alemany mania?'

'Alemany is almost an institution in the Jauma family. My husband's relations are all from Gerona, and most of them still live there. My father-in-law was a lawyer too, but he went into manufacturing way before the war. I think he was making cork stoppers. When he set up offices in Barcelona, he needed an accountant, and he chose one who was very well respected — Alemany. He was a kind of lucky charm. Firms that he was involved with were firms that did well. He was good for them. Then the war came, and Alemany had to go into exile, because he'd been the director of some workers' centre or something. My father-in-law also went into exile, although not for long. I doubt that Alemany's exile had anything to do with his professional activities. He was also involved in Barcelona Football Club, during the club's most political period. Anyway, in the end Alemany had to leave the country, and the business didn't do so well. He came back many years after the end of the war. The whole family used to consult him over business matters. He was an old firebrand, very tetchy, and consumed with hatred for Franco. He must be about a hundred years old by now, and he still works as an accountant, although he's not as involved as he used to be. He just handles a few accounts here and there, and to give you an idea of what people think of him, my brothers-in-law still come down from Gerona to consult him every now and then.'

'And Antonio consulted him too?'

'Yes. He was always making fun of the old man, but he said he had the best accounting brain he'd ever met.'

'Had he seen him recently?'

'It's possible. I couldn't say.'

'How can I get hold of Alemany?'

'I'll give you his address.'

The woman sat down at a hundred-and-fifty-thousand-peseta imported English writing desk and copied out an address. She was dressed in mourning, with an elegance that was excessive for a woman about to eat alone, and her make-up strove to hide the dark rings around her eyes. Carvalho's next question stopped her dead in her tracks.

'Did your husband leave you well provided for?'

'I've collected on two fairly substantial life assurance policies, and Petnay pays me a pension, which is decent enough by today's standards. We'll have to see how it stands up in the years to come, though. I need to invest the insurance money, but I'm not sure where. I've left it in Fontanillas's hands, but he says that this is a bad time. Nobody is investing. Everybody is waiting to see what's going to happen on the political front.'

'You've left it with Fontanillas? Why not Argemi?'

'Fontanillas has a lot of experience in these things. Argemi runs a wonderful business, but he's not strictly a money man. I have four children, señor Carvalho, and they're all at an age where they cost a lot of money.'

'How did the children take the news of their father's death?'

'Very badly at first. The two boys got over it fairly well. But the girls still miss him terribly. It's only natural.'

'And what about you?'

'What do you think?'

'I don't think anything. That's why I'm asking. I remember a French song I heard once. It said, more or less, "Even though I love you a lot, and we're in the same political party, if you should go one day, it'll leave me more time to read and to find myself."'

'That's not a very nice thing to say.'

'That's the second time someone's told me that today.'

'Antonio was a very suffocating person, very all-consuming, you could say. Egocentric, I suppose. On the one hand he could be infuriating, but at the same time he gave me a good life. The main thing that got on my nerves was the way he never used to stop talking, particularly about sex. It was all talk, though...'

'All talk?'

'Yes. At least, I think so. And even if it wasn't, I don't really care. It used to take the pressure off him when he talked, so I used to let him. I got used to it, although sometimes I found the stupid things he used to say in public quite unbearable.'

'In your opinion, why was he killed?'

'I think it was probably a revenge killing. This whole big-business world is full of gangsters and self-made types without the sensibilities of men like Antonio, Fontanillas and Argemi. I always tell them that they're the exception. Sometimes when we were at a cocktail party or something Antonio would point to a person and say, "That one would kill his own father for a hundred pesetas..." Or, "That one's a pig... That one's a criminal..." Antonio was very aggressive as an executive. He was always joking about it. He would look in the mirror while he was shaving and say: "I'm an aggressive executive — grrrr!" and he'd roar like the MGM lion.'

The widow Jauma was laughing and crying at the same time. Carvalho found the sight of her submissive breasts and her broad, earth-mother hips arousing. She had the face of a Castilian — with a mantilla, she would have been just right for the Holy Week procession in Valladolid.

'Was your husband a jealous man?'

'Very.'

'Did he have reason to be?'

'I am not a sex maniac. I have a house and four children to look after, and everything has always depended on me, because he never used to help in the house at all. I would never have had the time to go out looking for adventures.'

'Don't you still have friends from your younger days?'

'My friends were the same as Antonio's. I was still a child when I left Valladolid. Because of my father's profession we travelled a lot. I never had time to make friends.'

'Did none of Jauma's friends ever proposition you?'

'What are you trying to suggest? That it was a *crime*

passionel? Can you really imagine Vilaseca propositioning me? Or Biedma? Can you imagine Biedma making advances to me?'

'I can imagine it perfectly well.'

'Well, you must have a good imagination...'

Concha Hijar was now visibly uneasy, and wanted to terminate the interview. She looked at the Empire-style mantel clock and bit back the observation that it was almost dinner time, for fear that Carvalho might take it as an invitation.

'It's getting late. I have to help Vera with her homework.'

'I'll be leaving, then.'

'Have you discovered anything?'

'A range of possibilities has opened up, and one of them might be the light at the end of the tunnel. I've had a terrible day. I feel like an opinion poll interviewer working on piecework. I've seen too many people today — Gausachs, Fontanillas, Biedma, Vilaseca, Dorronsoro, and now yourself. Oh — and Argemi. I almost forgot the incredible Argemi.'

'Why incredible? If you ask me, he's the most normal of any of them.'

'Tell me honestly, what do you think of your husband's friends?'

'They remind me of a poem by Gabriela Mistral, which the nuns used to teach us. Three girls are playing at imagining the future. They all want to be queen.'

Pedro Parra wasn't making it easy.

'Who do you think I am — Milton Friedman? Those kinds of flow-charts are a visual gimmick — they're not scientific.'

'I need to have a visual idea of Petnay's operations in

Spain and how they connect up. Not just interlinking directorships and so on — I want a chart of all the companies that depend on Petnay for what they produce.'

'I can't do that under the counter. I'll have to give the figures to one of our graphics people, and if I give him the data he'll be able to draw you up a flow chart. You'll have to pay him something, though.'

'And I'll treat you to a good camping tent.'

'Drop dead!'

Having called Parra, he rang his office again.

'All quiet on the western front, boss. The German hasn't rung.'

A day late. Almost inconceivable. The hippy life has changed our Dieter, Carvalho mused. He'd had enough of the day's conversations, and of himself, and decided to get them out of his system, so he plumped for a cinema where they were showing *Night Moves*. Afterwards he'd get home sufficiently relaxed to cook himself something special — something slightly painstaking and packed with stimulation and small difficulties. The film was an excellent example of American cinema noir, with Gene Hackman brilliant in the role of a private detective in the introspective tradition of Marlowe and Spade. In addition, Carvalho felt a special attraction to Susan Clarke's chunky, angular eroticism, so the presence of this mature blonde, splendid in her spontaneous, animal beauty, was an added bonus. Yet more role models! Which should he choose? Whom should he copy? Bogart playing Chandler? Alan Ladd doing Hammett? Paul Newman as Harper? Gene Hackman? In the privacy of his car as it crept up the slopes of Tibidabo, Carvalho practised the mannerisms of each of them. Bogart's dewy-eyed look and the contemptuous curl of the lip. Alan Ladd, and the way he walked as tall as possible to cover up for how short he was. Then there was Newman, with his self-awareness of being so very good-looking. And Hackman, with the look of a man who's been jilted by his wife, weighs two hundred pounds, and is tired of life.

'No news, boss. Not a peep out of the German.'

'If he calls, whatever time of night it is, make sure he rings my place.'

To begin cooking duck at one in the morning is one of the finest acts of madness that can be undertaken by a human being who is not mad. The duck roasting in the oven, shedding its fat and turning brown as if it was on a simultaneous slimming and tanning course. In the meantime, Carvalho heated some bacon fat in a pan, and used it to fry onion and mushrooms. He then added white wine, salt, pepper, and a bit of sliced truffle. The truffles came from Villores, in the Maestrazgo, and they were supplied by a commercial agent, who was also a Latinist, and who lived alone a few houses down from Carvalho. Next to his kitchen the agent had a room in which he stored the treasures which his relatives brought from Villores, or which he brought back himself from his fortnightly trips. The Chaldeans believed that the world extended no further than the furthest mountains known to them; Fuster, the agent, believed in his heart of hearts, with all the faith of a primitive Christian, that the world extended no further than Villores, and that neighbouring populations such as Morella could be considered more or less as planets inhabited by alien beings. Since the agent and Carvalho were both eaters, drinkers, and bachelors, the pair of them often devoted their Sundays to matters gastronomic. Fuster's speciality was a rabbit paella with almost no onion.

'Because otherwise the rice goes soggy.'

When he was in a good mood, Fuster would recite from Caesar's *Gallic Wars*. Carvalho would allow the torrent of Latinism to pass, and would then join his friend in a medley of songs from the Castellon/Aragon border, or the songs of Conchita Piquer.

> Eyes that are green, green as the basil,
> Green as the green corn,
> Green as a green, green lemon tree.

Seven hours after having initiated the proceedings, there was always something left to try in one or other of their houses, and it was generally already morning by the time they decided to go to bed — Carvalho with his head full of stories of the Maestrazgo and Fuster with a superficial resumé of the cases that the detective had been involved in that week.

The duck had finished roasting. Carvalho separated off the legs, wings, and breast, and cut up the remaining bits of meat, including the bird's delicate innards. He mixed the meat back in with the duck's juices, and added a handful of stoned olives. Once the meat had blended with the juices, he mixed it in with the diced bacon, the mushrooms and the truffle, and added a couple of spoonfuls of grated breadcrumbs.

He let the mixture cook for a short while, and then sprinkled it over the larger pieces of meat, which he had already arranged in a casserole. The bird drank in the flavour of the sauce, and displayed on its brown-roasted surface a landscape of mushrooms, bacon, olives, breadcrumbs, and fragments of the meat sauce. He put it on the gas for five minutes, and then in the oven for a further five. A sublime, unfathomable smell of well-roasted meat assailed his nostrils as he opened the oven door. He felt that need of solidarity or complicity that takes hold of amateur cooks when they know they've cooked something rather special. It was half past two in the morning. Without a second thought, he returned the food to the scorching heat of the oven and leapt down the stairs that led to his dew-drenched garden. The night had stretched a canopy of deep coolness and solitude over the little village whose location seemed designed for the contemplation, on the one hand, of Barcelona, right down to the sea, and, on the other, the progress of a Catalonia winding its way to the mountains. He ran the few yards that separated him from the huge building that was shared by his three neighbours, but where only Fuster actually lived the whole year round.

He called up a couple of times, and suddenly a light appeared, announcing the apparition of Fuster on the terrace above. Sleep had left his blond goatee beard and his thinning but strategically combed hair ruffled, and had tilted the angle of his glasses to such an extent that one side frame was stuck in his left ear and the other was desperately seeking the support of his right.

'What time of night do you call this? What's up — is your house on fire?'

'No. A duck ragout.'

'A what?!'

'I've cooked a duck. It's not a very big one, but there's no way that I'm eating it on my own.'

'It's half two in the morning, though.'

'A duck ragout, friend.'

'A young duck?'

'A veritable duckling!'

'You sure of that?'

'Absolutely.'

'Go and get the wine open. I'll be right with you.'

Either Carvalho was excessively slow in returning home, or Fuster had run, driven by the cool damp of the night and his rekindled appetite. At any rate, by the time he arrived Carvalho had not had time to open the bottle of Montecillo. Fuster placed on the kitchen table a small basket that he had brought with him, filled with dried fruits from Villores, natural honey, also from Villores, and some strange pastries belonging to a species of popular dry pastries whose ingredients necessarily included egg and almond.

'My sister-in-law made these pastries. They're from Villores.'

'I suspected as much.'

'After duck there's nothing better than a few hazel nuts with honey and a pastry to settle a good meal.'

Fuster opened the oven, raised his head, and closed his eyes. His thin nostrils were quivering with anticipation.

'You've surpassed yourself.'

A celery salad was the perfect prelude to the duck.

'Now there's a fundamental contribution from Villores — you've put truffle into it.'

'Yes.'

'That's most unorthodox. You don't put truffle with duck.'

'You put what the bloody hell you want...!'

'Oh well, if that's the way you feel about it...'

Two glasses of chilled *eau de vie* were downed in the hope that they would create space in their respective stomachs.

'If this *trou normand* doesn't settle things, we'll be up all night.'

Fuster gently fondled his stomach.

'You're crazy. Or rather, we're crazy. It's four in the morning!'

'If you want to sleep easy, you have to vomit. The main thing is to have eaten the meal. Digesting it is wholly incidental to the exercise and quite pointless.'

'I'll go straight home and if I'm not asleep within five minutes I'll remember a restaurant in London where I used to wash dishes when I was a student, and that'll make me vomit. I feel like throwing up even at the thought of it. Thanks, Pepe. You've put an extra night into my life. I would have spent it just sleeping like an ox, but I've lived it instead. I'm grateful.'

> When the night comes and spreads its shadows,
> Few animals do not close their eyes,
> And the pain of sick people grows.

'My fellow countryman Ausias March would not have written those lines if he'd had a neighbour like you.'

Alone again Carvalho noted how objects in the room seemed to be creeping up on him again, and he wasn't sure if they wanted to protect him or suffocate him.

'Biscuter — I know this is a hell of a time to be phoning,

but it's important. Has anyone rung?'

'No one. I wasn't asleep, boss. So as to stay awake for your phone call I was reading one of the books off your bookshelf. It's a very sad book, but I'm getting through it.'

'Which book?'

'*The Heart*. I read one bit that was just like the serial on TV — *Marco*. Similar, but not the same. I've been crying, boss. Can't you tell it from my voice? And another bit — the story of the Sardinian drummer boy. Do you remember it? He must have been like the drummer of Bruch. It's true isn't it — that the drummer of Bruch doesn't die?'

'Not while he's playing his drum, no. But afterwards he very definitely does.'

'I've just got to the bit where Garrone's mother dies. Another bit of melodrama! It's a very good book, but everyone always seems to be dying.'

At a given moment, some designer must have decided that, given that Catalonia was trying to reconstruct a *raison d'être* for itself in the field of politics and culture, there was no reason not to do the same for interior decor. So they invented a kind of rural Renaissance style combining the much-vaunted Catalonian sobriety of taste with the lightness required for modern furniture. The result was a style of furniture called *renaixentista*, which was certainly good to look at, but which was a dog's dinner as far as its antecedents were concerned. From the moment you stepped into the hallway, Alemany's flat was a declaration of principle. Above a Catalonian flag hung framed portraits of Macia, Companys, and Tarradellas, the three presidents of the Generalitat in the twentieth century. Next to the photo of Macia, a frame transformed a letter into a holy relic. It was a handwritten note in Catalan from Companys to the master of the house: 'My dear Alemany, our friend Rodoreda tells me that you've been ill...'

An affectionate letter which reflected the older generation's fetish for formalities. The letter took on new meaning when señora Alemany, twenty years younger than her octogenarian husband, spoke in a subdued voice to inform him that Alemany was ill, very ill. Alemany was all skin and bone, with a pale complexion and grey hair that was neatly combed. Breathing through his mouth and peering at Carvalho with eagle eyes, Alemany told the detective to come and sit by his bed. He gave his wife just one look and she hurried from the room. Then the old man looked at Carvalho and asked him to be brief. The detective explained the reason for his visit. Had Jauma been to see him recently about anything to do with Petnay? If so, what? Was it something important? The old man said nothing. Carvalho explained that he was there on behalf of Jauma's widow, and the eagle eyes became more gentle. He shut his eyes as if to make them gentler still, swallowed his saliva by a motion of his Adam's apple that was almost audible, and a slight trembling movement indicated that he was gearing himself up to speak, in the way that Spanish toilet cisterns give a slight quiver just before the water begins its descent down the pipe.

'Señor Jauma and I — I've called him señor Jauma ever since his father died — had a fine friendship. He was from Vidreras, a village in Gerona, close to my own. I am from Santa Cristina de Aro. Señor Jauma, as I say, was alarmed when he saw that the figures that I prepared for him did not add up, but that the figures in the company's official audit did.'

'What was the discrepancy?'

'This will surprise you. Two hundred million. Yes — really, two hundred million pesetas.'

'Was this the first time?'

'No. Let me finish. That's what I was going to say. It

wasn't the first time. The accounts that I've drawn up and
the accounts prepared by Petnay haven't tallied since 1974,
but there's never been such a big gap before — usually it's
only been five or six million. On each occasion Jauma
informed the company's head office, so that they could
investigate the matter. The first two years they replied that
it had all been cleared up. But this year the amount was
too big to explain away. I advised señor Jauma to have the
figures double-checked by somebody else, because I was
worried by the responsibility involved. He made me run
through the figures again and again, and each time the
discrepancy came out at two hundred million.'

'What did Petnay say?'

'All I know is what señor Jauma told me. He rang me
one day and said: "Don't worry, Alemany. It's all been sorted
out." That was one week before his death.'

'Have you told anyone about all this since Jauma was
killed?'

'It was a professional secret between myself and señor
Jauma, and also a matter of friendship.'

'Have you kept a copy of your work?'

'Of course. I would only let it go into the hands of señor
Jauma's elder brother, though, and then only on condition
that he promised — promised — that he would never use
it against his brother.'

'I suppose we can presume that it wasn't Jauma who
had appropriated the money.'

'Obviously.'

'Didn't you think that Jauma's death might have been
connected with the business about the disappearance of
the money?'

'Of course. But since there's been so much garbage piling
up in this country, so much filth, during the dictatorship
of that petty crook, that scum... !'

The insults came from his lips like shells from a howitzer.
They gave him the energy to raise his head from the pillow,
with the aid of thin muscles that were white and fragile,

and which soon gave way, to let his head sink back, but not his anger.

'I let a few days pass and I saw that they were providing an explanation. Fine. It was none of my business. If anyone had raised questions about the money, or about the running of the firm, then Oriol Alemany would have gone straight to the board of directors and I would have told them a thing or two. But then I fell ill. I'm eighty-six years old, and I still do the audits for four companies. Look at those books, there.'

On the *renaixença* sideboard lay four large credit/debit books, an accounting pad with big lilac-coloured board covers, a classic Waterman's fountain pen, an ink rubber and a set of recently sharpened pencils.

'In the afternoon, when my head clears, my wife sets up a table for me, and I work for a bit until I get tired. Just a moment ago señor Robert rang to ask how I'm getting on with the accounts. He rings me every day. Not that he's trying to hurry me up — it's more his way of encouraging me. I used to do the accounts for his father. He was what I'd call a proper industrialist, of the sort we used to have before the war. He was a man of the centre-Right, but not one of those who went off to Burgos. I vouched for him several times during the war, and one day, when I realized that, for all my protection, they would be coming to look for him, to do something dreadful to him, I went to see him, and I said: "Señor Robert, I can get a car and take you as far as Camprodon. From there I know how to get you across the mountains." We'd always had a wonderful understanding, you see. He was in the League, and I was in the Socialist Union, but we were both Catalans, Catalans to the core. Señor Robert wouldn't listen to me, and a few days later they found him dead on a piece of waste ground over by Horta. His widow always used to say: "Ah, Alemany! If only he had listened to you!" You follow my meaning? Anyway, I didn't take on clients just because they wanted me to take them on — I took them on because *I* wanted to, and they were really more friends than clients, because it's a bad thing when an accountant thinks only of making money.'

He turned down the bedclothes and revealed a gold Barcelona F.C. shield embroidered onto the breast pocket of his pyjama jacket. He looked at the shield and then at Carvalho. 'If it hadn't been for those hooligans who took the club over after the war... I was one of the directors of Barcelona during the Republic, when the club was a *proper* football club. Because now those comedians, those crooks... You can't tell me that it's a proper club now! It's just another monument to Franco, and it will stay that way until they get rid of the dross — in other words, the Spanish Football Federation. I said this way back in the thirties, to Hernandez Coronado, a journalist who later became a director of Madrid Athletic. I said: "If it was up to me, Barcelona would withdraw from the Spanish league and join some other league — the French, maybe... or the Australian... it's all the same to me." "Don't take it like that, Alemany, old chap," he said. Don't take it like that! How am I supposed to take it when they rob us of match after match? All Madrid knows is how to rob us blind, and ever since the war they've been trying to turn us into a nation of shepherds and farmers, like Churchill wanted to do with Germany. Although I have to say that I would have done the same with the Germans. They'll soon be getting up to their old tricks again. I give it another five years. There's plenty of scope for wheeler-dealing, and what has foreign investment ever done for us except prop up the dictatorship that kept Catalonia down?'

'Oriol, don't talk about politics — you know it only upsets you.'

'Oh, leave me alone, woman! "Don't talk about politics," she says. Everything's politics!'

His wife handed him a little tray with a pill and half a glass of water on it. The old man concentrated his energies on a meticulous swallowing of the pill and then gave his wife a look which drove her from the room.

'Don't talk about politics, indeed... everything is politics!. Now they say that we're heading for democracy. And who's taking us there? The same traitors who had it good under Franco... First democracy, and then autonomy. Damn them all!'

'Señor Alemany, it is possible that the business with the missing money is important for the inquiries that I'm making. Could I count on you as a witness?'

'When the time comes I would consult with señor Jauma's elder brother, because he is now head of the Jauma family and holds the moral responsibility — at least, as far as I'm concerned.'

'I hope you get better; I hope Barcelona wins out; and I hope Catalonia gets its autonomy.'

'It won't happen in my lifetime. Are you from Catalonia?'

'I don't know. I'd say I'm probably one of the "traitors".'

'In Catalonia, the real foreigners are actually Catalans — people like Samaranch, Porta, and other moneybags who lined their pockets under Franco. They're your real foreigners.'

From the doorway Carvalho could see that the old man was still smouldering with anger. In the drawing room the widow-to-be had tears in her eyes.

'He's on the way out. He's very ill, poor thing.'

'He seems very well, considering.'

The wife gave him a look she'd copied from her husband.

'It's his character. It's his stamina that keeps him going. I think the only reason he's lived this long is because he wanted Franco to die first.'

The message from the Golden Hammer had been urgent, but the king of the pimps was sitting making inroads into a plate of cockles, which he then washed down with a tomato juice. He invited Carvalho to take a seat.

'I don't like it.'

'What don't you like?'

'This business you're investigating. For the past forty-eight hours they've been pulling all my pals in, trying to get someone to own up to the Vich killing. They tell me that some new boy who's been trying to make his mark round here has signed a bloody statement saying that *he* didn't actually kill Jauma, but that everyone's saying it was one of us who did. The next step will be to pull in some poor sod and get him to sign a confession. It looks to me as if someone's pushing very hard to get this case stitched up — someone with the power to be able to put pressure on. The civil governor leans on the chief of police, and the chief of police leans on someone else, and so on, down to the cop on the street.'

'You still say you don't believe the official version?'

'I know how these things work. I'll wait till they put the silly fucker inside, and then I'll know who's calling the shots, and whether he's signed with the fear of God up him, or whether he actually knew something. At this moment he'll be at the police headquarters. This evening they'll take him to the Modelo, and tomorrow I'll send in a lawyer to find out what's going on.'

'They might put him in solitary.'

'If they put him in solitary, I'll send the lawyer of one of the prison big-shots, because they can get to talk to prisoners in the punishment cells and they always know everything. By tomorrow we'll know something, for sure.'

'Would you be able to find out who's putting the pressure on?'

'That's none of my business. My territory begins and ends in Plaza de Catalunya, as you might say. Anything beyond that is up to you. It must be someone pretty big,

though, because we've been behaving ourselves, and for
the last two days they've been grabbing our balls with both
hands. Anyway, you'd best go now, because the less I'm
seen with you the better.'

The bar lay outside Barcelona's criminal quarter, and
had an air that suggested it served nothing but tomato
juices and camomile infusions for forty-year-old ladies lost
in the desert of the late afternoon. He returned to his office
on foot, mingling with the midday crowds on the Ramblas
and bathing in the innocence of the sun: students, office
workers, old-age pensioners, all looking to enjoy a stroll
and soak up the free nutrition of the spring sunshine.
Looking like a puppy thrown out of his kennel, Biscuter
was standing in a corner of the office which had been
invaded by one of the long-haired policemen of the previous
visit, and a gigantic inspector who looked like he weighed
a ton, and who seemed to have two moustaches, one over
his mouth, and another between his eyes.

'You've been out early this morning, eh, dick-sniffer.'

Without replying, Carvalho settled himself in his seat
and swung it to right and left. Biscuter slowly recovered
his confidence to the point of taking a step forwards and
coming to stand at his side.

'We've come to save you a bit of work.'

Carvalho's silence caused the two policemen to look at
each other. The older man leaned the full weight of his
thorax over the table and propped his hands on the edge.

'It's all been cleared up now. A pimp has owned up that
Jauma was killed because he was going too far with one of
the girls. It wasn't him who killed him, and he doesn't know
who did, because he's new on the scene. But a lot of his
associates are talking about it. Our chief says that we
should call on the dick-sniffer and tell him to take a
vacation. The police have got things in hand.'

'So there's no need for you to go wasting your time,' said
the younger man, in a conciliatory tone.

'No point in cutting up meat that's already been sliced.

One of these days we'll pick up the murderer, probably on some minor charge, and that'll be that.'

'If you insist on carrying on with this wild goose chase, it must be because you're a workaholic, or you're trying to bump up your client's bill.'

Carvalho's state of having apparently been struck dumb was accompanied by a semblance of being lost in thought.

'Would you happen to be trying to get rid of us? You haven't even said good morning, yet. Did you hear this gentleman say good morning?'

'He doesn't have to if he doesn't want to.'

'I'd like to hear the sound of his voice, though. I don't usually talk to people just for the fun of it.'

He lowered the weight of his half ton of thorax further in Carvalho's direction, and the chair suddenly stopped rotating.

'Biscuter — did you offer these gentlemen something to drink? Would you fancy something, gentlemen? It's easier to talk with a glass in your hand.'

'Ah — at last — things are looking up! He spoke! Did you happen to take in what we've just been telling you?'

'Yes. I understand that sometimes you have to do things that you don't like doing, and that often you don't even know why you're doing them. You're just obeying orders.'

'That's right. Spot on!'

'It's obvious that someone, somewhere, is very keen for this case to be closed, and they've come up with some half-starved trainee pimp with more fear than pride.'

'Ah, so that's what you're thinking — that we force confessions out of people by beating them up and waving guns at them.'

'There are people in this world who shit themselves just at the sight of a police station — give them half a chance and they'd happily sign their own death warrants.'

'You're talking about the old days. Police training is different these days. I myself have studied scientific methods for observing a criminal's behaviour without having to get physical with him. I won't deny that the police *used* to beat people up, but things are different nowadays.'

The older man seemed not very amused by his long-haired associate's attempts to dissociate himself from the old days.

'Don't go teaching your grandmother to suck eggs. A criminal is still a criminal. Always has been and always will be.'

'People can change.'

The younger man stuck to his guns, encouraged by Carvalho's comments on humanity's potential for transformation. The larger policeman disagreed vigorously.

'If you go through life thinking like that, you'll never get ahead in this profession, and you'll just find people taking advantage of you.'

'I observe an interesting difference of opinion between the two of you,' Carvalho commented, in a neutral tone. 'In *your* case it's the voice of experience speaking... years on the job.'

'Twenty-five.'

'That's a long time. And in *your* case it's technique that's talking, and that also has its value.'

'I don't deny that you can learn through science — you learn a lot, in fact — but I believe in calling a spade a spade.'

'Would you like a drink?'

'Thanks, but not while we're on duty.'

The caveman with the double moustache calmed down and switched police roles, from the aggressive to the paternal. He smiled at those present and turned to his young assistant:

'If you carry on thinking like that, you'll find criminals getting away right under your nose. You *have* to be distrustful, because prevention is better than cure. My father was a *guardia civil* in a small village during the Depression, when everyone was hungry. People were thieving every day. Chickens, corn, rabbits, potatoes. And every day people came complaining to the *guardia civil*.

Whenever my father picked up a suspect, crack! he'd stick his fingers in the door and crunch them till he confessed. Obviously, he didn't always get the right man, and more than one person ended up with his fingers crunched even though he'd never stolen a thing. But he certainly stopped the chicken-stealing. Now there's food for thought!'

Biscuter gripped his hands and closed his eyes, as if, through the tunnel of time, he was communing with someone else's pain, or as if he was scared that at any moment somebody might jam *his* fingers in a door.

'Who was it rang you within the last couple of hours to insist that the Jauma case is now closed?'

'Who told you that?'

'Did they tell you to ask me to call off my inquiries?'

'Yes. Don't worry, though. You'll get your money.'

'That's not the problem. The hard bit is making your first million — after that, it's plain sailing. I can't talk openly over the phone, but you still haven't said who rang you.'

'They told me that some young criminal had confessed to the killing.'

'They should be so lucky! Either under threats, or under some pressure — probably the former — he sang like the proverbial canary. Do you follow me?'

'I think so.'

'Give me three more days on this case and I think I can crack it. Tell me, though, who was it who rang?'

'Gausachs, Fontanillas, and Argemi.'

'In that order?'

'No. Gausachs phoned today. Fontanillas and Argemi called last night. In that order.'

'There's been nothing in the papers, so how did they find out?'

'They were my two representatives during the police investigation. I wasn't actually there myself, so the police dealt through them.'

'The police will come knocking at your door in a few hours, trying to put pressure on you to close the case.'

'I don't know what to do.'

'I repeat, just give me three days and I'll be able to prove that things aren't as simple as they say they are.'

'OK. Three days — but that's your lot.'

Nuñez was sceptical about his chances of convincing Jauma's widow:

'Sometimes she prefers Vilaseca, Biedma, and me, but when it comes to what she considers "serious" things, she'll only trust Fontanillas and Argemi. She thinks they're more reliable. I'll do what I can, though.'

Biscuter arrived from the market, puffing and carrying a basket full of treasures. He put the day's papers on Carvalho's desk before going to unload his wares in the kitchenette next to the toilet. As Carvalho cast an idle eye over the headlines, his attention was suddenly drawn to a picture with a caption that said, 'Identikit portrait of Peter Herzen'.

The Avis car-hire staff in Bonn had given the police a description of Herzen, which matched a description given by two waiters at a motorway restaurant just a few miles from where the German's car had been found. The likeness was startling. It was Dieter Rhomberg, without a doubt. Carvalho had a half-hour wait before getting through to Berlin. Rhomberg's sister didn't seem particularly worried at first.

'Have you read anything in the papers about the disappearance of a German subject in Spain, by name of Herzen?'

'I think I read about it.'

'Didn't they publish an Identikit picture in the German press?'

'I don't know. I don't usually read the news pages.'

'It's a fact, isn't it, that your brother actually left Germany four days ago.'

Her silence confirmed that he was on the right track.

'Look, lady, let's not play cat and mouse. This business is serious. There are people's lives at stake, possibly including your brother's.'

'Yes. Dieter turned up a short while after you phoned. He was in quite a state. He said goodbye to the boy, and to us. He was going away on a long trip, he said.'

'Did you give him my message?'

'Yes. He wasn't surprised. In fact he seemed to be expecting it. He said he was going to get it all sorted out.'

'I don't want to alarm you, but you should go out and get yesterday's and today's papers. Get the picture of Herzen, get a photo of your brother, and go to your local main Avis office.'

'What are you saying? Are you suggesting that this Herzen was in fact Dieter?'

'I'm sorry, but I see no other explanation.'

'But why would he go and hire a car from Avis? He's got a perfectly good car of his own — he hardly ever uses it.'

'Please do as I say. I only hope I'm mistaken.'

'I must say, you're very Spanish in your way of doing things. All high drama. You shouldn't go round frightening people like this.'

She was about to cry.

'Listen, lady, do as I say. Get the papers, and a photograph of Dieter. My way of doing things is actually like a harp player. Very gentle. And I've never played castanets in my life.'

'Fuck you,' he thought, when he heard the woman start to cry. Her suggestion of his conformity to a national stereotype had infuriated him.

'Come in,' he shouted, in a voice that carried sufficient irritation for the two people entering his office to do so rather gingerly, with all the caution of soldiers in a minefield.

'Does a detective live here?'

'No. This is just where they hang people. There's no detective living here. This is just where a detective works.'

'That'll do.'

The young man was evidently not amused. He had short hair, a musketeer's moustache, a Mexican white-wool cardigan, jeans, and ibex sandals worn over thick woollen socks. The girl only came up to his chest, but in that short distance she contained an impressive geography of mounds, valleys and dips, beneath a small roof of blond hair piled up like a coolie hat with loose curls hanging below it. All in all, her bizarre hair-do was a ploy to distract the viewer's attention from the marvel of her minuscule body. The attempt failed. He ran his gaze over the girl, until his eyes met hers. She smiled back mischievously.

'We want to consult you about a case.'

'You've lost half a kilo of hashish and you want me to find it?'

'It's more complicated than that.'

The girl let the male take on the active role, which he played very correctly, in a well-educated accent and a modulation to match. His gesticulatory style was convincing, as was the way she hung on his every word, and devoted equal attention to the way that Carvalho's eyes were fixed on her cleavage as it thrust out of the square décolleté of a tight-fitting dress.

'My brother has been under psychiatric treatment for the past two months. If it was a normal sort of case, we wouldn't have come to you, because these days who doesn't need psychiatric treatment? At least, you need it if you're caught up in the cogs of a system of life based on production and reproduction. My brother was a rationalist. He was a member of the PSUC — he was a communist — and he wasn't the sort of person who believes in witches and fairies, if you know what I mean. As far as he was concerned, one and one made two, and two and two made four. He's the sort of person who was always having a go at me because, according to him, I'm a good-for-nothing layabout. My girlfriend and I are actors. You might have spotted us on one of the demonstrations on the Ramblas, seeing that they pass right under your windows. There are so many demonstrations these days that you're bound to have seen us.'

'How on earth could I ever have missed this mini-marvel,' Carvalho thought to himself as he looked at the girl, and she knew what he was thinking, because she sucked in her cheeks to try to hold back a smile, but the smile still showed in her eyes.

'But then this bastion of Marxist rationality came crashing down.'

'Why? Did his wife run off with the local party chief?'

The girl stifled her laughter with her hand, and her companion tried to rise above Carvalho's vulgar sarcasm.

'No. Nothing like that. That would be a material explanation, but what I have come to tell you about does not belong to the material world. I'm talking about the supernatural.'

'Shame I can't provide any special effects. If you'd warned me in advance, I could have prepared a few rattling chains, whistling winds, that sort of thing.'

Biscuter poked his face out of the kitchen, from where the sound of frying could be heard. He had heard the word 'supernatural', and his eyes took on a greater than usual fixity and betrayed his total absorption.

'My brother is an architect. You must admit, that's a fairly realistic, materialist sort of job. He drives around all day visiting building sites. Two months ago he was driving back from Sant Llorenç del Munt just as it was starting to get dark. He picked his girlfriend up at Sabadell, because they wanted to go for a meal in Barcelona and then go to the pictures. He then drove on towards Molins de Rei, where he had to do his last visit of the day. All of a sudden he saw a woman standing by the road, thumbing a ride. He stopped the car. Was he going towards Molins? "Yes." "Me too." "Get in." So she got in, and sat in the back, and my brother drove on again. It was raining a bit, and both my brother and his girlfriend were watching the road. There wasn't a word out of the woman in the back. Then they came to a bend in the road, and she suddenly said:

'Watch out — there's a dangerous bend here.'

'My brother braked, and skidded a little. Afterwards he commented that it was indeed a dangerous bend. Since there was no reply from the woman, he turned round to repeat what he'd said, and he was completely thunderstruck. Imagine it! There was no sign of her. The two of them went hysterical. The girlfriend started screaming, "She's fallen out, she's fallen out!" but that was impossible, because the door was shut tight. Anyway, my brother reversed back to the bend and stopped the car. The two of them got out, and they searched the roadside inch by inch. They used the car headlights, and a camping torch that my brother always keeps in the glove compartment. No sign of the woman! Maybe she'd fallen down the embankment? They weren't equipped to go looking for her, so they decided to go and inform the local *guardia civil*. They went to the nearest station. A sergeant was on duty. He listened as my brother told his story, in as matter-of-fact a way as he could — in other words that the woman had definitely fallen out, and that, maybe because of the wind, the car door had closed again of its own accord. The sergeant didn't say a word. He went over to a desk, opened a drawer, and took out a photo which he showed to my brother and his girlfriend. "Is this the woman," he asked. They looked at it carefully. Yes. Not that they'd got a very good look at her, but it was definitely the same woman who had got into their car. "This is the seventh time I've heard this story," he said. "It happens the same way every time.

The amazing thing is that this woman died in a car accident, four years ago, right on that bend."'

'Jesus!' Biscuter shouted from where he was half hidden in his corner, thereby prompting the couple to look up anxiously.

'That's my assistant. Don't worry, he's flesh and blood — not much flesh, in fact, but you know what I mean...'

Carvalho lit up his favourite everyday cigar, an undeniably material Condal number six.

'Neither my brother nor his sister had known the story of that woman's accident. This knocks out the possibility of autosuggestion. We went and saw a reputable lawyer, and he confirmed what the sergeant had said. I myself, together with my father, have tracked down the seven other people who had picked up the woman, and they said that, just like in my brother's case, she had been hitchhiking, and then disappeared. They confirmed the story down to the last detail, and only one of them had already known about the accident previously, because he was from the same village as the woman.'

'What about your brother and his girlfriend?'

'She's in a psychiatric hospital undergoing treatment, and my brother's a complete wreck. He's tried everything from pills to alternative psychologists.'

'I'm not a shrink. Neither am I a voodoo doctor.'

'We want you to take this case on, using your normal processes of logical deduction, and see if you can make some sense of it.'

'You say your brother is a communist. Is he a rationalist communist, or a Catholic communist?'

'None of us at home are Catholics, my brother least of all.'

'Is he a mystical communist?'

'I don't follow you.'

'Does he believe in the communion of the Marxist saints, and in the resurrection of the flesh in an earthly paradise?'

'My brother is — or was — a man with both feet on the ground.

'Has he ever read Hans Christian Andersen? Or the *Tales of Hoffmann*?'

'His reading consisted of the set books for his exams at school, textbooks for quantity surveyors, Carrillo's *After Franco — What?*, and the party press.'

'Does he write poetry? Play the flute? Or the guitar?'

'I don't know whether it would help if I said that he and I are complete opposites. I *could* play the flute and write poetry, even though I don't in fact do either. But him — never!'

'So here we have a level-headed man who suddenly sees the ghost of a dead woman, right at a time when Francoism is being dismantled. A conspiracy. There's something very appealing about it, I must say. But there's no way I can take it on at the moment. Maybe I could once I get my present commitments out of the way — if I live to tell the tale. Biscuter, make a note of how we can get in touch with these good people.'

Biscuter went to take down the man's address and phone number. Carvalho turned to the girl:

'Do *you* have a phone number?'

'She's nothing to do with all this. She just happens to have come along with me. Anyway, you can find us just about any night in El Sot.'

'I see — you are part of Nuñez's entourage.'

'He was the one who suggested getting in touch with you.'

So, Carvalho thought to himself, Nuñez must have staged this little joke. I bet he's laughing like a drain at this very moment.

'I don't come cheap, you know.'

'I'm prepared for that.'

'Are you paying?'

'My father's paying.'

'What does your father do for a living?'

'He's a building contractor. Don't worry — he's got money.'

'And would he agree to my taking on the case?'

'I'll bring him here in person, and you can ask him for
yourself.'

'I'll keep in touch.'

A portable woman. As she disappeared in the wake of
the man, Carvalho imagined her on top of him, with her
sex locked onto his, her hands resting on his chest, her
head up, her eyes closed, her tongue just showing as she
begins breathing heavily, and her hair-do going up and
down as if it was being pumped from somewhere inside
her delicately-featured head.

'What do you make of all that, boss?'

'Nothing... Nothing at all.'

'Is it possible, though?'

'It's a story for winter, not for spring. Like stories about
bears and drowned people living at the bottom of seas and
lakes and garden ponds...'

'It makes my flesh creep just to think about it.'

'If you ask me, it's a plot. The bishops have teamed up
with Christians for Socialism, to make sure the Church
keeps a bit of the action. Forget it, Biscuter — I want to eat.'

'Shall I heat up last night's supper? Kidneys in sherry
and rice pilaff, remember?'

'What are you cooking now?'

'Chicken with artichokes.'

'It'll be fine heated up tomorrow. Give me the rice and
kidneys. But if the rice has gone lumpy, throw it away and
make some more.'

Rhomberg's sister wouldn't come to the phone. Instead he
got her husband. Sure enough, Peter Herzen was Dieter
Rhomberg. The photo had been identified by the Avis
employee who had rented him the car.

'I'm sure you'll appreciate that we're terribly upset. We just don't know how to tell the boy that his father's dead.'

'He might have decided to disappear as a safety measure.'

'Safety? Why safety?'

'What are the German police saying?'

'Nothing. They've taken a note of your information, and I imagine that Interpol will be in touch with the Spanish police so that you can tell them what you know.'

'I would be grateful if you could keep in touch...'

'I'm afraid I'll have to ring off now. I hope you understand... We're shattered.'

The aftertaste of the kidneys was suddenly sour in his mouth, and his stomach sent up a warning signal in the form of a sherry-flavoured burp. He had an uneasy feeling that he was out of his depth — on a voyage of no return that promised to be full of unpleasant surprises. Carvalho had to take several deep breaths in order to restore his disintegrating peace of mind. There was no match between the major crime he had got involved in and his recent past as a small-time private eye — a very different person from the ruthless cynic who had once been in the CIA, and who wouldn't have thought twice about terminating heads of state. Dieter had been driving the car when they arrived in Los Angeles that night to look for a hotel in Beverly Hills. They had come very close to crashing into a Buick that had skidded across the road, and they had driven into town slowly, with their nerves on edge. Fear had abandoned the city to the night, and the restaurants, cinemas, shops and stores were all asleep. All of a sudden they saw a man in a tracksuit top and running shorts coming up the pavement towards them, pacing himself with the regularity of a long-distance runner. He had a crew-cut and was breathing rhythmically.

'Looks like a zombie on a keep-fit kick,' Jauma said, and the three of them relaxed. Dieter pulled up, to see which way the night-runner was intending to go. A police car was following a few yards behind.

'He's got an escort.'

'Keeping an eye on him, more likely.'

The runner drew level with Dieter's car, but he didn't deign to register their presence. The driver of the police car raised one finger to his forehead to indicate 'this guy's nuts'. Then, as if determined to exercise their authority in the presence of these unaccustomed witnesses, the police drove past the runner and suddenly braked in front of him. They got out of the car and rounded on him aggressively.

'Stop right there, buddy!'

The athlete halted in his tracks, but continued running on the spot.

'What are you doing?'

'Running.'

'I can see that. But why? This is no time of night to be out running.'

'I work during the day, so I run at night.'

'Are you in an athletics club?'

'I don't run with other people. I run on my own. Is there some law that says I can't run on the sidewalk?'

'No.'

'So?'

'You're going to get yourself shot at this rate. People don't like other people running round the place at two in the morning.'

'Do you have proof of that?'

'Of what?'

'That people don't like other people running at two in the morning.'

'It stands to reason.'

The man continued running on the spot, and the cops glared at him for a moment or two. Then they glanced over to Dieter's car, and signalled to the runner that he could go. Seeing that he was already running on the spot, he took off like a rocket, accelerated as if he was using starting blocks, and used this burst of speed to regain his breathing rhythm and get back into his stride. The cops came over to the parked car and asked to see their papers. While one of them checked them, the other kept one hand on his gun and a frown in his eyes as he followed the runner disappearing into the distance.

'You planning to sleep in the car?'

'No. We're on our way to the Golden Hotel.'

'Down this street, and then take a left. Don't hang about, though. This is no time to be taking the air.'

'Do you get runners like that every night?' Jauma asked, pointing after the athlete, who was just about to be swallowed up by a dip in the road.

'Never seen one in this part of town. He must be crazy. He'll end up getting shot.'

'Why?'

'People don't like unusual things round here. Unusual things scare them, and when they're scared the first thing they do is get their guns out.'

Jauma went up the hotel stairs as if he was jogging, and entered the reception area breathing like a seasoned athlete. The receptionist didn't bat an eyelid. He helped them load their luggage into the lift, and came with them to unlock their rooms. The only thing missing in each of them was a Gloria Swanson or a Mae West in lace lingerie. Carved wooden bedheads painted cream and picked out in silver. Spiral bedposts supported a canopy that was gathered over the headboard in such a way as to reveal a large plaster rosette in the shape of a crown. An ostentatious sky-blue carpet; pink, silver-flecked furniture; a bathroom with an Empire-style bath tub; marble and chrome fittings in the shape of various exotic plants and animals; and a colour TV the size of a travelling trunk.

'Is the bar open?'

'If I decide so, yes,' replied the receptionist-liftman-telephonist-nightshift-bartender.

'I hope you'll be up at once, then. I want chilled French champagne and a hot chick.'

'I can bring the champagne at once, but you'll have a two-hour wait for the girl.'

'In that case I'll settle for the champagne, for now.'

Long voyages tend to aggravate the sexual member. Each man's favourite son was stirring in his trousers. While the others stayed awake and prepared for a two-hour wait, Dieter fell fast asleep — a solid sleep as befitted his solid stature. Jauma had donned a loose-fitting pair of silk pyjamas and was absorbed in examining the geometric variations on the test cards of the various TV channels.

'Come in, Carvalho. I'm trying to find one of them that is sufficiently hypnotic to send me to sleep. The buzzing tone helps. I'm a bit on edge.'

He told him what the bartender had said about the girls and the champagne.

'Two hours? That's a pretty lousy service. They must live on the other side of Los Angeles.'

The receptionist arrived in person, bringing champagne and a glass. He wasn't amused when they asked for a second glass, but his irritation seemed to pass when Jauma handed him a five-dollar tip.

'And what about my girl? Why so long?'

'At this time of night you'll only get a black girl or a chicano, and most of them live forty miles away, down by Watts, on the other side of town.'

Jauma looked at his crutch and commented:

'A lot of things can pass through a man's soul in the course of two hours.'

The police were hot on his heels. Gausachs wanted to see him. Fontanillas had rung: 'Must speak to you, urgently.' And Concha Hijar too: 'If necessary I can call at your office.' Gausachs received him in his office, seated in an executive chair made of high-quality tooled leather, and flanked by three men who were obviously foreigners and who observed Carvalho as they tried to figure out what made him tick.

'You've stirred up a fine mess, here.'

Despite the raised voice and the tone of reproach, Carvalho noted that the more or less polite approach made a pleasant change.

'If you hadn't started poking your nose in where it didn't belong, Dieter Rhomberg would still be alive today.'

'It wasn't me who tipped his car into the river and "disappeared" him.'

'Nobody tipped that car into the river. It must have crashed, and the body's bound to turn up one day. Anyway, the only reason why Dieter was on the move was because you were stirring everything up with this ridiculous investigation.'

Gausachs turned to the three men and said, in English:

'Do any of you want to say anything?'

The one with the commanding features who looked like he might have turned down the post as vicar of Wakefield turned to Carvalho and said, in an impeccable, slightly lilting English:

'I know that you understand English. My company is very concerned about this business, and wants it cleared up as soon as possible. You know how these things are — if there's a scandal in the milkman's house, sooner or later the whole street knows, and then the whole neighbourhood, and the milkman loses his customers. If there's a scandal in a company like Petnay, the whole world knows about it. At this point nobody wants to continue with this ludicrous investigation, particularly not now that it's indirectly claimed another innocent life. We realize that you have economic and professional interests at stake here, and we are prepared to compensate you for the loss of the case. How would two thousand pounds sterling sound — what's that in pesetas?'

Gausachs calculated the rate of exchange, and then said

in a generous tone:

'Upwards of three hundred thousand pesetas. A very fair offer, señor Carvalho.'

'Supposing I asked for ten thousand pounds? What would you say?'

'Probably nothing, but we would think the worst,' the 'vicar' replied, sarcastically.

'Would you pay, though?'

'It would be dishonest on your part to ask.'

'Petnay has nothing to say on the subject of honesty.'

The vicar blinked and looked to see what his colleagues were thinking. The two Englishmen shrugged their shoulders. Gausachs asked them:

'Leave me alone with señor Carvalho.'

Three pairs of shiny shoes disappeared. Gausachs offered Carvalho a malt whiskey.

'You could probably get more money than they offered, but not as much as you seem to think. Do I make myself clear? Given that we want to get the business settled, and given that you need to make as much as you can out of it, we could settle on four thousand pounds — sorry, I mean six hundred thousand pesetas. But don't push your luck, Carvalho. Petnay is an understanding firm, but it is also powerful. What's more, at this moment the Spanish police are very angry with you.'

'How come Dieter Rhomberg disappeared so abruptly from Petnay's payroll? Why did he sound like he was on the run? Why was he travelling under an assumed name, and not in his own car but in a hired car? Why did that car show up in a river that had almost no water in it? Why did he take that weird detour off the motorway? How come, if he was "drowned", no body has been discovered? Why are you all so keen to let everyone think it was an accident? Why are you prepared to give me six hundred thousand pesetas to get off the case? I think that just about sums things up.'

'In a few hours from now this will be the official version

and therefore the correct one. Rhomberg was going through an acute personal and professional crisis. In fact he had still not recovered from the death of his wife. Not only did he leave Petnay, but he underwent a personality change and decided to set off on a voyage of self-discovery. You turned up on the scene, mixing Rhomberg up with the Jauma case, without any proof that the two were connected. Rhomberg decided to come to Barcelona to settle the business for once and all, so as to do what he considered his duty by his good friend Antonio Jauma. As he's driving down, for reasons that we don't yet know, his car crashes into the river and he disappears. Maybe he'll turn up again in a few months' time, or even years, alive and well, having used this fake death as his way of getting away from everything as only a presumed corpse can. I think this also just about sums up the situation, and I think this explanation is far more likely to be accepted than yours. At the level of public opinion, it's more than adequate, particularly if people aren't inclined to see ghosts where there are none.'

'And what about Jauma's widow? And Rhomberg's family?'

'They accept Petnay's version, which is the only possible version. Tomorrow morning I shall be waiting for you, here, at ten. I want a signed statement from you, recognizing that the Jauma case and the Rhomberg case are both now closed, and accepting the official version. I shall hand over, with this very hand, over this very table, a cheque for six hundred thousand pesetas.'

'Did you know that Jauma had discovered an "oversight" of two hundred million pesetas in last year's accounts?'

'That's ridiculous! Where did you get that from — from one of Jauma's do-it-yourself accountants?'

'Petnay was informed about this missing money, so how come you weren't told? Why don't you ask the vicar of Wakefield?'

'What vicar are you referring to?'

'The slimy one out there who was trying to bribe me. Ask him, and tomorrow morning, here, at ten, have the reply ready for me. "In that very hand."'

Gausachs was plainly put out. Carvalho turned on his heel, walked off, and left Gausachs, muttering as he went:

'Petnay version, indeed!'

And he burst out laughing. The laughter came back to him several times as he proceeded on foot to the office of the lawyer Fontanillas.

'Damn you — you're getting me mixed up in a hell of a mess.'

'Don't get all worked up, señor notary.'

'What do you mean — I'm not a notary.'

'You look like a very notorious notary to me, and it doesn't suit you when you get angry. Calm down, friend. Take it easy!'

He sat down, without first asking if he could, and placed his hands on his knees. Fontanillas had pressed the button on his intercom, as if to send a message, and took a moment or two recovering from his surprise at Carvalho's abrasive manner.

'Go ahead — say it. I've done nothing but stir up trouble. But everything's sorted out now, and my services are no longer required.'

'We'll pay what we owe you.'

'And more besides...'

'If that's the problem, and more besides.'

'Why?'

'Because people need to be left to live their lives in peace, and ever since you started rooting around in the Jauma case, there's been no peace for anyone. Poor Concha, for a start. Then there's the wretched business about Rhomberg, which was indirectly caused by you, with these investigations of yours.'

'And what about you? Do you want a quiet life again, too? Were you the one — the prestigious lawyer and future leader of the Centre Right, from what I read in the papers

— who put pressure on the Civil Governor to find Jauma's killer come what may?'

'I have friends among the powers-that-be, and I did what I could to move things along. I saw it as doing a favour to Concha, so as to put her mind at rest. I know her, and I know that she won't rest until everything makes sense. Anyway, Carvalho, everything now fits. The police now have a statement that says that, unfortunately for Concha, Antonio died without his Y-fronts on. And Rhomberg has nothing, absolutely nothing, to do with it.'

'Did Jauma ever tell you that over the past three or four years million and millions of pesetas have disappeared from Petnay's accounts in Spain? Did you know that this year the figure ran to two hundred million?'

'This is the first I've heard of it. I'm surprised that Petnay weren't aware of it.'

'They most certainly were. Jauma informed them, year after year, and this year in particular.'

'Ridiculous! How could a company like Petnay permit a situation like that to continue?'

'That's precisely what *I* want to know.'

'Sit here and wait, please.'

A light that seemed to offend the eyes, or warn them of fearful things to come. Office furniture that encompassed three distinct epochs: from neo-classical polished wood, to metallic furniture that made hollow noises, and all this framed in that curious style that attempts to make all offices look like the offices of Hollywood films of the 1940s. Typewriters on metal trolleys. And, above all, people. People passing through and people sitting there with an uneasy feeling that perhaps it's going to be for ever.

The police themselves give the impression of being in historical accord with the furniture. There are some on the verge of retirement, with the faded, opaque luminosity of years and years of service, with little moustaches which they learned to trim during the War and which they still tend carefully, grey hair by grey hair — a strange but cultivated insect with rectangular wings pinned to a leathery upper lip. Then there are the forty-year-olds, athletes to a man, and all with pot bellies and an ideological formation dating from the Franco era, the only one they have known. They all have to hold second jobs in order to make ends meet, and they're fed up and angry at the way they have to spend the hours of their working lives among a defeated and ill-fated humanity. Finally, the young ones, really young, long-haired and looking like young bank clerks, with a certain metallic naturalness, and with provincial university law degrees, but who failed to disguise sufficiently their opposition to Inspector So-and-So. Or ex-Falangist youth who have converted into a profession the mystical notion that life should be an act of service. There are also the ones who have learned everything from North American TV films, following the style of the FBI agents like the kids of Hamelin followed their wise piper. The gestures of office workers, a mechanical aggressivity that is part of their stock-in-trade, and an ability to pass from a blow to the forgetting of that blow in an instant, in the confidence that the person on whom it landed has no choice but to play along. Young car thieves, pickpockets, shoplifters, prostitutes, gays with plucked eyebrows and false eyelashes, quarrelling neighbours with tears in their eyes and the marks of blows on their faces, an old man who has stabbed his luscious niece, and a hunter who shot his wife without waiting for the hunting season to begin. The lucky ones make a statement and leave, but there are some who remain at the end of the corridor, and through a chink in some door that has not been closed in time, you hear their screams and protests, the threats made in a room without windows and with no light other than what hangs over the loser like a noose. When they return from the end of the corridor — maybe bruised and maybe not — with their hands handcuffed and looking contrite, they look like they're returning from an enforced first communion. Carvalho watched them as they reached the last opaque glass door, which was as far as he could see. But he knew what came after. A sudden end to the labyrinth of offices, and the start of the cement. Stairs that plunge down to a damp, cold hell which is accessed by a barred door which then leads to a corridor with cells on either side, and the toilet-cum-shower at the end, where the shit makes it impossible to take a shower and the smell of the disinfectant never succeeds in overcoming the smell of the most wretched, desperate piss in all the world. 'Door!' they shout from above, and from below a uniformed guard moves calmly and deliberately to open the door to receive the prisoner and the accompanying instructions. Put him in solitary. The prisoner will regain his identity in the cell and will discover how far he has been defeated, with the clear awareness that in this game it was impossible to win anyway. Even if you're only in for a few hours, it strips you of something that nobody will ever be able to give you back. You're left with the dizziness of the leap that you have to make between the reality of what you think you are and the reality of what the police want you to be.

'Well... Carvalho! We meet again...!'

Somebody gave him a slap on the back that felt almost friendly. Raising his eyes he saw the face of a Spanish police inspector who could have come out of a foreign film that Spanish National Radio would have described as anti-Spanish for the simple fact that it was anti-Franco. Then the second-rate Hollywood actor left him. Several minutes passed, and Carvalho sensed that he was in for a long wait, a black sheet of a night without sleep, which he would have to spend either pacing up and down the painfully short corridor or sitting on an uncomfortable chair with hard edges. They left him in the company of the man who had shot his own family. A mediocre Sunday-driver sort of a man, who stared at his handcuffed wrists and sobbed incessantly, as if his nostrils were being torn apart by the crying.

'Remei, poor Remei!'

'Poor Remei, eh? You should have thought of that before you shot her.'

'Remei, poor Remei,' the hunter wailed, ignoring the admonitions of a passing police officer. The hunter raised reddened eyes and looked at Carvalho:

'Twenty-five years, and never a bit of trouble. I've never been here, even to get a passport. Why would I want a passport — I've got a nice little villa, and we go there every Sunday.'

'Did you kill her?'

He bowed his head and said he hadn't, and sobbed sobs that were trying to drag tears up from unknown depths.

'And the kid. I shot my daughter too.'

By now his crying seemed more substantial, or at least it had increased in fluency and mucosity. He poked around looking for a non-existent handkerchief. Carvalho handed him a sheet of white paper that was lying on one of the tables.

'They're going to do for you.'

'Here, use this.'

The handcuffed man contrived to blow his nose.

'Poor thing! She was complaining. I wanted to build a barbecue in the garden, a silly thing, so's we could have meat grilled on proper charcoal, because we've got butane gas indoors, and meat grilled over gas just doesn't taste right. I bought some of those heat-resisting bricks... what do they call them...?'

'Refractory.'

'That's it, refractory. And I ordered a good solid iron grid from the ironmonger's, big enough to grill meat for a regiment, because sometimes there are twenty or twenty-

five of us, what with the girl's fiancé, and my brother and
his kids. Anyway, I wanted it to do paellas too. I don't know
how people manage to cook these days.

'People forget that every once in a while you might need
to make a paella. And what are you going to cook it on?
Remei always used to say: "When you have to do a paella
for more than six people, this cooker's not big enough. A
paella needs to be kept moving, otherwise the rice cooks
unevenly." "OK," I said, "I'll build a barbecue outside." I
started cementing the bricks in, and she starts fussing:
"No, I don't want it there, because all the smoke will go into
the house, and then it's me who has to clean up afterwards."
And so on, blah-blah-blah, and so there I was, with the
cement already mixed, and half the wall already built. I gave
the bricks a kick, and she started saying I was crazy. "You're
mad. Mad. Just like your mother!" And out it all came. First
she had a go at my mother. Then my father. And then the
girl joined in. And then, I don't know, I just wanted them
to stop, I wanted an end to the boom-boom-boom going on
in my head. I turned on them, and they ran over to the
garden gate, and carried on — blah, blah, blah. And I swear,
sir, I swear, as I sit here now, I have no idea how I ended
up coming out of the house with the rifle. I just wanted
them to stop. And Remei was shouting at me from the gate,
"Look at the bastard — now he's got his gun." And I fired.
And fired again. And they tried to run away, and I didn't
want them to, so I fired again, and again, and they both
fell. Oh, mother of God!'

'José Carvalho Larios?'

'Yes.'

'Follow me.'

Eleven o'clock at night. A three-hour wait.

'Has he just killed his wife and daughter?'

'No — wounded them.'

'Seriously?'

'The daughter, yes. The wife only slightly, but she's in
a state of shock. Come on in.'

The inspector who had slapped him on the back was now sitting at the end of the room.

'We can get this over with very quickly if you co-operate. I want a complete statement regarding your relations with Rhomberg, and the reasons why he was travelling to Spain under an assumed name, or at least as much as you know.'

Carvalho began back at square one, in the United States. The officer was peering over the top of his glasses at a bundle of documents which presumably had to do with Carvalho.

'Don't you know that it's against the law for a Spanish subject to enrol in organizations like the CIA without authorization?'

'I started off giving Spanish lessons, not realizing that it was the CIA. Then I found it amusing, so I carried on. When I left, I clarified my position with two ministries — Foreign Affairs, and the Home Office.'

He continued his account up to his latest phone conversation with Rhomberg's brother-in-law and showed them the telegram that had arrived from Bonn, signed 'Dieter'.

'You're going to find yourself in big trouble if you carry on with this case. The Jauma case is now closed. The murderer has been arrested. We have his confession. A young man from Vich. Jauma arrived at a roadside bar run by the boy's mother-in-law and started flirting with the lad's wife. We happen to know that the girl's the village prostitute, and that the husband lives on her earnings. Anyway, Jauma made a pass at the girl, and she complained to the husband. There was a fight, and you can imagine the rest for yourself. As for Rhomberg, either he has faked his own disappearance or he's at the bottom of a river somewhere.'

'You couldn't drown a cat in that river!'

'Don't you believe it. There's been a lot of rain this year, and the water level was up. Anyway, my job is just to warn you. The case is now settled. You'll now make a statement as regards Rhomberg. I'll read it back to you, and if you agree it's a fair representation of what you said, then you can go. I repeat, I'm not speaking for myself; I'm passing on orders from above.'

He pointed upwards at the ceiling, and the eyes of those present followed his finger. A young policeman was at the typewriter, typing with two fingers, evidently a prisoner of a set of expositional formulae that were insufficient to translate what Carvalho was trying to say. He tore up sheet after sheet in order to start over again, and the frustration only increased his nervousness and aggressiveness. In the end Carvalho had to dictate his statement himself, complete with punctuation, and an hour later, with the witching hour past, the policeman embarked on a meticulous reading of the document, which was followed as attentively by the typewriting constable as it was by Carvalho himself.

'Fine. You can go now. But remember what I told you.'

'Is Jauma's killer in the building, here?'

'They've just finished questioning him.'

'Have they taken him down to the cells?'

'Not yet, no. He's got a visitor. His mother-in-law.'

'Could I see him?'

'You can see him, but not talk to him.'

In one of the offices the tearful hunter was talking with a middle-aged woman. He introduced her as his sister. A fifty-year-old woman who was still fresh and goodlooking, with twenty excess kilos very well distributed about her person. In another corner, a smiling and disdainful Paco the Hustler was talking with his mother-in-law. A faded denim outfit and long, curly hair. The features of a hardened wide-boy. He saw Carvalho looking at him and stared him out defiantly. Cool, confident, and sure of himself.

'Why do they call him "The Hustler"?'

'He says that's been his nickname since he was a kid. He used to steal chickens in the village in Andalusia where he comes from. Then his folks came to live in Catalonia.

He had a bit of a record as a small-time hustler, but then he married the daughter of a woman who ran a bar, and seemed to settle down. At least, he gave up thieving, although the *guardia civil* reported that he'd put his wife on the game.'

'A village pimp, eh?'

'There's a lot of it about.'

Carvalho bade the young police officer goodnight, and passed under the eye of the vigilant guard at the front door, to reach the fresh, black air of the street outside. He had a hunger and a thirst as if he hadn't eaten for days and he felt like he hadn't shaved for a week. And all this for four hours' detention. He went to get his car from where he'd left it parked next to his office in the Ramblas, and fifty metres into his freedom he heard the sound of voices. Someone was running up behind him. It was Biscuter and Charo. They fell on him hysterically.

'Was it all right, chief? Did they treat you OK?'

'Oh Pepe, poor Pepe, my Pepe...'

Charo's mouth kissed the entire geography of his face in minute detail.

'Don't go mad — I was only in there for four hours!'

'In that place you always know when you go in, but you never know when you're coming out again.'

'Biscuter's right. He rang me, and I've been out worrying about you all night.'

'What about your clients, Charo?'

'To hell with my clients!'

'I've got a meal ready for you, chief. It'll make your mouth water.'

Propelled by Charo and Biscuter, Pepe reached his office in a good frame of mind, even though the day's events had left him with many unanswered question. Supper was a squid casserole with potatoes and peas, washed down with a bottle of Montecillo. Charo ate the squid, but without the sauce. She drank the wine too, despite Carvalho's observations about the irrationality of her diet. Biscuter and Carvalho smoked two cigars. Montecristo Specials.

'The widow's been ringing. Every half-hour. I've lost count...'

'Whose widow? Franco's?'

'No, boss — Jauma's. She said it's urgent she sees you today.'

'It can wait till tomorrow.'

'Nuñez phoned too. He was pretty insistent. He said he'll be waiting for you at El Sot if you get out of prison before three o'clock.'

'I haven't been in prison, Biscuter.'

'I say it's the same thing. I've never yet set foot in a police station without ending up with at least six months inside.'

'I'm going for a talk with Nuñez, and then I'm off home. I'm missing my creature comforts.'

'I won't leave you tonight, Pepiño. I'm coming up with you.'

'Do what you like.'

She kissed his shoulder under his shirt and hugged him round the waist as they went down the stairs. He drove up right outside El Sot, and told Charo to wait in the car. Nuñez rushed across to meet him, and they went to find themselves a quiet corner to talk. Carvalho told him the latest, namely that somebody had provided the police with a suitable murderer for Jauma, and that it looked as if Dieter Rhomberg's body had disappeared for ever.

'The widow's the key to it all. If she pulls out I have no authority to carry on.'

'I'll try to put pressure on her.'

'Just a few days. A week. I need just one week. At least

so as to know if I'm on the wrong track.'

He saw a girl standing among a group of people. It was the same girl who had been with the young man of the hitchhiking ghost.

'Where's your boyfriend?'

'I don't have a boyfriend. That was just a friend of mine. He's not here.'

'What a shame — it would have been a golden opportunity, except that I'm busy tonight.'

'The year still has another two hundred nights in it.'

'How about we eat out tomorrow?'

'Hey — you're quick! I don't know... I'll have to think about it.'

'Ring me.'

As Carvalho was about to leave, the girl gave him a big smile. Nuñez was clucking around like a solicitous host.

'Pretend you don't know what's going on. Don't phone Concha. I'll ring her myself and tell her that you're out of town pursuing your investigations.'

'That will be true enough, as it happens.'

'How do you mean?'

'I'm taking a trip. I want to see a river, and a reactionary town.'

'Vich?'

'Precisely.'

Charo devoted herself to a detailed foreplay that lasted the entire drive back. Having arrived home, Carvalho made his way, naked, down the darkened hallway of his apartment, and his cock was warmly welcomed, first by her lips and then by her tongue, as it pressed hard against her teeth and her mouth opened to make way for it. Charo proceeded backwards on all fours, sufficiently slowly so as not to interrupt her oral caress of his cock, and when they reached the sofa she gently made him sit down, maintaining the contact all the while. Then she swiftly exchanged the warm damp protection of her mouth for that of her sex, which opened its tender slit to him. As Carvalho came, his attention was divided between her thighs and a buzz of thoughts that was refusing to take solid shape.

'Did you like that?' Charo whispered in his ear, aware of a job having been well done.

'Not bad.'

'You have such a way with words.'

In order to have reached the river at that point, Dieter would have had to leave the motorway at Junction 6, taking the A-road towards Barcelona, and then decided to drive round a maze of cart tracks. Or, even more bizarre, he would have had to come off at Junction 5 and double back towards Gerona. The idea that he'd been looking for a place to eat didn't hold water, since he'd already eaten at the Jacques Borel restaurant at Exit 7, in the company of a second person.

'Did they leave together?'

'That I can't say. I'll tell you the same as what I told the police. First this German was sitting there. I remembered him because I remember thinking that the Germans had started coming early this year. Then this other man came over and seemed to be asking if he could join him. He was thin, dark-haired, and a bit on the short side...'

'Were the other tables all taken?'

'A bunch of tourist coaches had turned up from somewhere, and the place was fairly full, but it wasn't packed. Incidentally, the other gentleman paid the bill.'

'Did the German try to pay?'

'I wasn't looking, so I can't say. The short gentleman came over very determinedly, asked me for the bill, paid it, and went back to the table. When I looked round again they'd gone.'

'So they didn't arrive together?'

'No. Definitely not. But as to whether they left together, I really can't say, because as you can see, from where I sit you can't see the car park. All you see is the first car parked next to the door.'

'What did the police have to say about the German's eating partner?'

'They asked a lot of questions about him. He was one of those short, thin types, and he had a lot of facial hair. He was clean-shaven, but you could see that he was the hairy sort, and he had sort of a big face, if you know what I mean. He wasn't from Catalonia. He spoke Castilian. Very dry — very Castilian, you might say.'

'Did he leave a good tip?'

'Not exactly. Fifty pesetas.'

'Was he a regular customer, maybe? Did you recognize him from before?'

'No. And I'm an old hand here. There's a big turnover of waiters in this place, but I've been here for three seasons now.'

Carvalho decided to drive the route that Dieter must have taken to get to the river. The very idea that he'd have made such a detour was patently ridiculous and would only have made sense if he'd been a nineteenth-century violinist with a passion for listening to murmuring streams and poplars with their flashing white leaves rustling in a gentle breeze. What's more, there was nowhere near enough water to drown a giant of a man like Rhomberg. On the other hand, if you accepted the idea that he'd faked an accident so as to disappear from history, the river Ter was only a few miles further on — a far more substantial river — not to mention all the rivers that he'd have had to cross as he sped across Europe from Bonn to the Tordera. Carvalho struggled down the riverside, along paths that were no more than muddy tracks and occasionally turned into little streams where the recent rains had washed down. He came to the point where the German's car must have dived off.

You could still see the track marks of the crane that had
lifted it out, and the broken vegetation that marked where
the car had gone down. Carvalho returned to the main road
and made for Vich, travelling along the northern slope of
the Montseny range. He was an urban creature by nature,
and all this gave him an inexplicably pleasant sense of
nostalgia and euphoria — the clarity of the air at this
altitude; the luxuriousness of the woods which were
becoming daily more lush ever since the decline in use of
wood charcoal and the subsequent eradication of the small
brushwood-collecting industry; the constant presence of
the three peaks of Montseny, which changed in form and
volume as your viewpoint shifted; and the green of a
countryside that was well watered by small rushing rivers
that hurtled towards fusion with larger rivers. He had never
lived in the country, and in general his links with nature
extended little further than his garden in Vallvidrera and
the occasional contemplation of Valles from the windows
of his apartment. This, on the other hand, was serious
countryside, with farmhouses, woods, farmland and here
and there small islands of summer residents observing the
principle that mountain air is healthier than the seaside.
Some had built themselves Swiss-style chalets, with almost
vertical slate roofs designed to cope with a snow which was
never much more than an optical illusion in that part of
the world, and which generally ended up as a dirty layer of
frozen slush on the ground. The Ibiza style was also in
evidence, as was the style which provides a showcase of all
the building materials known to man, from brick to slate,
and taking in wood and artificial stone en route. The petty
bourgeoisie has bad taste the world over, but the twentieth
century has the honour of having conceived a specimen of
bourgeoisie that is more than usually cretinous, with a
level of earnings enabling them to live in splendid isolation,
but with a cultural formation that extends no further than
mass consumerism. Still dizzy from the curving mountain
roads, he finally reached the plain of Vich, with its

landscape dotted with little hillocks of grey volcanic earth. He drove into the town, where the big old houses provided an austere central nucleus surrounded by modern housing consisting for the most part of small brick-built town houses, or two-storey apartments whose scale was constrained by tight budgetary considerations. He parked the car in the main square and went in search of small shops from whose ceilings hung salami sausages, dry, smoked sausages and cured pork fillets that looked as if they were made of china. He stocked up with two huge salamis, five smoked sausages and a gammon ham, and refrained from buying *butifarras* in order to observe the ritual of buying them in La Garriga. He bought a box of Vich sponge cake for Charo, and the third passer-by he asked was able to inform him where to find La Chunga, the dive that belonged to the mother-in-law of Jauma's alleged murderer.

'It's shut down, though. You know what happened?'

'Yes.'

'When the two women were left on their own, they decided to shut up shop.'

'Are they living in Vich?'

'No, they've got a flat over the bar. Who are you after, the mother or the daughter?'

'Which would you recommend?'

'The mother, without a doubt. She's divine. Got such an arse on her... save you the price of a mattress!'

He recalled a half memory of the woman who had been talking with Paco the Hustler. He went on to fill in the outline with imagined fleshy pleasures as his eyes scanned the horizon in search of the roadside bar. In front of a furniture showroom, at the end of a long stretch of road, just at the point where the ridge of tarmac begins to turn off towards Tona, La Chunga finally appeared. A flat, whitewashed, tile-roofed building. An illuminated Tio Pepe billboard, plastic multi-coloured Coca Cola and Pepsi signs, and a curtain of plastic strips hung over a door that was very definitely shut. There were signs of life coming from the back, though, and from the one-room flat over the bar. As he came round the front of the building he saw a pick-up truck with its doors open, loading goods and chattels from a side-door of the bar. A man was doing the loading, and Paco the Hustler's mother-in-law was telling him to be careful as she passed out the boxes. The woman had twenty-five years in each of her well-rounded breasts and fifty combined in an arse that was a sight to see. As her eyes turned to meet those of the stranger, the faded beauty in her generous features still possessed a come-hither quality that was concentrated in her impertinent lips.

'The bar's shut.'

'It's not a drink I'm wanting. I want to talk with you and your daughter.'

'If you're a journalist, you can go right back where you came from. I've had enough. Go away and leave us alone!'

'That's right,' said the man. 'Go away and leave us alone.'

He jumped down from the truck and stood between Carvalho and the woman, legs apart and menacing. Carvalho waved his ID card under their noses, and when the man read the word 'detective' he relaxed.

'He's the police.'

On the balcony of the flat appeared a girl who was fifty per cent the image of the woman below.

'More police?'

The girl was crying more than shouting. Carvalho nodded his head in an attempt at an authoritative gesture, and walked towards the house without turning to see if they were following.

'How much longer are we going to have to put up with this?'

The woman gave Carvalho a threatening look.

'It's all been signed and sealed. In God's name, why do you have to keep bothering us?'

The man gave her a look that told her not to say too much, and at that point the girl arrived from upstairs, with her teenage streetwalker's breasts showing under a thin woollen jumper.

'Is he your husband?'

'No. My brother. I'm a widow. And if they think that just because I'm a widow they can intimidate me, they're very much mistaken. Take it from me, I'm no push-over, and everything I've got in this life I've earned with my own two hands.'

'The gentleman, Antonio Jauma...'

'Gentleman, you call him! Are you referring to the one who was killed? Because he was no gentleman. At least, not what I mean by a "gentleman".'

'Did you know the man?'

'No. What I know is what the kids told me.'

'What kids?'

'The girl, here, and Paco, her husband.'

'So you never actually saw Antonio Jauma?'

'No. On the night he turned up I'd gone upstairs to watch TV. My favourite comedy was on.'

'According to the police, Jauma went to a bedroom with your daughter, and a short while later the girl came out again, half naked and screaming for her husband.'

'So they say.'

'Is it true?'

The girl lowered her eyes.

'Don't you say a word, you! She's still a minor. She's only eighteen.'

'So who's going to answer my question?'

'Me, if I feel like it.'

Carvalho went up to the woman and reached out and tweaked her nose.

'Turn down the volume, lady, it's giving me a pain in the head. Now, you're going to answer. Fast, and politely, because if you don't, you're going to get a kicking right where it hurts.'

The anger on her lips and in her eyes expressed itself only in a quiet sob and a couple of impotent tears.

'Is that a proper way to talk to a woman?'

'I talk to you the same way you talk to me. Like a truck driver. So get on with it. Enough pissing about. You — why did you run out screaming?'

'Because he was wanting to do filthy things with me.'

'What kind of filthy things?'

'All sorts. He wanted to beat me. He wanted to see me piss. I called my husband. I managed to push him out of the room, and that was the last I saw of him. Then I heard a shot. Paco came back, very nervous, and said that the man had pulled out a gun.'

'So where did he find a gun? From his navel? I thought he had no clothes on when you pushed him out of the room.'

'He was dressed.' The mother spoke up.

'That's right, he was dressed,' the daughter confirmed, staring at the ground.

'What happened then?'

'I don't know. Paco did it all. He drove off with his pick-up, and came back three hours later.'

'I heard the truck driving off, and I thought, "Where's that waster going at this time of night?" Because Paco is a waster. He's done whatever he's done, but I don't blame him, though, because bastards like your "gentleman" don't deserve to live. If a man likes women, that's fair enough. But he should be straight about it. I can't stand perverts.'

'Why are you leaving?'

'Because there's too much scum around here. From first thing in the morning it never stops — journalists, sightseers and nosey-parkers. It's like living in a zoo.'

'My sister has sold the bar, and she's leaving. I say she's doing the right thing.'

The woman glanced at her brother with a look that could kill.

'Sold the bar, have you? Well fancy that! Your son-in-law gave himself up yesterday. The news wasn't in the papers till today. They must have come pestering you all morning, and by midday, lo and behold, the bar's sold! Who bought it?'

'Well... it was only a verbal agreement.'

'With whom?'

'I don't know. He said he'd be in touch. I gave him the address of a cousin of mine who lives in Barcelona. We're going to stay there for the time being so that we can be closer to Paco, and then, depending on how things go, we'll probably come back to the village.'

'Do the police have the address of this cousin of yours?'

'Why should they? The lawyer has it, and that's good enough for when they need me as a witness.'

'Well I want the address too.'

The man pulled a ballpoint out of his jean jacket and wrote the address on a page of *Interviu*.

'How many punters do you reckon to get in a day? One? Two?'

'That's none of your business.'

'What do they pay for a screw?'

The girl broke into hysterical crying. The woman slapped her and pushed her into a corner of the room. Then she turned on Carvalho in a blaze of fury:

'Why didn't they come asking questions when my son-of-a-bitch husband left us in the shit in the first place? Why didn't they ask me *then* how much money I had tucked away? No chance! Anyway, here, nobody's been sleeping with anyone. The girl sleeps with her husband and I sleep with myself. That's my story, and if you don't like it...'

'But did she go to bed with Jauma? Because if she did, that's prostitution.'

'Go to bed? What on earth are you talking about? He told her: "Come in here, I've got something to show you."

And this poor innocent followed him, and that's when the trouble started. Is that good enough for you? Because it's the best explanation I've got. And now you can hit me and kick me as much as you like, because that's all you're getting out of me.'

'Sir...'

The man cleared his throat. He was slow, thin, and his huge hands were covered with traces of cement and plaster.

'Let's be civilized about it, sir. You have to understand, sir, that we've been through bitter times here, very bitter, and my sister has her ways, but that's because she's had to make her own way in life from a very early age.'

'Don't waste your breath on him, Andres, they're all the same.'

'No, Fuensanta, no. When people talk, it helps them understand each other. Isn't that right, sir? You understand what these two women have been through, don't you?'

Carvalho walked between the obvious fear of the brother and the raging fury of the sister. He was furious with them, and furious with himself. The fear and anger of poor people, he thought to himself.

'I'm going. But I haven't finished with you yet. You're not making a single move unless I know about it. Tomorrow I want the name, nationality and date of birth of the man who bought this Ritz, together with his address and the size of his trousers. So watch out!'

In the nearby furniture showroom they told him that La Chunga had been open for five years. The girl had still been in plaits and the woman had been living with a Catalonian gypsy who earned his living gathering mushrooms. He'd pick them and dry them, and during the season he'd sell them to packers in Granollers. One day the gypsy disappeared, and within a week or two he'd been replaced by a self-employed truckdriver who worked for an artificial-stone factory in Aiguafreda. The truck driver was the last of the regular men about the place. The bar didn't earn a lot. The regular clientele were mainly immigrants, and the bar served the occasional wayfarer with alcohol, coffee, cold drinks, or a snack. The woman began waving her breasts around, and the place began to liven up. One day the girl went on the game too. Always trouble in the place, one of his informants observed. Punch-ups galore. No-hope whores. Then the girl took up with this pimp, an evil little bastard, but at least he knew how to keep the clients in line.

'They were up to their necks in debts. I think one of her boyfriends got involved in some shady deals, and she got landed with the bill and didn't have the money to pay. He'd used her signature in some fraud or other.'

At the petrol station they filled in the rest of the details for him. Fuensanta's brother worked as a bricklayer for one of the big building contractors in Centelles.

'He was the first of them to leave the village. Then it was the usual pattern — the rest of the kids followed, and then the parents. The parents are dead now. With the exception of the bricklayer, none of the kids will have anything to do with the woman at La Chunga. If you ask about her, they say, "She's not one of us." They're ashamed of her. The bricklayer still shows up every now and then. One day he told me, "What do you expect — she is my sister, after all, and I'm the eldest brother. I've got certain responsibilities, wouldn't you say?'

He waited at the petrol station for the pick-up to pass. The old man was driving, his hands still covered with plaster and cement. At his side, bolt upright, in the full consciousness of her volume, sat Fuensanta. From between them peered the contrite face of the adolescent prostitute. The bricklayer acknowledged Carvalho with a slight nod of his head, but Fuensanta dispatched a visual thunderbolt that cracked against his windscreen.

He bought his *butifarras* in La Garriga. They were freshly cooked, and made with blood and eggs. Catalonia is next in line after the Germans when it comes to extracting the best gastronomic advantage from pigs. Leaving aside the hams, which are always too soft and lacking in flavour, the local pigs had the honour of contributing a range of really splendid sausages. An excellent display — the proof of Carvalho's observations on the matter — appeared on the serving-counter of the Fonda Europa, a restaurant in Granollers that Carvalho would escape to every once in a while, to confirm, with surprise and admiration, that it still maintained its high culinary standards. On the food counter there was a pile of sausages on a dish which featured in the menu under the heading *plat du jour*. Looked promising. Next to excellent local sausages, which probably came from Llerona, were factory-produced sausages and specimens of the damp-looking local ham, which seemed to have been cured by immersion in the sea rather than hanging in the air. The local ham had some distant family relation to Parma, but without achieving the latter's savoury tenderness. To have ordered the chef's special for a starter was an act of Pantagruelian caprice that closed down subsequent options. He thought it advisable to pass over the hams and *chorizos* and settle on the pork sausages which ranged from everyday salamis to the ethereal lightness of egg sausages or *fuet*. The waiter left at the side of his table the trolley which came with a range of serrated knives and a large basket for rind, skin, and other detritus. When Carvalho came to the Fonda Europa, he always ordered a special tripe dish consisting of tripe and pigs' trotters, which had a honey sweetness similar to what the Andalusians achieve by adding pig's jowl to the austere tripe dishes of Castille. He found himself comforted by the fact that he was not alone in his desire to eat everything the Fonda Europa had to offer, a tendency also observable in his fellow diners, especially on market days, when the dining room was packed with dealers and reps, concentrating their energies in the search for the deepest and broadest dishes. It was also a restaurant with space, so that each table could create its own environment and lose itself in the operation of eating, without being watched by the people at an adjoining table with that look of superficial curiosity characteristic of people who like to spy enviously on what other people are eating. The simplicity of the late modernism of the decor was also appealing — walls that were painted in colours that were also gastronomic. Themes and colours that were digestive, either because metaphysically both can exist or because a satisfied diner will accept any murals, even those cooked in the sauce of late modernism. The wine was not up to the standard of the food, and if the choice of a Rioja was a choice of the lesser evil, Carvalho once again mused on the disparity that exists in Catalonia between an excellent popular style of cooking and the lack of finesse of its more popular wines. The *mel i mato* dessert offered by the Fonda Europa was up to the standard of the rest of the meal, yet Carvalho ordered it more out of respect than because he really wanted it. As one who appreciated the tragic side of eating, it seemed to him that anything other than fruit for dessert implied a reprehensible frivolity, and cakes in particular ended up annihilating the flavour of quiet sadness that must be allowed to linger at the end of a great culinary performance.

With his hunger completely vanquished, Carvalho chewed on his Montecristo. As the smoke began to rise, he found himself musing on how things were going — or, rather, not going. Somebody was trying to establish a rationale for the killing of Jauma, and it was obvious that it was a fabrication. Why? Jauma's discovery of the shortfalls in Petnay's accounts could have been the reason, but then Petnay had been informed about them. In fact they had seemed to respond to his revelations by hushing the whole business up. Who had handled that money? Why? On the one hand there was the political pressure to get the case shut, and all the expense involved in buying a killer who could claim that he had been defending his honour, and who would be freed in another couple of years, several million pesetas the richer; then there was the ruthlessness with which the people behind all this had acted in the case of poor Rhomberg. In the face of this great wall that was moving to block him, Carvalho only had the fragile pretext of his commission from the widow, a commission that was looking increasingly tenuous in the light of the pressure that was undoubtedly being put on Concha Hijar at that very minute. If the widow pulled out, his only remaining option would be to stoke up a political scandal with the aid of Alemany the accountant and the leftwingers among Jauma's circle of friends. And who would pay him for that? He wasn't after the satisfaction of a job well done, but at least he liked to see a job finished, and it worried him to leave a problem unresolved, in the same way that he didn't like to see a job around the house left undone for want of a suitable screwdriver or because he'd forgotten to buy a roll of insulating tape. The only emotional factor in it for him was the question of Rhomberg's son. With Jauma he felt a professional solidarity, but the solidarity that he felt for the German kid came from somewhere in his blood. It came from the depths of a childhood terror of being orphaned. It came from having seen the wretchedness of kids in the *barrio* who had been left fatherless by the war, or by prison, or by shootings or the post-war tuberculosis. The fragility of those orphans who poked their shaved heads through the geraniums on balconies that were as rusty as the collective spirit of the *barrio* aroused in his stomach the anxiety of the young animal that discovers in others' misfortunes the possibility of its own.

'For the working class, everything is tragic,' his father used to say, 'whether it's a sickness, a divorce, or a death in the family. The rich always have a mattress ready so that when they fall they don't get hurt.'

The German kid probably had a mattress soft enough

to protect his little bones, but not to protect against the damage to the esteem he felt for the father he idolized. Once again Carvalho regretted the poverty of his emotional upbringing, with its basis in absolutes. In Japan a dog had apparently died of a broken heart because its master had not come home: he'd read this on a caption to one of the agency news photos displayed in the windows of the offices of *La Vanguardia* on calle Pelayo. A man had stabbed another man because he was trying to steal the woman he loved: he'd heard this recited by a balladeer on Radio Barcelona. A little girl died of grief because her parents had had a baby boy and he was going to inherit the family's wealth: he'd heard it, and seen it, acted by a lousy tragic actress at the Sala Mozart. Probably the German boy would grow up strong and confident, freed of the authoritarian presence of a castrating father. But then again, maybe not. He could end up suffering the same fate as Tyrone Power in *Son of Fury* — sadistically enslaved by his uncle and tutor as played by George Sanders. He'd taken an instant dislike to the voice of Dieter's brother-in-law. Prussian, he'd thought to himself. Or rather, a Prussian-sounding voice according to what conventional wisdom thinks Prussian-sounding voices sound like. But the kid would grow up. He'd emigrate to the South Seas. He'd go pearl-fishing. Then he'd hire other people to do the pearl-fishing for him. He'd get rich on the proceeds, and come back to Berlin and humiliate his uncle. Or he'd grow up living in the past, a failure, who would fall in love with strong women who'd ignore him totally, and he'd end up committing suicide by swallowing all the records of his favourite singer, dissolved in acid.

'We shouldn't bring children into this world. No matter how much we do for them, we can never compensate them for the dirty trick of having brought them into the world in the first place.'

So said his father, particularly when he became obsessed with the prospect of the impending nuclear destruction of the world. Every time a nuclear mushroom cloud appeared in the pages of *La Vanguardia* or the *Diario de Barcelona*, Don Evaristo Carvalho would point an accusing finger at it and embark on a Malthusian tirade for which the young Pepiño was the sole audience. The boy soon became aware that his very existence was a lamentable error which (for his own good) his father now deeply regretted.

'If humanity just made up its mind not to have any more children, in fifty years the human race would die out, and the earth would revert to the forces of innocence — water, sun and minerals.'

Right up to his death, Evaristo Carvalho had a feeling of remorse every time he saw his son, and he tried everything possible to purge the boy's brain of any instinct towards paternity. From his habitual vantage-point on the balcony he would watch as the cars and the generations passed. Cars were the symbol of human madness — a machine designed to speed up mankind's absurd progress from birth to death. And for him the kids that emerged from the bellies of the girls in the *barrio* were victims — losers of everything and winners of practically nothing.

'I ask you! The woman in number seven's had another kid, for God's sake! Needs her head examining, bringing more victims into this world...'

Carvalho had always meant to ask his father if he'd have thought the same way if he hadn't lost the Civil War.

He'd invited Pedro Parra up for a meal at Vallvidrera. He managed to find time to go to the Boqueria to buy the essentials for a spare but wholesome menu designed to replenish the energies of a colonel who had still not abandoned his dream of storming the Winter Palace. A leek soup and a freshly-caught steamed turbot. Parra was pleased to find a meal that was not going to jeopardize his life's struggle against cholesterol and uric acid.

'So this is how you live! A proper little hideaway!'

'North, South, East or West, my home is wherever I happen to be at the time...'

'You bachelors can always afford to leave the cage door open.'

Parra ate sparingly, drank just one glass of chilled Perelada, and was enchanted by the dessert of yoghurt, orange juice and grated orange peel. He was rather put out when he discovered that it also contained Cointreau and a triple sec, but was placated when Carvalho assured him that the quantities involved were minute. He declined the offer of a coffee and took a small packet from his pocket.

'I'm sorry to be a bit of a bore, but I'd be grateful if you could do me an infusion with these leaves. If you'd rather, I could do it myself.'

'What is it?'

'A mixture of what Catalonians call *puniol y boldo*. Excellent for the digestion. And for the liver.'

From the same pocket he produced a small dispenser which disgorged two small saccharine tablets which he placed within reach for when the infusion was ready. Carvalho poured himself a coffee, and two glasses of *orujo*, and prepared to counter Parra's ironical comeback.

'To think that I was counting on you for the revolution! You'll be too unfit when the time comes.'

'You still on about the revolution?'

'My old plan still holds. I've just adapted it to changing circumstances.'

Twenty years earlier Parra had calculated how many activists would be needed to occupy the nerve centres of the country's four or five principal cities.

'All we need do is wait for the cracks to start appearing in the state apparatus. Then we move in and seize the time.'

Parra was appalled by the Left's growing willingness to

negotiate electoral alliances, and had been obliged to postpone his plan of action to some future date when the vanguard elements of the working class would hopefully have regained their historical lucidity and thrown off that sense of self-pity that led them to want to be accepted by the bourgeoisie.

'Here's your flow-chart. If you ask me, this kind of thing's more for visual effect than for serious study: they're more graphic art than economics, really.'

'In this case I'm more interested in the graphic art than the economics.'

'The picture is fairly complete. It shows the relationship between Petnay and its various associated companies, at several levels: (1) companies that are directly linked because Petnay owns shares in them; (2) companies that are indirectly linked because people from the boards of directors of directly linked firms are also on the boards of firms that are indirectly linked; (3) companies that are indirectly linked via family connections — parents, children, marriages, that sort of thing — the list isn't completely up to date because our research department can't afford to spend all its time reading the gossip columns; and (4) companies that are indirectly linked because their survival depends on selling to Petnay itself or to one of its subsidiaries.'

'It looks more like a swamp than a flow chart!'

'Don't start complaining — we did it for you in record time. And don't forget, you owe the lads five thousand pesetas for doing all the fancy work with the coloured pens. Now, how about telling me what this is all about? Would I be right in thinking it's to do with the stories in the papers, about Antonio Jauma and Dieter Rhomberg?'

'Could be.'

Carvalho's eyes flicked from name to name, and from time to time he recognized names that he'd seen in the papers. Present-day members of the government; yacht-owners who tended to come fourth or fifth in international races; noted socialites from Fuengirola, Torremolinos, Puerto Banus and S'Agaro; and sundry notables from the national Chamber of Commerce.

'I'll take a closer look at this later.'

'If you'll excuse me being nosey, I'd say you're dealing with some pretty big fish here. Jauma was by no means a nobody. I've copied you an article from *Time* magazine, to give you an idea. It gives a list of the leading political and financial figures in Spain at the time it was written, together with their future prospects. Jauma's right in there. They describe him as having strong prospects at the international level.'

'They're a bit wide of the mark with the politicians, though.'

'The article's from the Franco period, and they underestimate the staying power of some of the old guard. But if you take a close look you'll see that the financial list isn't so wide of the mark. Maybe you don't follow these things, but today you'll find all these characters holding key positions. There's been a change of faces among the politicians, but in the world of industry and commerce everything's stayed just as it always was — in fact the Young Turks of the economic sector are increasingly tending to take on political power. It's a phenomenon typical of periods of crisis. Big capital feels confident for as long as it has the back-up of the repressive power of the fascist state. As soon as that state starts losing its grip, big capital goes through a phase of dissociating itself from the political forces that might previously have represented its interests, and in part takes on that role itself. This also happens in countries with a formal tradition of democracy. Look at Italy. The Agnellis never took on a directly political role for as long as the Christian Democrats were strong enough to do their dirty work for them. But as soon as the political forces representing their interests began to disintegrate, the Agnellis started getting involved in politics themselves. The elder one dabbled in conspiracies, and the younger one stood as a member of parliament and tried to advance his interests inside the Christian Democracy.'

'So what's big capital's game in Spain right now?'

'They're moving on several fronts at once. I don't believe that Spanish capital is divided into one bloc that's nostalgic for Francoism — the so-called economic "bunker" — and another bloc that favours change as long as it can control it. I think they're all banking on a controlled changeover, but at the same time they're keeping one hand on their guns. In other words, they hand out a hundred pesetas to the neo-Francoites, a hundred to the Centre Right, and another hundred to the far Right and the secret police.'

'A hundred pesetas! We're talking about five million, rising to two hundred million...'

Some impulse prompted him to get up and begin pacing round the room like the proverbial caged animal, or, in Carvalho's case, like an ex-prisoner pacing round his cell in voyages through a geography of the imagination.

'Now, they're not that generous just for the hell of it. In order to have coughed up two hundred million, either they must be very strong undertakings or they must have a very strong hand to play.'

'Two hundred million, in 1976 to be precise.'

'What are you talking about?'

'You could do a lot with money like that. Finance a sympathetic political party; hire a bunch of armed mercenaries; or even buy top-level government decisions.'

'Yes, two hundred million's not bad. But that would have to be just for starters.'

At four in the morning Carvalho finally fell asleep. The sheets that the 'colonel' had given him fell to the floor like a gentle flight of clumsy, ingenuous animals. He dreamt of having a strange erotic relationship with Fuensanta, which began with a plate of sausage and beans served at the counter of a bar which was too flashy to be La Chunga.

'Are they real?' Carvalho asked, pointing to her breasts.

'Touch them.'

He did. They were big, soft, and hot.

'If my son comes back, we're done for.'

They found a hiding place among some plastic drainpipes in the moonlight, but the woman still wasn't satisfied.

'They can see us from the house.'

'Which house?'

In the background you could see the outlines of a terrace roof, and the shadow of a guard with a rifle slung across his shoulder.

'It's my son. Can't you see him?'

'I thought you had a daughter.'

'No, no, a son.'

Carvalho seemed to have no strength left to finish pulling her skirt off, even though he could already see in the moonlight the promise of a white arse with its soft cleavage appearing between two cool, spherical globes of flesh.

He suddenly found himself awake, with his cock at half mast and a sex urge somewhere in his nether regions. He made his way to the toilet, unsure whether to piss or masturbate. As he pissed it relieved the pressure on his sex organs, but not on his imagination, which was still a jumble of carnal images of Fuensanta and her daughter. He cleared the dirty dinner plates off the table so as to make room for the carefully detailed sheets of paper that Parra had given him. The name Gausachs cropped up five times in firms that had links with Petnay. The lawyer Fontanillas was on the board of directors of two companies with rather remote connections, and Aracata Milk Products Ltd turned up in the list of firms supplying raw materials.

'Boss — señora Jauma has been chasing you for two

days now. She wants you to get in touch with her, urgently. Should I give her your Vallvidrera number?'

'Certainly not. If she calls again, tell her I'm out of the country.'

'As it happens, I already have.'

The seven minutes that it took him to get from Vallvidrera into the centre of town seemed longer than usual. He decided against waiting for the slow, asthmatic and over-ornate lift, and walked up the worn pink marble steps that led to the flat of Alemany the accountant. He was met by a tearful señora Alemany, and all she could say was:

'He's dying. He's dying.'

It did indeed seem that Alemany had decided to die. He lay there with his yellow blotchy face more or less sunk into the pillow. He tilted his head slightly at the sound of his wife's voice, and his eyes still had the fierce look of the badly wounded eagle that senses the mystery of its own death approaching.

'Alemany — I wanted to ask you something else about señor Jauma.'

'The father?'

'No, the son.'

'Ah, the son.'

His eyes returned to the ceiling as if he was washing his hands of the business, but the way he tilted his head slightly in Carvalho's direction indicated that he was all ears.

'About the money that was missing from the Petnay accounts.'

'I will only discuss that with señor Jauma.'

'He's dead, Alemany. Remember? He was killed because of something to do with those accounts.'

'So many people dying, so many...!'

'Alemany, how was that money channelled out of Petnay? What company did it go through?'

'They've taken all of them. My collection. My books.'

'He's dying, he's dying!'

'What are you talking about? Who's taken them?'

'He's getting confused. Señora Jauma rang me yesterday, and she had a very good offer to make me. A friend of hers was interested in buying my husband's accounting books. You see, he used to keep copies of all the most important accounts for his archive, and this gentleman told me he wanted to buy them all for the library of some business college he's involved with.'

'You sold them?'

'Yes. Yesterday. Two gentlemen came to look at them, and they said they definitely wanted them. I asked my husband what he thought. They made us a very good offer, and they told me that if I sold the accounting books they would also make me an offer for our collection of posters of the Generalitat, and for my husband's correspondence with Macia, Companys, and Pi i Sunyer.'

'Who made this offer?'

'One of them was called Raspall, and I don't remember the other.'

'Did they pay you?'

'Yes.'

'How much?'

'A decent figure. It pained me to sell them, but what would I have done with them otherwise? All I have is this flat, a pitiful pension, and a few shares that are worth nothing. They wouldn't have been any use to the children either.'

'Who signed the cheque?'

'Mr Raspall. My eldest son paid the money in this morning.'

'Does Alemany know that you've actually sold them?'

'I told him. At first he said no; then he agreed. At the moment he's grumbling and shouting at me every now and then, but then he says it was a good idea because that way I end up with a bit of money.'

Alemany was sleeping, or pretending to sleep. Carvalho raised his voice, to wake him.

'Alemany, you've got to tell me — who was responsible

for siphoning off that Petnay money?'

The old man was like a block of marble — either deaf or fast asleep. He didn't respond to Carvalho's shouted questions, and the noise brought his children running. Politely, at first, and then with growing anger, they asked Carvalho to leave so that the old man could die in peace.

'So many people have died — so many...' the old accountant murmured, evidently aware that he was about to become the next in a string of dead acquaintances, and that nothing and nobody was any longer worth opening his eyes for. The approaching footsteps of the Alemany children more or less drove Carvalho out, and when he found himself alone on the landing he had the sensation of other steps sounding behind him too — the same footsteps that were dogging his trail and always seemed to get there before him. First there was the buying of the bar, and now buying up Alemany's papers. Maybe Concha Hijar, unbeknownst to herself, had done a deal with her husband's murderer. There would be no point in confronting her and demanding to know the name when he only had a hunch to go on. Tense with fear and anger he arrived at the Petnay offices. Gausachs's secretary stepped out of the way just in time to avoid being pushed and Gausachs himself spluttered a protest and made as if to get up, but then sank back into his chair under the pressure of the inevitable. The inevitable, in this instance, was Carvalho, standing in the middle of the office, with the secretary at his side spluttering accusations at him and apologies to Gausachs.

'It appears that you learned your trade from American gangster movies.'

'It's not often that I get to deal with big-time crooks. Like yourself, for example.'

Gausachs closed his eyes wearily and gestured to his secretary. She was evidently well trained, and withdrew, shutting the door as she went. Carvalho picked the chair that was furthest from Gausachs, sat with his legs hanging over one of the arms, and from this sprawling position waited for Gausachs to emerge from his puzzlement.

'Well, I mean... This is unheard of!'

'Choose your words carefully, Prof. For something to be unheard of means that it has to be said, and up till now I haven't even said good morning.'

Gausachs came round his desk and stood in front of the detective. He ran his hand through his thick, blond hair, and the same hand then fumbled in the breast of his waistcoat, ending up finally in the pocket of his trousers. By this time Gausachs had mustered up a smile.

'What have you come for? The cheque or an explanation of an alleged embezzlement dug up by some amateur accountant?'

'As far as the cheque goes, don't rule it out, and as for the accountant, he can't be so very amateur if someone's seen fit to buy up his records for a seven-zeroes figure.'

'He must have written his accounts in illuminated lettering! Anyway, as regards the alleged embezzlement, you can relax. Head office in London has explained it all to me. You must have got the figure of two hundred million from *Ali Baba and the Forty Thieves*, though. Every year small amounts of money go unaccounted for. These are moneys spent by Petnay in direct contacts between the company and its subsidiaries or associated companies — technical training courses, public relations, entertainment expenses and so on. Jauma was surprised when he discovered this expenditure, which is controlled from London, and which is authorized by special managers that Petnay maintains in its subsidiaries. If he hadn't then started going round like a bull in a china shop, he would have waited for the company's world-wide accounts to arrive from London, and he would have discovered that there was nothing to get alarmed about.'

'In other words, he wouldn't have found out about the wheeler-dealing.'

'Don't be so childish, for God's sake. What wheeler-dealing?! Do I have to spell it out in words of one syllable?'

Gausachs's reaction betrayed impatience, surprise, and a measure of irritation.

'Somebody's psyched up a village pimp to get him to own up to the Jauma killing.'

'Would you mind translating that into Castilian?'

'You know what I'm talking about. Somebody has bribed a small-time pimp to confess to Jauma's murder. And that same mysterious somebody has bought up the lifetime records of the accountant Alemany, which include, among other things, the trail leading directly to the person responsible for laundering this missing money from the Petnay accounts.'

'You're the kind of person who thinks that the Jesuits put poison in our water.'

'Somebody has been putting tons of bromide into our water, so that we all go to sleep, and you must either be a cynic or a halfwit if you don't smell the immense amount of shit around you. Or maybe your nose has just got used to it.'

'I'm asking you this as a favour. Accept Petnay's offer and leave us in peace. For your own good. And for mine. And for Concha's. Stop trying to play James Bond.'

Nuñez looked as if he'd slept the night with his clothes on. He opened the door with a damp floorcloth in one hand. In the middle of the room — which, judging from the shelves full of books and the table piled with papers, was a hallway, a bedroom, a dining room, and a work room all rolled into one — a bucket of dirty water seemed to be contemplating its existential condition as a bucket of dirty water. Nuñez wrung out the floorcloth and put it on the floor next to the bucket. He took a bottle of cologne from a shelf and sprinkled it on his hands, flapping them around and waiting for it to evaporate.

'My lady friend is out at work, so I was cleaning the flat.'

A long, silent pause. Time for mutual observation.

'Concha wants to call it off. She's been trying to get in touch with you. I haven't been able to dissuade her.'

Slowly Carvalho unfolded his version of what had been happening:

'That money must have been destined for some illegal end. If it had been a case of personal embezzlement, Petnay wouldn't have been in such a hurry to cover it up. This was money that was disappearing with the company's consent. Jauma must have suspected something. He felt isolated, surrounded. So he consulted someone he thought he could trust. He went along with the company's explanations at first, but this year either the amount was too big, or Jauma discovered something that made him particularly uneasy. Deciding to kill him was a very serious step. There's only one real explanation. Jauma was becoming a threat. The conclusion is obvious. They decide to kill him, and then bring all their political and economic influence to bear so as to cover their tracks. What I don't understand is why Jauma was so naive. He knew perfectly well who he was dealing with. Either he was trying to make a quick buck by blackmailing Petnay, or he was too free with someone he thought he knew and trusted. The former possibility fits perfectly with how things have turned out. The latter makes things a bit complicated. Jauma would have to have told someone what he had found out, but perhaps he told the wrong person. Or maybe he went directly to the person responsible and came right out with it. Either way it suggests that he trusted the person he contacted. Whether he was opening his heart or accusing him, he would have to have known the person quite well. He is then betrayed. And murdered. My hunch is that the murderer comes from your group, one of the high flyers in the photo. Logically it

would have to have been either Fontanillas or Argemi. Both
men had direct links with Petnay, the first because he was
an advisor to various Petnay subsidiaries, and the second
because he owned a company that was dependent on
Petnay. On the other hand, we can't rule out the possibility
that it was one of the others in the group — the lifelong
reds. They kill Rhomberg because he knew something, and
they were afraid that I would talk to him. There's a lot of
potential in all this — perhaps too much potential for a
person like me. I could get a lot of money out of it. The
widow will pay me very generously to prevent me from
jeopardizing her rather handsome company pension.
Petnay is also willing to pay me to drop the case. Never have
I been within reach of earning so much money in such a
short space of time, and that worries me. What can I do?
We live in what's almost a democracy. Maybe I should go
public with it. Tomorrow I arrange a meeting with a few
journalists, and I openly accuse Petnay. There's a big fuss,
and a public inquiry, which concludes that a tenth-rate
private detective was trying to use a public scandal to
advance his own personal position.'

'The way you put it, there's no way out.'

'There *is* a way out. It all depends on you, and Jauma's
other left-wing friends. You could give the case a political
dimension.'

'I don't know about that. I don't think I could create
complications for my party at a delicate time like this. Can't
you see that it would be a disaster for the party to take the
side of a sex maniac who was light-handed with women's
knickers? Because that's what would come out at a public
inquiry. We're just coming out of years of silence and
persecution. You don't really think we could afford to get
involved in a scandal like this, do you?!'

'What about the others? Vilaseca and Biedma?'

'Vilaseca doesn't come into it. He would be of no use to
you. Biedma, on the other hand, would go along with you,
I'm sure, but he'd be your worst ally. Like David against

Goliath, a raving red and a down-at-heels private investigator teaming up to take on a respected multinational and drag its name in the mud...'

'So what do I do — take the money and run?'

'That's your problem.'

'What would you do?'

'If I were in your shoes, I wouldn't do anything at all. I'd just go home and wait for a more propitious time, when the balance of power was more in my favour. One of these days Petnay is bound to put a foot wrong, and that will be the time to revive the case. If you want to leave it for a bit I might even be able to give you a hand.'

'One evening, when all the various occupants of the building where I have my office have gone home, a couple of unpleasant characters will come up the stairs. They'll take advantage of the fact that Biscuter is out, probably on a shopping expedition. When Biscuter returns he'll find me as dead as a doornail, and the papers will call it: "The curious case of the killing of a detective who flirted with the underworld." My curriculum vitae doesn't read too well. An ex-communist ex-member of the CIA with a girlfriend who's a prostitute and who's not so much select as selective. Or maybe they'll kill me in my house at Vallvidrera and then set fire to it. I generally have a fire in the house, even in Spring. It helps me think. You got me into all this...'

'So what do you expect *me* to do? I could arrange to be with you when they come so that they kill me too. If it makes you any happier, I could come to your office every evening to keep you company, or to your house every night. I'm game. I can understand positions of individual morality. Mine, however, begins and ends with myself.'

'To tell you the truth, I don't fancy dying. Not even in the company of the likes of you.'

'I feared as much.'

'The problem is that I think I'm going to have to follow this through.'

'You're prepared to go it alone?'

'I'll find out who murdered Jauma, and I'll get my money off the widow. I need to. I'm saving for my old age.'

'I'm not. I do just enough translation work to be able to smoke without getting cancer. At the moment I'm working on Karl Marx — *The Critique of the Gotha Programme*.'

'Be sure to send me a copy. I'm in the habit of lighting my fire with transcendental books. The more a book has pretensions to being transcendental, the more guilty it is. At some point in its life it must have conned someone.'

'You're one of those who reach for their guns when they hear the word "culture".'

'No. I reach for my lighter. Culture means cooking with or without sauces, living like a mortal or an immortal, worshipping your own wife or someone else's wife. Culture is either French or English, Spanish or American, Eskimo or Italian. What *you* call culture is just verbal orthopaedics.'

'All those years of learning German, and now it turns out it was all a waste of time!'

'The tongue has offered you no sexual satisfaction?'

'Are you referring to the spoken tongue, or to the tongue as a muscle?'

'For the moment, the spoken tongue.'

'I can't complain. Even though I was living in a country as puritanical as East Germany, I was still having a girl a week. Beneath the semblance of the nation's Marxist rigidity vibrated a deep romanticism. One of them insisted on cutting a lock of her pubic hairs, and gave it to me as a souvenir.'

'Do you still have it?'

'I left it there. Imagine what would have happened if they'd found it when they searched me at the border!'

'You communists are the world's reserve of puritanism.'

'One day we'll be vindicated.'

It wasn't easy to prise the widow Jauma out of her territory of children deprived of a father and a flat where even the windows were starched and ironed. Carvalho's solution for a situation that was threatening to get out of hand was to arrange to meet her down by the port, to ignore her remonstrations, and to put her in a position where they had to continue their conversation in a pleasure cruiser that toured one of the dirtiest harbours in the world. Maybe it was going a bit far to invite her for *moules marinières* in a cheap restaurant beneath the lighthouse.

'Just exactly who do you think you are? Stop thinking you can treat me like a dog on a lead. Don't forget, you're working for me.'

Carvalho downed his mussels and then used a mussel shell to raise spoonfuls of the sauce to his lips.

'They're disgusting. I don't know about "*marinières*"... they taste of petrol and they look more like they've been shipwrecked... Look how many cloves they've put in. The cook must have been a Murcian. Murcians put cloves in their food the way the Jews put nails into Christ on the cross. My grandmother was from Murcia, and she used to make fish soup. It was cheap but good. She used slices of swordfish, a green pepper, onions, tomato, and cloves.'

'Will you stop fooling about and get to the point?'

'It's time we talked about money. I want thirty per cent of what they've given you for being an accessory to your husband's murder.'

'If you carry on like that, I'm going to hit you.'

'Please suppress the army colonel side of you. You know perfectly well that you've been playing along with the people who killed your husband. The final stroke was fixing up that deal with Alemany's wife and persuading her to sell the account books. You can tell the crook who bought them that I'm preparing the documentation, and that I intend to call a press conference about it.'

'Everything I've done has been for the good and protection of my children. The case is closed, the murderer has been arrested, and you've been overstepping the mark. I have no problem in coming to a financial settlement with you, so you need have no worries on that score. Dropping the case will not cause you any financial inconvenience.'

'Did they threaten to withdraw your pension?'

'Nobody threatens me with anything.'

'Or did they promise they'd pay you money?'

'Nobody buys me.'

'Your husband was killed by the same person who is now insisting that you bury the case.'

'You're crazy. You're like an actor who plays Napoleon once, and ends up thinking he *is* Napoleon.'

'Pass the word on. I'm out to get him. He'll be front page news in all the papers.'

'Here, take this. I want no further dealings with you, and from now on I accept no responsibility for your actions.'

A folded cheque was deposited next to the pile of empty mussel shells. Carvalho licked his fingers, dried them, and reverently picked it up.

'Two hundred and fifty thousand pesetas. Not bad.'

'It would buy more than a year of your time.'

'My father retired on a pension of eight thousand pesetas a month after having worked for sixty-five years — or rather seventy, because at the age of five he was already looking after the cows. If I had pursued my career as a professor of sociology and literature, I would now be earning thirty thousand pesetas a month, plus yearly bonuses. No less than four hundred and fifty thousand pesetas a year. So you see — you got your sums wrong. It's too little. That said, though, it's not bad.'

'Are you in need of help, señora?'

It was the long-haired policeman again, and at his side a colleague, dressed like a specialist in Peruvian agrarian reform.

'Señora Jauma, do you always travel escorted by the Sixth Fleet?'

'Drop the wisecracks. We've been very patient with you.'

'He wasn't bothering me. I came of my own free will, and we've finished now.'

'Don't forget — tell your protector that I'm gunning for him.'

'You're gunning for nobody, friend. And don't go acting flash, because we might just decide to pull you in.'

Concha Hijar was already a drumming of heels in the middle distance. The two policemen wavered, and then went and parked themselves at the bar so as to keep an eye on Carvalho. The detective got up and went to watch the queasy movement of the leaden sea. It was raining. The sea seemed offended by the scant contribution of the falling celestial waters. He took several deep breaths to empty his stomach of the malodorous vapours of anxiety. Close to his heart lay the undeniably comforting presence of a fat cheque, which might not buy out one's fear of death, but would make a decent addition to the savings account which Carvalho kept as a protection for his old age. If he ended up as one of those old men who wet their beds, the thousand-peseta notes would make an excellent absorbent mattress.

'It looks like we've wet the bed again, señor Carvalho...'

Or:

'You disgusting old man — you've pissed yourself again.'

All that stood between these two comments was the insurance of a lifetime's savings, religiously buried under the grey tombstone of his Savings Bank paying-in book.

'Steer clear of banks, Pepe. Avoid them like the plague. Banks go bust and take your money down with them. Savings banks are more reliable.'

'But they give a lower rate of interest, dad.'

'They're safe, though.'

Or maybe he would buy a piece of land, with a view to reselling it when he retired. If the country went democratic, though, it would be harder to speculate in land. And what about if socialism came? Then they'd have neat, clean old people's homes everywhere. They'd connect a plastic pipe to his cock, and when he urinated in his sleep, it would end up in a collective reservoir of purified piss which would then go out into the city's water supply as privatized water fit for public consumption. The Antonio Gutierrez Diaz Gerontology Centre. They would cremate his body in the La Pasionaria Crematorium, and then they would scatter his ashes in the Friedrich Engels Eternal Matter Park. It would be a real drag if they killed me right now, he thought, with the town hall in a mess, and a shortage of grave spaces, and with Charo and Biscuter following the coffin and crying all over the place. And what would become of Biscuter then? He'd have to teach him a few things. Biscuter's best chance would be to try and get a job in a restaurant somewhere, because he had all the makings of a good cook. But then he was so sickly and stunted that the only feelings he inspired in people were pity and disgust, and racism doesn't operate only on the colour of your skin, but also on how you look, how tall you are, what kind of nose you have, what kind of hair, and so on. He'd make out a will, so that in the event of his dying unexpectedly his savings and the house at Vallvidrera would go to Biscuter and Charo. He'd leave his wine cellar to Bromide so that he could die with his liver pickled in good wines. Within a few hours the threat he'd made to Concha would provoke a reaction. Carvalho decided to meet it armed. He left the restaurant purposefully when he heard the siren of the approaching ferry. The two policemen boarded the boat behind him and took up seats where they could watch him. Neither of them spoke. They observed the passengers on the boat as if they were mentally classifying them into active criminals and latent criminals. When the boat docked, Carvalho set off to the local branch of the Savings Bank to pay in his cheque.

'Look, I don't have my savings book with me. I'd like to put two other people's names on the account. They'll come in to sign later.'

'Fill out this form, please.'

He had to write out Charo's and Biscuter's proper names,

but he suddenly remembered that he hadn't the faintest idea what they were. The counter clerk didn't look like the type who would willingly accept diminutives or nicknames. A savings-book made out in the name of José Carvalho Larios, Charo and Biscuter would have prompted at the very least a meeting of the board of directors of the Savings Bank Association. Shit! He set off on foot to the office to ask them for their proper names and also to get his gun. He sat in his swivel-chair. Biscuter was preparing beans, and raised an inquiring eye when he saw Carvalho examining the mechanism of his Star handgun.

'Do you always carry a gun?'

'You have to, in this country.'

They had taken off their jackets as they climbed up the paths which led to the heights overlooking Death Valley. Jauma made the point that he wasn't big on landscapes, but he accepted that the place was impressive. This was the third time that Carvalho had visited the high, red-earth plateau from which you can see, almost at arm's length, the white, curving undulations of Zabriskie Point, with the sun setting on them. Mountains where you could very easily kill yourself as you set off in pursuit of the unknown — of some place that you would never want to return from, a place of total oblivion, where you could enjoy being the sole living particle in a totally uninhabited world, a particle freed from fear. Meandering trails at the bottom of the wind-blown valley — yellow, black, blue, green and red — as the early evening shadows settle in.

'If we don't get a move on, we'll be too late to take photos at Zabriskie Point, and we'll be late getting to Vegas, too.'

'I want to see the Ann Margret show. It's her first show

since the accident and the plastic surgery.'

Dieter was wanting to take photos, and Jauma wanted to see one of his erotic fantasies in the flesh. They raced off to Zabriskie Point. Rhomberg's camera just had time to photograph Carvalho pretending to stride off to the horizon, which by now was turning mauve with the setting sun.

'I suppose the trip's over for you now. You only came out here to see these hills again, didn't you.'

'Yes.'

'Doesn't Vegas tempt you?'

'Not really. This was what I came for.'

Dieter continued driving, partly because Jauma was ill at ease with automatics, and partly because he didn't enjoy the passivity of being a passenger. Darkness was settling on the desert, but you could still see the dry, rolling countryside, the old abandoned wooden houses, and the distant silhouette of the road to an Indian reservation which Jauma decided against visiting.

'I want to see Ann Margret and I want to gamble. Tomorrow I have to do the rounds of the shops to see how business is going. Both Dieter and I have come here to work, but in Las Vegas real life begins when the sun goes down. What'll you be doing tomorrow?'

'I'm going back to San Francisco.'

'Only staying one day?'

'I like seeing Death Valley.'

'I've only ever seen it from the plane, and in the Disney film *The Living Desert*.'

'If you've got a couple of days to spare, why don't you hire a light aircraft and take a flight over the canyons. Do the Colorado canyon first. Then there's another canyon nearby, with a forest of phallus-like pillars of rock left by the erosion. You should find the spectacle stimulating.'

Jauma promised to do the trip, even if only to check out the phalluses.

'I'll kneel before them and pray for mine to be as big and eternal as theirs.'

Las Vegas suddenly came into view like a brightly-lit mirage in the middle of the desert. Dieter put his foot down. In Jauma's sephardic eyes the reflection of the approaching lights mingled with the sparkle in the eyes of a man eager for a party. They drove into the midst of a kind of multi-coloured electric sun dedicated solely to the promise of happiness to come. Vegas still managed to amaze them, even though all three of them were regular visitors — Carvalho because he was a training instructor at a CIA base near the city, and Dieter and Jauma because this was a fabulous world of social relations created by the industries that they were involved in. Jauma had reserved rooms for them at the Sands Hotel, and what they got was a bungalow each, fronting directly onto the sands of the desert and backing onto lush monumental gardens which were criss-crossed by youthful hotel porters driving baggage trolleys.

'Don't be too long dressing, Carvalho. The show's at Caesar's Palace, and I want to eat first.'

An assortment of smoked savouries, accompanied by a Moselle wine, and followed by fresh lychees flown in from Thailand and a Calvados of exquisite aroma and proper strength. He gazed at the women dressed in curtains and their menfolk in fancy dress: green Prince of Wales check suits, yellow shoes, red shirts, and solid gold pendants in place of ties. The waitresses were wearing the sort of clothes that Cleopatra might have worn at the moment of her death, if we suppose that Cleopatra would have worn a skirt so short as to present the invading Romans with the full spectacle of her royal arse.

'You've not still got your gun with you...?!'

'It's become part of me.'

Ann Margret's floorshow was opened by Sergio Mendes and his Brazilian band. A professional perfection tailored to the receptive capacities of an audience that was split more or less evenly between rich people, adventurers, and newly-weds. Everyone was wearing evening dress, and the men's suits and women's dresses bought in Paris or in branches of Parisian stores in New York and Los Angeles had been adapted to the calculatedly 'casual' tastes of the North American market. Ann Margret came on-stage with her perfect little body and her new, improved face, looking like a mischievous street-urchin: Her voice was childlike, but she handled it well. She was one hell of a dancer too, as Jauma never tired of saying. She had the audience on their feet when she announced that at one of the tables in the immense hall was Elvis Presley in person. The one-time youthful rock and roller got up to acknowledge the enthusiastic screams of the middle-aged women in the audience. Everyone was on their feet scanning the aisles for the island where their hero exhibited a corpulence corseted in an adolescent costume. With a final wave he left, surrounded by bodyguards who unceremoniously shoved aside the women pressing forward for an autograph. With Elvis out of the way, everyone calmed down again, the house lights dimmed, and the show continued. Jauma wanted to get closer to the stage. He came back enthusing.

'She's perfect! Perfect!'

They headed for the exit, to get out before the rush and find a seat at one of the gaming tables. The one-armed bandits were looking like robots in electronic evening dress. But the green baize covers of hundreds of gambling tables introduced a vice of another era multiplied by the demon of present-day prósperity. Dieter settled himself among the serried ranks of fruit machines. Jauma took possession of a seat at a table where baccarat was under way. Carvalho inspected the small stage of an Egyptian barge on which an orchestra of first-century BC Romans was playing. However, the solid policemen protecting the casino safes were dressed in colours that were very much twentieth-century: grey, khaki, beige and camouflage. Brown-skinned policemen with big guns in white leather thigh holsters. Carvalho ventured five quarters on the fruit machines, and then resigned himself to a long wait, given the obsessiveness with which Jauma was following the game and losing his money. Dieter was doing the *via crucis* of every fruit machine in the place, with the methodical rigour of the German engineering inspector that he was. For a while Carvalho exchanged glances with a small, shapely Jewess surrounded by her menfolk, who were gazing ironically at a game in progress. He took advantage of her temporary separation from the clan to inquire whether she wasn't thinking of trying her luck.

'My religion doesn't permit me to gamble,' she said, through moist lips, but to Carvalho it was as if the voice was coming from the two compact globes that stuck out over the *décolleté* of her pink tulle dress. Her whole group was staying at the Holiday Inn, and Carvalho offered to take her back to the Sands, to show her the desert.

'The hotel's owned by Sinatra.'

The dark-skinned woman spied movement among the clan. A man with crinkly black hair and heavy features looked over at her from the midst of the clan.

'I can't. We're leaving now.'

'Are you from San Francisco?'

'No, Owosso. It's hardly on the map even. We're here to celebrate my in-laws' golden wedding anniversary.'

'It's a shame you can't come to the Sands. From my room you can see the Sahara Desert.'

She returned to her family and friends with a look of immense satisfaction on her face, and hooked herself onto the arm of the hard-faced Jew, looking as if she'd just returned from crossing Sinai. Dieter had another two hundred and thirteen fruit machines to go, and Jauma wasn't even noticing Carvalho's attempts to attract his attention from across the table. At one point he looked up, and his eyes met Carvalho's. He had the glazed look of a man in the grip of gambling fever. He looked at Carvalho as if he was a stranger. Carvalho raised his arm in a half-hearted wave. He paused at the door for one last look, but Jauma was sitting with his chin resting on folded hands and totally engrossed in the game.

Biscuter had finished slicing the beans, and he offered him a handful of the tenderest ones. Carvalho took a mouthful and savoured their agreeably bitter taste. At that point the phone rang. He curbed Biscuter's impatience, let it ring, and then picked it up cautiously, as if it was a time bomb waiting to be defused.

'Is that you, Carvalho?'

'Who's that?'

'Look, we're over at your girlfriend's, and we're having a bit of a party. We'd like to talk with you, though. Come over straight away, on your own, and leave your hardware at home. We'll be waiting for you at her flat. Don't hang about, because otherwise we might decide to have a bit of fun with her, and we're very demanding.'

They hung up. He put his gun in a drawer and slipped a flick-knife into his pocket.

'Call Charo's flat in one hour from now, and if you notice anything unusual, ring these two numbers — Nuñez and Biedma. Tell them where things are at.'

'I'm coming with you, boss.'

'You stay right here — and lock yourself in.'

'Should I call the police at any point?'

'Only ring them if someone steals your beans.'

He arrived at Charo's staircase, panting. He tried to calm his breathing in the lift, and by the time he put his key in the door he imagined that he had the look of a man capable of handling himself. Inches away from the door stood the owner of the voice that had phoned him. Judging by the broken nose, he thought, he must have been a boxer, and the nose was flattened even more by the smile that spread across his halfwit features.

'Now that's what I call punctuality! Come in, with your hands up.'

At the end of the hallway another man was waiting. He was short, with trousers that were baggy at the knees and a jacket with shoulder pads so thick that they grazed his earlobes. They searched him, checking under his armpits and in his pockets.

'So what's the flick-knife for — trimming your nails?'

Propelled by the heat of the boxer's breath on his neck, Carvalho walked past the short man and entered the living room. Charo was there. She had been stripped to the waist, but still had her skirt on. Two men were holding her by the arms. When she saw Carvalho, she began to cry. Carvalho made as if to turn, but just at that moment he received a heavy kick to the leg that was supporting him. He lost his balance and fell flat on his back. The boxer went to kick him in the balls, and the short man kicked him in the side. As he sat on the floor trying to protect his genitals with his hands, they kicked his arms and then put a scarf round his neck and pulled on it so that he fell backwards. Balanced on one buttock he lashed out, kicking with both feet together and trying to make contact with the one standing nearest. The boxer reeled and grabbed at the sofa to prevent himself falling. By now Carvalho was on his feet again. He aimed a punch at the short man, who staggered back under the impact. Still staggering, he opened the knife that they'd taken from Carvalho. Charo screamed, and as Carvalho turned he saw a hand squeezing one of her breasts as if it was trying to strangle it. He dived towards her, but collided with the bulk of the boxer, who was now on his feet again. The boxer punched him, first in the kidneys, then in the chest, and then full in the face. Stunned, Carvalho lashed out at the boxer's face with two fists clenched together, followed by a head-butt to the mouth. Carvalho's momentum sent him sprawling to the floor on top of the man. One great paw flattened his nose and pulled his head backwards as if trying to wrench it off his body, while the other was delivering piledriver punches to his ribs. He managed to press his thumbs into the eyes of the fallen man, and he let out a yell, causing the other three to come running to his rescue.

'Run, Charo, run!'

But Charo was paralysed — she was crying, with her fists clenched and her lips bruised. Carvalho lashed out blindly, oblivious to the blows raining down on him. They hauled on his jacket and dragged him over to the radiator. Two of them sat on his back, and the other two gripped his arms. He felt the cold metal of a handcuff click round one wrist. A few more punches and they drew back. As he tried to raise himself he realized that the other handcuff was locked round the radiator feed-pipe. An irrepressible aesthetic instinct led him to lift himself up, and he sat there, powerless, looking from one face to the other and trying to contain the sob that came welling up from his stomach at the sight of a terrified Charo, her breasts covered with bruises. He tugged at the chain of the handcuffs to see if they were loose. Everyone and everything was out of reach. He lowered his head, settled his back against the radiator and tried to gather his thoughts. There were burning stabs of pain coming from various parts of his body. He moistened his top lip with his tongue and found that it was soaked with blood. The others were checking their bruises. The boxer's eyes were streaming with the pain.

'You scratched me, cocksucker. Now we're going to show you something.'

The boxer turned to Charo and gave her two hefty blows which knocked her to the floor. He grabbed her short hair and dragged her up, mauling her breasts with one hand and choking her screams with the other.

'If you scream I'm going to castrate this queerboy pimp of yours. You — cut his balls off.'

The short man moved across to Carvalho with the flick-knife open. Charo stopped screaming and began sobbing.

'Take a look at her, ponce! The only reason we haven't screwed her is because we prefer virgins, and this one looks like she's done the rounds. But we could burn her tits with cigarettes. We're all smokers. Or we could mark her face by scoring it with sugar lumps.'

He had taken a lump of sugar out of his pocket and was removing its paper wrapper with a slowness that suggested hesitation. When he had it unwrapped, he pushed it abruptly against Charo's face. She jerked back in panic, like an animal facing death and with no possibility of escape. Carvalho was sobbing silently, through gritted teeth.

'We won't mark her. At least, not today. It's up to you, cocksucker, whether we come back another day to give her a seeing to. A whore with gashes all over her face earns fuck-all. And then we have the acid treatment. But we reserve that for really obstinate cases, and it looks like you're starting to see sense, arsehole. You'll get there. OK, let's go.'

The other three filed towards the door and turned round to watch. The boxer was standing in front of Carvalho, with his legs apart.

'Look what you've done to my eyes, cunt! Why don't you try it again, eh?'

One, two, three punches sent the detective to his knees, as he tried to prevent the blows from smashing his teeth.

The boxer seemed sated. He showed Carvalho an envelope, which he then tossed onto the sofa.

'Read it carefully and make sure you do what it says. Otherwise we'll be back, and today's little episode will look like a picnic.'

He removed Carvalho's handcuffs and backed off to join his associates. Their footsteps echoed down the hallway and the door closed behind them. The only other noise in the flat was the sound of Charo sobbing quietly. They avoided each other's eyes. Carvalho was on his knees. Charo was sitting in a chair with her hands in her lap, her cheeks red and tearstained, her breasts livid with bruises, and her body bowed under the weight of an invisible disgust.

Feeling like a man who has survived the end of the world, Carvalho rang Biscuter and told him to come as fast as he could, and to bring a big bottle of liniment. He still hadn't said a word to Charo. She was still crying quietly to herself, but when Carvalho went over and put his hand on her head, the tears suddenly turned to bitter sobbing, as if the floodgates had been opened for everything that was welling up inside her. Carvalho stroked her reddened cheeks and looked worriedly at the bruisemarks on her breasts. He went to the bathroom and stuck his head under the tap, suppressing the spontaneous shouts triggered by the pain spots all over his body. He soaked a towel in water and went back to the front room. He wrapped the wet towel round Charo's head and cradled her head in his arms, feeling her warmth as it penetrated the cloth. When he took the towel away, the swellings on her face had gone down and the bruise-marks were more clearly defined. He put the towel gently onto her breasts and crossed her arms across it to hold its soothing coolness next to her bruises. He exercised his arms vigorously, and then felt his ribs. He flexed his knees, despite the pains shooting through his muscles. He had no bones broken, and this cheered him up. Charo had arranged the towel around her like a shawl, and was trying to see to her hair. Some part of her scalp was obviously hurting, because she was feeling her head gingerly and grimacing when she hit a tender spot. Carvalho took a jug of water out of the fridge and downed half of it. He filled a glass with iced water, got a couple of aspirins from the bathroom cabinet and made Charo swallow them.

'Is this all they did to you?' he said, pointing to her face and breasts. She nodded. Then she examined Carvalho's bruise marks and closed her eyes in horror. Carvalho realized that he hadn't yet seen himself in the mirror. He went back to the bathroom. His alter ego looked frightening. His upper lip was a mass of cut, swollen flesh. He had cuts on his right cheek, big bruises on his cheekbones, a bloody graze in the middle of his forehead, and from some hidden point in the forest of his hair a trickle of half-coagulated blood traced across his brow. He raised his shirt to find his ribs a dark purple colour. He pulled down his trousers. His testicles had swollen to the size of blackened tennis balls. He removed his trousers completely, filled the bidet with cold water, and bathed his genitals. Someone was knocking at the door. He shouted to Charo not to open. He arranged a small hand-towel as a moist dressing between his legs, pulled up his trousers, went into the kitchen to pick up a large pair of scissors, and moved towards the door. The spyhole revealed the face of Biscuter, distorted into a great yellow blob.

'For God's sake, boss! For God's sake—what happened!'

Biscuter hopped nervously around Carvalho, checking the damage. The detective took the bottle of liniment from him. They went into the living room. Carvalho lifted the towel from Charo's shoulders. Biscuter blushed and looked away. Carvalho poured the liniment into his hands and delicately rubbed it into the girl's breasts. He replaced her damp towel with a dry one and then returned to the bathroom to bathe his entire body with the lotion. He was beginning to feel better, as he sank into the other chair and relaxed. Charo had put on a silk dressing gown and was sitting quietly. Biscuter looked at them, obviously wanting to say something but not knowing what.

'Put up a sign saying we're shut for holidays, and come up to Vallvidrera with me. You too, Biscuter.'

'If you need me, boss, I will. But if not I'll hold the fort here, and God help them if they dare show their faces in the office.'

'Well said, Watson — but I want you to come to Vallvidrera. Go and get my car from the parking lot, and park it just by the front door. I don't want people seeing me in a state like this.'

'I've got beans on the stove. What should I do with them?'

'Take the pot and bring them along. We'll finish off cooking them at Vallvidrera.'

'Anything you say, boss!'

Biscuter went off, making his brrm brrm noise as he went, and Charo couldn't help laughing. Carvalho picked up the sealed envelope and put it in his trouser pocket. One half of him was dying to open it, but the other half wasn't. Charo followed the transfer of the envelope, and the look of fear returned to her eyes. She and Carvalho looked at each other. Wanting to ask, but not wanting to answer. Carvalho went up to the roof terrace where Charo was in the habit of sunbathing, at the top of a modern building constructed in a gap in the rotting structure of the old *barrio*. As he leant on the railing he saw Biscuter arriving. Charo was putting some things into an overnight bag. She turned off the electricity in the hallway. When she turned round after locking the door she was wearing a pair of sunglasses. Biscuter opened the car doors like a chauffeur in a film. They drove towards the Ramblas, down to Paralelo, then along calle Urgel, to the old part of town and the slopes of Tibidabo. The fighting was beginning in the Ramblas. The armed police were forcing the demonstrators up neighbouring side-alleys. They gave more determined chase to some demonstrators rather than others, apparently motivated by random degrees of antipathy to their prey. One of the fugitives stumbled against the bonnet of Carvalho's car, and at the speed of light a large black truncheon shook his shoulders with a series of blows that whistled down as the air was sliced by the hurtling rubber. Behind the plastic visor protecting his face the policeman had his eyes shut and his teeth clenched. The sound of the cars hooting infuriated him still further. He turned round and began lashing out with his truncheon at the cars nearest to him. Two or three of his associates joined in his insensate bludgeoning of the cars, and when the traffic began to move off, the truncheon blows rained onto their boots as if lashing the hind quarters of fleeing animals. Biscuter was driving with his head down and the tip of his nose virtually between the spokes of the steering wheel.

The scene of violence outside the car had Charo clinging to Carvalho and periodically closing her eyes in horror.

'Let's get out of this shit country, Pepiño — please, let's go away somewhere.'

She cried for virtually the whole of the drive. Carvalho held her in his arms as he went up the steps to the apartment. Biscuter followed, with Charo's bag in one hand and a china cooking pot tied up with string in the other. Once inside, Charo settled herself into an armchair. Carvalho began his fire-lighting ritual, deciding this time to use Alfonso Sastre's *Anatomy of Realism* as kindling. Biscuter undid the web of knots and stuck his nose into the cooking pot to check the state of the stewed beans.

'I've put mint in with them, boss. I bought a packet at the chemist's. It's dried mint, but it still gives a good flavour.'

He was whistling to himself in the kitchen.

'Now this is what I call proper conditions to cook in. If only I had this gear in the office...'

The smell of the cooking relaxed them. Even Charo sniffed appreciatively, and although she said repeatedly that she wasn't hungry, and that Pepe and Biscuter were two savages who thought of nothing but their stomachs, and that beans made you fat and she had no intention of ending up like a balloon, moments later she lifted the lid of the pot, smelt the aroma with evident pleasure, and had Biscuter almost passing out with delight when she said:

'Your cooking's as good as Pepiño's.'

Carvalho took the envelope out of his pocket. First he put it on the mantelpiece. Then, fearing that the sight of it would give Charo the horrors again, he put it in a drawer in the sideboard and began to lay the table.

The room smelt of the camphor in the liniment. The rest of the house smelt of bean stew. Across Charo's bared chest the bruises had formed into capricious *fleurs du mal*. Carvalho didn't wake her. He shifted the unwashed dishes, sat himself on the one corner of the sofa that wasn't occupied by the sleeping Biscuter, and wrote something on a piece of paper, choosing his words carefully as he wrote. Then he put it in the envelope that his assailants had left him. He put his jacket on and put the envelope in one pocket and the note that the boxer had given him in the other. He shook Biscuter to wake him.

'I'll be out all day. Don't let Charo go out.'

'I'm getting up now, boss. This house needs a good clean-up.'

'This house needs nothing of the sort. It's fine as it is. You just keep your eyes open, and stay with Charo.'

His somnolent major domo had bloodshot eyes. Carvalho felt his gun where it sat in his pocket. Biscuter's eyes followed the gesture, and it seemed to shake him awake.

'I'm not letting you go on your own this time.'

'Don't worry — this time I'm taking my little protector.'

The sun was barely up. The damp night air gave everything an early-morning smell — the earth, the pine trees, and the gravel as it crunched beneath Carvalho's feet. The roads to the city were empty. The comanches were still sleeping in their lairs, or were just starting their daily gargles in the bathroom. The traffic lights saw that he was in a hurry and duly obliged. He arrived at Nuñez's house just as the concierge was opening up, put the envelope in Nuñez's mailbox and left again before the man could question him. He checked to make sure the boxer's note was still in his pocket, took it out, unfolded it and put it on the passenger seat.

'It gives me great pleasure to invite you to my estate at Palausator (Gerona) for an exchange of views. I shall be expecting you at midday on Saturday, and I would be

delighted if you could lunch with me. You can inquire
for the whereabouts of my house in Pals or La Bisbal,
but I enclose a map anyway, in case you need it.'
Signed: Argemi.

The motorway seemed built for him alone. He devoured
the miles, driven on by the emptiness of it all and the gentle
coolness of the morning. As he crossed the Tordera he gave
a moment's thought to Dieter Rhomberg, and how he had
died for the greater glory of universal stability. He came off
the motorway at the Gerona North toll and took the road
to Palamos. The countryside was slowly yawning into life.
Tractors were working the fields. A van was going round
picking up its daily harvest of dead dogs run over by passing
cars. Groups of children in single file were walking to the
local high school.

'The van picks up its daily harvest of dead children run
over by passing cars, and dogs are walking to school in
single file,' Carvalho said to himself, out loud, and then,
at the top of his voice, he started into a romantic aria.

> You're the woman I love best,
> The only one to whom I gave my heart

Then he let rip with 'Faithful triumphant sword', and
half strangled his vocal chords when he tried his luck with
the tune:

> I love you
> Like a man loves his mother,
> Like a man loves his girl,
> Like a man loves mo-o-o-o-ney
> I lo-o-o-o-ve you.

In La Bisbal they told him that the only place he would get
something solid to eat was at La Marqueta. A small
restaurant with oilcloth-covered tables, the wife in the

kitchen, and a cylindrical giant of a man listing what they could heat up for him at that hour of the day: chicken with crayfish; spidercrab with snails; pigs' trotters; roast kid; stuffed squid; baked snails with a vinaigrette or garlic dressing; turkey with mushrooms; stewed veal; sausage and kidney beans; an assortment of home-made sausages; *butifarras*; pork fillets; pork chops and steaks. The man completed his recitation, confident of the overwhelming effect of such a litany. Carvalho chose spidercrab and snails.

'It's more snails than spidercrab, really. The crab is for the flavouring.'

'I suspected as much. After that I'll have the kidney beans and *butifarra*, with a side-dish of garlic mayonnaise.'

Slices of bread that still had the smell of the wheatfield about them. A thick, dark red wine of the sort that turns your ears red in winter.

'Where do you get the wine from?'

'We make it ourselves. I've got a cellar on the other side of the river.'

'Could I buy a few bottles?'

'I don't know if I'll have time to get them ready for you. I've got a lot to do first.'

'Call me at the Argemi estate, in Palausator. Ask for me by name — Pepe Carvalho — and tell me if you can manage it. I'd like to pick up thirty or forty bottles on my way back.'

The man offered him an almond pastry which he said was called a *rus*, and placed at his elbow a big bottle of *garnacha*, from which Carvalho filled his glass three times. He came out of the La Marqueta having decided that the world was a wonderful place after all, and at the same time stressing to his host that the best time to call him chez Argemi would be between twelve-thirty and one. Then he wandered through La Bisbal looking at the ceramics shops, and went into one to order himself a tiled picture that showed the points of the compass with the names of the local winds — Gargal, Tramontana, Garbi. Once again he said that they should phone the Argemi establishment, without fail, between twelve-thirty and one, because then he'd be able to tell them if he needed two pictures instead of just one. Next he went into an antique shop and bought an old oak chest.

'It's a present for someone. I wonder, could you ring me at the Argemi estate in Palausator, because I don't have the address that I want it sent to...'

'I know the people. Señor Argemi's house is full of furniture that has been bought at our shop.'

'Call me at around one. Maybe a bit before. Ask for me — Pepe Carvalho. Then I'll be able to give you the exact address.'

'Don't worry, I will.'

In a fish shop recommended by the man at La Marqueta he ordered a fair-sized *rascasse*, a kilo of small squid, and a further kilo of rock fish for making soup. He asked could they please keep them in the fridge for him, and be sure to phone him at Argemi's half an hour before they closed for lunch, to remind him to call by and pick them up.

'I've got so much on my mind that I'm quite capable of driving back to Barcelona and forgetting all about them.'

'No problem, sir.'

Like Hansel and Gretel, he was dropping bits of bread en route to the ogre's castle, to mark his way. He returned to his car and set off for Palausator, calling in at Peratallada on the way, to ask a few questions about the Argemi estate. He made a point of telling various people his name, and made inquiries as to Argemi's personal standing in the area and the physical layout of the estate. He was told that he could get there directly from the road that ran through the ricefields around Pals, or he could go the roundabout route via Sant Julia de Boada. Carvalho checked out both routes. He climbed to the top floor of an abandoned rectory in order to get an overall impression of the estate. The grounds were overlooked by a large, solid country house set on a gently sloping green ridge. A trail bike was being put through its paces on the path leading to Argemi's private forest. There was a bustle of people in the vicinity of the house, and the smoke rising from an outdoor barbecue indicated that an al fresco lunch was being prepared. Carvalho decided that the time had come.

A groundsman came out to meet him at the iron gate. He was old and Andalusian. He made inquiries via a phone concealed in one of the square stone columns that supported the iron gate. The gate opened to reveal an enormous lawn stretching away to the house. A de luxe lawn which had grown, in the space of a few years, as much as a normal lawn would grow in thirty. As if his entrance had been a signal, a thousand small jets of water started up and wove a cool, sparkling web in a fine spray across the lawn. The installation covered more than half a hectare of lawn in a display of hydraulics that bordered on the aesthetic. An expensively dressed servant was taking two Afghan hounds for a walk, and they were busily engaged in barking at the detective's wretched little car. The path left the lawn behind and continued over a gravel esplanade that was dotted with magnolias, acacias, and laurel bushes. The walls of the house were covered with wisteria, alternating with bougainvillea and Virginia creeper. This vegetal mass was scrupulously respectful of the windows of the house, which were conspicuously Gothic, evidently stolen by antique dealers from old churches in the Pyrenees that had been abandoned to the mercies of bats and antique dealers. A roofless Gothic cloister surrounded a forged iron outdoor grill set on large chunks of masonry. The spit-roast on its own engaged the efforts of two women and a man who were preparing the charcoal for a barbecue that was evidently expected to be perfect and well attended. Beneath an arch of recently-hewn stone stood Argemi, waiting to greet him, in a short silk dressing gown and with a big Havana between his fingers. He had placed himself in the centre of the doorway in such a manner that the keystone with the date of the building on it acted as a frame for his neatly-trimmed grey hair.

'Carvalho — you don't know how much pleasure this gives me.'

'Hi, dad!'

The shout came from an Amazonian female motorcyclist on a trail bike as she roared past the front door of the house. Carvalho just had time to register a slender blonde body encased in leather and a toothpaste smile.

'That's my daughter. We call her Solitud at home, in honour of the great novelist Victor Catala.'

'She's some girl! Is she for real?'

'I believe so.'

'Are you sure you didn't have a PR company create her? I remember an advert that was very popular when I met Jauma in San Francisco. A blonde girl, looking unmistakably American, smiles out from a street hoarding and announces to the world at large: "Everybody needs milk".'

Argemi laughed as he inclined his short, well-fed body to usher Carvalho in. The entrance hall was about half a kilometre square, and provided a showcase of some of Europe's best antique shops. From there they went into an open-plan living room, passing beneath a pair of Catalonian vaulted arches, which also looked like the result of a competition to find the biggest and the best preserved. There were three seating areas, marked off by oriental carpets. One for watching television, another for reading, and a third for conversation, which was where Argemi took Carvalho, and where they sank into carnivorous sofas that seemed to swallow them up with the smooth, sucking motion of shifting sands.

'A prince among houses, Carvalho! If this house could

only speak. It used to belong to the richest landowners in this part of the world. They went bankrupt during the first Carlist war, and the eldest son took off for Cuba. He made his fortune there, and returned home. He decided to buy back the house, and set about making it habitable again. The family went bust again, though, after the Civil War. At that point the house was bought by my father-in-law, and he started the work which has led to this being the jewel that it is. What you see here is ten years of work and the entire imaginative effort of my life devoted to creating a house that would reflect my cultural tastes and my taste for good living. I'll show you my wine cellar later. And the indoor swimming pool. And the little mini-golf course I have in the west wing. As you see, I have a splendid oak forest, which I have stocked with my favourite animals, deer and squirrels. Do you know what excites me most about forests? The mushrooms that pop up at the end of August. Here they call them *flotes de suro*. I don't know their name in Castilian. Perhaps they don't even have one. Castilians don't go in for mushrooms much... In fact they're useless with them. By the way, can I count on you for lunch?'

'All depends on what we're eating.'

'Barbecued meat. All local meat. Everyone knows about Gerona veal, but I can assure you that the best thing about Gerona is its lamb, its *butifarras*, its fresh dripping, and the rabbits which I raise on the same food that they'd eat in the wild.'

'I see that you enjoy eating all kinds of animals, señor Argemi. Calves, rabbits, pigs, lambs, Germans, and even your own best friends.'

'I gather you're wanting to get down to business. Your bruises must still be hurting. Believe me, I was very worried that my men might have overdone it. However, I must say, your face looks very presentable.'

The expensive-looking servant came in with a message for Carvalho.

'There's a señor Savalls on the phone for you, from La

Bisbal.'

Argemi obligingly excused him, and Carvalho took the
phone, spoke to the man from La Marqueta, and remarked
pointedly what time it was, whose house he was at, and
that he would be there to pick up the bottles by four that
afternoon.

'Your business with the bottles seems rather urgent...'

Argemi's comment was accompanied by a slight
puckering of the brow and the beginnings of a broad smile
on his muscular face.

'So, let's not beat about the bush. Yesterday was just a
warning. You've overstepped the mark. I realize that your
threat to Concha was some sort of bravado, but I decided
that the time had come for action.'

'When I made that threat I still hadn't made up my mind
between you and Fontanillas.'

'Carvalho, the very idea of Fontanillas is absurd. It does
your professionalism no credit at all, I'm afraid. Fontanillas
is a politician, of no great aspirations and no great qualities,
but who is likely to end up in the government some day.
You should have known at once that it was me. When you
leave this house, you may find you don't have long left on
this earth.'

The servant reappeared with the phone.

'A call for you, from Terra i Foc, from La Bisbal again.'

Carvalho repeated almost exactly the formula of the
previous call. Argemi had allowed himself to be swallowed
further into the sofa. His eyes were twinkling.

'That's a rather expensive life insurance you've taken
out, there.'

'You've not seen the half of it.'

'Don't worry. I'm enjoying it. Anyway, to continue. As
you know, officially speaking the loose ends have all been
tied up. Jauma was murdered. Rhomberg was going
through a personal crisis and disappeared. The authorities
think that you're just a troublemaker trying to stir things
up. So there's nothing for you to do, now. I suspect that

you're not a moralist — in fact I know you're not. So I'm going to give you exactly what you're looking for: the satisfaction of knowing that you were on the right track, and also a few details that you don't yet know. For a start, I didn't actually kill Jauma with these hairy hands which the good Lord gave me. To be honest, I couldn't have done it. I was terribly fond of him, and in fact I still am. For instance, I'm seriously worried for his family's future, so I've just found a buyer for his yacht. It's not easy to sell a yacht these days, particularly when everyone's expecting tax reforms that are going to hit luxury items in particular. Incidentally, my own view is that this is only fair. The keystone of any radical democratic reform has to be progressive taxation. As I was saying, I didn't kill Jauma personally, but I did give the orders for him to be killed. Jauma was an excellent manager, but he lacked a proper global overview of Petnay's role in the world. I, on the other hand, was Petnay's political confidant, and a number of decisions passed through my hands. There's a good cover for all this, since my company has production links with Petnay. My real functions, though, were rather more complex. For example, Petnay is very worried about Spain's political future. Not simply because the company itself could lose out, but also for what a chaotic political situation in Spain could mean in the context of politics and economics at the international level. Reasonably enough, Petnay has been trying to influence the political situation in Spain, and will play a part in any solution that is progressive, yet doesn't fundamentally change things. The Lord moves in mysterious ways, however. Petnay considers that a powerful democratic Right is needed in Spain, to prevent a revolutionary free-for-all. For that to happen, there needs to be a permanent threat of destabilization. I'm sure you take my meaning. Petnay is banking on a democratic solution, but at the same time they are financing far-Right violence so as to generate fear, which in turn will guarantee order. Let's be frank, Carvalho. Franco taught us a very basic lesson. Under a strong hand, a country produces. Democracy cannot permit the use of a strong hand, but in order to succeed it needs terrorism in the background, a dirty war, which drives people into the arms of stabilizing forces that appear to have clean hands. Petnay started off, rather tentatively at first, directing funds to this end. When Franco died the caution vanished, and that was when Jauma and his picturesque accountant discovered that two hundred million pesetas had disappeared somewhere along the line. Petnay's explanations only made Jauma even more suspicious. He carried on investigating, and discovered that my company had been the channel by which Petnay had funnelled the money to its unknown destination. He approached me. At first he came right out and accused me of embezzlement, on the assumption that I had been in cahoots with some senior Petnay executive to defraud the company. I decided to give him the whole story. But then something happened which I hadn't anticipated. Jauma began to feel the call of his political past. It got particularly bad after the right-wing violence at the start of this year — labour movement people being killed, kids shot in the street, and so on. Jauma was going off the rails, and I could see it. In the end he rang me and gave me an ultimatum. I was to make a public statement about Petnay's financial arrangements. I warned him that it would all end in tears. He, personally, would be socially and financially ruined, and there would be a political scandal which would do nobody any good. After all, it suits the centre parties to have a bit of right-wing violence about, because it makes them look like the lesser of two evils. The same goes for broad sections of the Left. The ultra-Right provides the Left with a useful alibi: they can't afford to overturn the centre parties, because the fascist savages would step in and occupy the resulting political vacuum. And of course all this is great for the ultra-Right, because they get the chance to crack a few heads and kill someone every once in a while, and this keeps the Left right back at square one and does any reformist government a tremendous favour.

'Now, I didn't offer my services in all this without a lot of reservations and soul-searching. In the end, I think that what I have done has been justifiable even from a progressive point of view. Jauma refused to understand, though. I had discussions with Petnay, and we concluded that there was no choice but to kill him. Then you came along and started sticking your nose in — or rather, you, and Concha with her idiotic puritanism, and Nuñez and his having nothing better to do with his time. It was all the fault of you three that I had to kill Rhomberg, and it cost me a lot of money, let me tell you. You can't imagine what it costs these days to hire a killer who's willing to go through a trial, plus three or four years in prison, and everything that it entails. It costs a fortune. In comparison, Alemany's archives worked out cheap. And, as it turns out, Carvalho, getting rid of you is going to cost me even less. Almost nothing, in fact.'

This time it was the fish shop ringing. Carvalho was becoming uncomfortably aware that Argemi had good reason to laugh.

'What other guarantees did you set up?'

'What I want from you is a complete explanation of what has happened, to be deposited with a mutually trustworthy person.'

'Very literary. I'd almost be tickled to oblige. Anyway, as I was saying, getting shot of you isn't going to cost me a lot. The price of a good lunch, in fact — to which it gives me great pleasure to invite you. I also wanted to invite you to share a really special moment with me.'

He rang a small gold bell to summon his servant.

'I bought this in Vienna. It's the bell that the emperor Franz Josef used to use when he fancied sex with Sissi. Ding-ding, and she'd come running like a little dog. Ah, Miguel — would you please bring us the bottle I told you about.'

'And what about Rhomberg? How did he die?'

'There's no point you talking in front of the servants. I pay them so well that they'd kill for me if I told them to. Anyway — Rhomberg... The main thing is that he's dead. There's no point in your trying to find the body. We learned from the Jauma case, and decided to cover our tracks. I don't know the details of how he died, but I gather that the people who do this sort of thing can be pretty ruthless. I don't know the men involved personally. I rely on middlemen. Raspall, for instance. He was the one who bought Paco's mother-in-law's bar to set up a discotheque, and he was also the one who bought Alemany's papers, with a view to presenting them to the Institute of Business Management library — purged, needless to say, of anything that might incriminate me, but in such a way that the figures still add up.'

The servant carried the silver tray at a perfect right angle as if it were an extension of his arm. On the tray were a dust-covered wine bottle and two slender cut-glass wine glasses.

'Look at that. It's a '66 Nuits Saint Georges. Exactly a year ago I brought ten crates back from France, and the producer there told me that I had to lay it down for at least a year before I touched it. And now you and I are about to have a well-deserved first tasting.'

The servant opened the bottle. Argemi immediately took the cork, closed his eyes, and savoured the bouquet. Then he tossed it over, and Carvalho caught it.

'Smell that — this is a superb wine.'

Carvalho smelt it, and immediately regretted having entered into the game.

'Well, say something! It's excellent, isn't it!'

The wine occupied the transparent belly of the glasses, and as it lay there it took on a redness that was the most basic red in all the world. The servant handed one glass to Argemi and another to Carvalho. He nodded deferentially and withdrew to where he had come from.

'Drink, Carvalho. It's a wonderful wine.'

They looked at each other across the room. The only one smiling was Argemi, but his smile suddenly evaporated as Carvalho slowly emptied the contents of his wineglass onto the carpet. The detective got up, making no attempt to conceal the pain in his muscles. He turned his back on Argemi, went towards the door, and continued walking as Argemi commented in a calm voice:

'Jauma didn't deserve the sacrifice you've just made for him. Nineteen sixty-six was a great year for Bourgogne wines.'

Carvalho went down to his car. He waited for the motorbike to pass one more time, to get another view of the strong, young body that needed milk like the whole world needs milk. He started the car, drove past the iron gate, which was solicitously opened for him by the groundsman, and made his way mechanically down the driveway that connected with the main road. The entire geography of his brain was taken up with the phrase 'the angst of the senior executive', and minutes later he found himself heading for home, humming those six little words to the backing of a tune which he had never heard before, and which would never be heard again.

Also by Manuel Vázquez Montalbán and published by Serpent's Tail

Murder in the Central Committee

'A sharp wit and a knowing eye' *Sunday Times*

'Montalbán is a writer who is caustic about the powerful and tender towards the oppressed' *TLS*

'I cannot wait for other Pepe Carvalho titles to be published here. Meanwhile, make the most of *Murder in the Central Committee*' *New Statesman*

'Montalbán writes with authority and compassion — a Le Carré-like sorrow' *Publishers' Weekly*

'A thriller worthy of the name: a taut, intelligent tour de force set in the shadowy minefield of post-Franco Spanish politics' Julie Burchill

'Splendid flavour of life in Barcelona and Madrid, a memorable hero in Pepe and one of the most startling love scenes you'll ever come across' *Scotsman*

'Tightly plotted, very funny, not a one-dimensional character in sight. What more can you ask?' *Tangled Web*

The lights go out during a meeting of the Central Committee of the Spanish Communist Party — Fernando Garrido, the general secretary, has been murdered.

Pepe Carvalho, who has worked for both the Party and the CIA, is well suited to track down Garrido's murderer. Unfortunately, the job requires a trip to Madrid — an inhospitable city where food and sex is heavier than in Pepe's beloved Barcelona.

Southern Seas

'Pepe Carvalho is a phlegmatic investigator. His greatest concern is with his stomach, but when not pursuing delicacies, he can unravel the most tangled of mysteries'
Sunday Times

The body of Stuart Pedrell, a powerful businessman, is found in a Barcelona suburb. He had disappeared on his way to Polynesia in search of the visionary spirit of Paul Gauguin.

Who better to find the killer of a dead dreamer than Pepe Carvalho, overweight bon viveur and ex-communist? The trail for Pedrell's killer unearths a world of disillusioned lefties, graphic sex and nouvelle cuisine — major ingredients of post-Franco Spain. A tautly-written mystery with an unforgettable — and highly unusual — protagonist.

Off Side

To revive its sagging fortunes, Barcelona FC has bought the services of Jack Mortimer, European Footballer of the Year. No sooner has Mortimer taken possession of his company Porsche than death threats start arriving. Are they a hoax, the work of a loner or are they connected to the awesome real estate speculation that is tearing Barcelona apart?

In a period of turmoil where Catalan pimps and racketeers are being hustled off the streets by crime syndicates from the Middle East, Pepe Carvalho is thinking of retirement, but the need to save the soul of his beloved Barcelona forces him to take on a case that can only end in disaster.

An Olympic Death

Translated by Ed Emery

'Montalbán's Barcelona has a truly great sense of place. Essential reading' *Northern Echo*

As Barcelona prepares for the Olympics, the city is turned over to make way for new roads, new stadia and the giant prawns of Mariscal.

Pepe Carvalho who remembers the good old days when a hammer was always to be found with a sickle is forced to work for Olympic entrepreneurs whose only game plan is to make a fast buck.

As Carvalho tries to come to terms with the new values of the present, his life — gastronomic, amatory and professional — confronts the disillusion of middle age.

Also published by Serpent's Tail

Landscapes After the Battle

Juan Goytisolo

'Juan Goytisolo is one of the most rigorous and original contemporary writers. His books are a strange mixture of pitiless autobiography, the debunking of mythologies and conformist fetishes, passionate exploration of the periphery of the West — in particular of the Arab world which he knows intimately — and audacious linguistic experiment. All these qualities feature in *Landscapes After the Battle*, an unsettling, apocalyptic work, splendidly translated by Helen Lane' Mario Vargas Llosa

'*Landscapes After the Battle* . . . a cratered terrain littered with obscenities and linguistic violence, an assault on "good taste" and the reader's notions of what a novel should be' *Observer*

'Fierce, highly unpleasant and very funny' *Guardian*

'A short, exhilarating tour of the emergence of pop culture, sexual liberation and ethnic militancy' *New Statesman*

'Helen Lane's rendering reads beautifully, capturing the whimsicality and rhythms of the Spanish without sacrificing accuracy, but rightly branching out where literal translation simply does not work' *Times Literary Supplement*